Hearts
MADE FOR
BREAKING

ALSO BY JEN KLEIN

>>>>>>

Shuffle, Repeat

Summer Unscripted

Hearts

MADE FOR

BREAKING

♥ ♥ ♥ ♥ ♥

JEN KLEIN

RANDOM HOUSE 🏠 NEW YORK

Text copyright © 2019 by Jen Klein
Jacket photograph copyright © 2019 by Getty/Xsandra

All rights reserved. Published in the United States by Random House Children's Books, a division of Penguin Random House LLC, New York.

Random House and the colophon are registered trademarks of Penguin Random House LLC.

Visit us on the Web! GetUnderlined.com

Educators and librarians, for a variety of teaching tools, visit us at RHTeachersLibrarians.com

Library of Congress Cataloging-in-Publication Data
Names: Klein, Jen, author.
Title: Hearts made for breaking / Jen Klein.
Description: First edition. | New York : Random House, [2019] | Summary: Challenged by her best friends to break her serial dating patterns, eighteen-year-old Lark gets to know transfer student Ardy and learns about broken hearts and the power of real love.
Identifiers: LCCN 2017051554 | ISBN 978-1-5247-0008-9 (trade pbk.) | ISBN 978-1-5247-0009-6 (lib. bdg.) | ISBN 978-1-5247-0010-2 (ebook)
Subjects: | CYAC: Dating (Social customs)—Fiction. | Love—Fiction. | High schools—Fiction. | Schools—Fiction.
Classification: LCC PZ7.1.K645 He 2019 | DDC [Fic]—dc23

Printed in the United States of America
10 9 8 7 6 5 4 3 2 1
First Edition

>>> for my writer village <<<

CHAPTER ONE

Yesterday, my heart was "broken," which is why today I'm sitting on a glossy but practical daybed with hidden drawers for extra storage. The mattress is firm, the spread is a bright floral pattern, and the throw pillows are wide and comfortable.

Yep—IKEA on a Saturday morning. That's me. It's not exactly something I like to publicize, but this is what I do every time I fake a heartbreak. What better place to try to forget what's wrong with me than here: a collection of perfect rooms, just like the rooms in the houses I want to design someday. Perfect houses for perfect families full of perfectly normal people.

That's the dream.

I stay where I am through visits from a handful of other families who are interested in outfitting their homes. In the past, I've gone to a compact kitchen or one of IKEA's cleverly designed space-friendly living rooms, but yesterday's relationship dissolution propelled me here. There's something comforting about the idea of eventually owning a home that I might want other people to visit. A place to be peaceful, a place to be proud of . . .

Until there's an earthquake.

At least, that's what I first think when I jolt awake, startled by the bed's movement beneath me. Horribly aware that Southern California is a hotbed of geologic activity, I grab for the frame, jerk to an upright position, and scramble to remember the closest exit.

Except then the fog wisps away from my brain, and I realize three things all at once:

1. I was asleep in IKEA.
2. There was no earthquake after all.
3. Undateable Ardy Tate is sitting on the end of the bed, looking at me with undisguised curiosity.

"Sorry, Lark." His eyes are wide and brown and blinky behind his dark-rimmed glasses. I notice the light freckles scattered across the pale skin of his nose. "I didn't realize you were actually asleep."

"I wasn't." Lie #1.

"I wasn't trying to freak you out."

"You didn't." Lie #2. Ardy is all kinds of cute and lanky and—let's be honest—a little awkward as he perches beside me in his screen-printed tee and skinny khakis. I realize I have no idea what to say to him, and that's the part that's freaking me out because usually I know exactly what to say to a boy.

No, not usually. *Always.*

This double standard is how I know the universe is unfair: because Ardy Tate is labeled Undateable, when, despite all appearances to the contrary, it should be a description for *me:* Lark Dayton.

My third and fourth fingers are tapping against the bed frame, so I make a tight fist to still the movement. "What are you doing here?" I ask, before thinking the question through, because it's definitely not one I want to answer in return.

"My mom sent me out for candles." Ardy looks rueful. "And, yes, I know I'm nowhere near the candles. This place is a maze."

"Tell me about it," I say, grasping the lifeline he's unintentionally thrown out for me. "My parents wanted me to get . . . napkins."

"Napkins?"

"The cute striped ones," I say, remembering a package my mother bought one time. "I ended up in Guest Rooms and needed to take a break."

"It's not for the faint of heart," Ardy agrees. "I think napkins and candles are both in the Marketplace. You want to go find it?"

I nod because what else would I do, and moments later we're winding our way past closet storage systems and toward the staircase. My fingers tap against the leather strap of my messenger bag, and I hazard a sideways glance up at Ardy. He's tall—much taller than I am—with a sharply angled jawline and the finest dusting of shadow around his mouth. Maybe he doesn't shave on weekends. I wouldn't know, because this is the first time I've seen him outside of REACH High.

It's October now; Ardy Tate transferred to my school at the

beginning of our senior year, so I've only been aware of him for a couple of months. When he arrived, even though I was newly flirting with Rahim Antoun, I noticed that (a) Transfer Boy existed and (b) Transfer Boy was quirky-hot and seemed smart. At first I didn't pay much attention to him because Rahim and I soon were finding places to make out on campus, and I was enjoying that New Boy rush. By the time Rahim and I stopped hanging out (after I invented superstrict parents who would never let me go anywhere with him), two new things had come to my attention: (c) Transfer Boy's name was Ardy Tate, and (d) Ardy Tate was Undateable—something about an event that occurred at his old high school—plus, he was basically stapled to Hope Burkett's side. Hope's boyfriend, Evan, is stapled to her other side, so supposedly she and Ardy aren't together, but they *seem* like they are, and that's enough for me. Although I may mess around with lots of guys, I do not go after those who belong to other people. Not by a long shot.

A girl has to maintain *some* ethics.

As we reach the bottom of the stairs, I can't help asking the question. "What's Hope doing today?"

Ardy looks confused. "I don't know, homework or hanging out with Evan, probably. What's Dax doing?"

His question throws me for a loop. Sure, Dax is the boyfriend who fake-broke my fake heart last night, but our short-term dalliance wasn't front-page news or anything. Has Ardy been paying attention to who I date?

Or, rather, "date"?

"I don't know," I tell Ardy, because I don't want to go there.

We step into the controlled chaos of the IKEA Marketplace: a tangle of aisles filled with interesting, low-priced items. The shelves closest to the stairs are brimming with galvanized metal wall letters, the type you buy separately so you can assemble them into words like *FAMILY* and *LOVE* and *TOGETHER-NESS* to decorate your home.

There must have been elementary school–aged kids here earlier, because the top row currently spells out the word *BUTT*.

Ardy stops to play with the letters. "What should we say?" he asks, picking up an *R* and an *E*. "How should we leave our mark on the world?"

"I don't know why we'd even try." I point to the *BUTT*. "We can't top that."

"Clearly." Ardy sets the *E* down and finds an *L,* then hands it to me. "Okay, just our names, then."

Two minutes later Ardy's name is spelled out in block letters on the upper shelf, and mine is along the left side, vertically, one letter to a shelf. Ardy nods approvingly at mine. "Top to bottom, I was not expecting that."

"It's more visually interesting," I tell him, and then we leave our names there. Not together . . . but close.

When we find the candle section, Ardy grabs two of the wax pillars—a yellow and a blue—and juts them toward me. "You're an excellent judge of beauty. Which color?"

Instead of looking at the candles, I gaze up into his dark eyes, deciding to fall back on my old comfortable standard: flirtation. I give him a wide smile. "What makes you think I know how to judge what's pretty?"

I assume he's going to say something about how I look—because that's what boys do—but he doesn't. Instead, his eyebrows make a tiny dive toward each other. He shrugs, taking a step back.

"You drive a pretty car, you have pretty hair, you date pretty boys."

It's not that he says it rudely; it's that . . .

Well, maybe he *does* say it rudely. I can't tell with Ardy Tate.

My face must give my thoughts away, because suddenly he looks awkward, maybe even a little concerned. "Sorry. Did I make it weird?"

"No—" I start to say (lie #3), but then stop because Ardy has raised both candles to the top of his head and is waggling them like alien antennae.

"This would be making it weird," he tells me, solemn. It's so stupid that a burst of laughter comes out of me before I can stop it. Ardy lowers the candles, grinning at me in return. "I'm going with blue."

As he starts gathering blue candles, I quell my laughter, feeling unbalanced by the encounter. I point to another aisle. "Found the napkins. Thanks for the navigational assistance. I have to run. Meeting someone at the mall."

And I escape. But not without looking back at Ardy . . . who hasn't stopped looking at me.

Really? Ardy Tate?

» » « «

I shove the bag of IKEA napkins into my messenger bag as I push through glass doors into the air-conditioned glossiness of the Burbank mall. We never came here last year while it was under construction, but since it's become a sleek, modern building, the teens (and, sadly, the tweens) flock to it on weekends. Cooper is waiting for me right inside the entrance. His outfit—white trousers and a white Oxford—makes me roll my eyes. "Let me guess," I say, and then switch to an overly polished British accent. "Brunching on the green with Ian?"

"You can stop that." Cooper knows exactly what I'm doing. "There's no brunch, there's no green."

"You look like you're trying to make a sale at the Gap." Which is true. This is my friend who's been known to set off his Persian skin tone by lining his huge dark eyes with turquoise. I've seen him with a Mohawk, with a nose piercing, and, at one momentous middle school event, in a leopard-print tuxedo. But today he's the buttoned-up version of himself. Even his hair has been slicked down with some sort of product. It's as if his entire personality has been muffled.

"I happen to like the way I look." Cooper strikes a pose. "I think I'm quite dapper."

"True . . ." I take a quick visual survey of the nearby stores and then grab him by the shoulder, spinning him in the direction of a little indie clothing shop: Cali-Cool. "But usually when you want to be dapper, you wear something like *that*."

Cooper's eyes light up at the sight of the black T-shirt in the window. A bright rainbow soars across the chest, and underneath are the words *NOT STRAIGHT*.

"Oh, I would rock the pride out of that."

"I *know*." I motion to the Every Guy in the World outfit he's currently wearing. "And yet . . . this."

"There are many facets to my personality," he tells me. "Sometimes I like to blend in."

A voice comes from behind us: "Only when you're with Ian."

Cooper droops but stays where he is, continuing to face in the direction of the rainbow shirt. I spin to see my other best friend, Katie Levitt. Her creamy cheeks are brushed with peach blush, and her long blond hair has been newly blown out. I smile at her. "Cooper didn't tell me that you were here, too."

Beside me, Cooper exhales a short puff of air. "I was pretending it wasn't true."

Katie makes a face at the back of his head. "I ran into Captain Crabby at the food court. He let it slip that you were coming, so I stuck around."

Cooper finally turns to look at both of us. "It wasn't an invitation."

"You don't need one," I assure Katie.

"She's crashing our party," Cooper insists.

As always, Katie is unfazed by him. "I'm invited to all the parties," she tells us.

She's not wrong. Not that I'm complaining. It doesn't hurt my own popularity that one of my BFFs is absurdly gorgeous and has an unspoken season pass to everything.

Everything except—as far as Cooper is concerned—my friendship with him.

"What's your problem with Ian, anyway?" Cooper asks her.

"I don't have a problem with him." Katie's violet eyes go purposefully huge as she slides them toward me. "Do you, Lark?"

Well. That's hardly fair. Cooper doesn't need to hear a pile-on about Ian. "He's fine," I say. Cooper's new boyfriend is so basic it hurts, but the last thing I want is to start a fight.

"That's a lie," Katie says.

"Speaking of lies . . ." Cooper pops his fists onto his hips and stares at me. It's a challenge. "How's Dax? Still hooking up with him?"

"No." I lift my chin, knowing where this is going. "He broke up with me last night."

"How could he break up with you?" Katie asks. "You weren't really dating."

Cooper doesn't say anything, continuing to stare at me until—because he knows me better than anyone—I cave. "*Fine.* I might have given him a tiny push."

"Please." Cooper snorts. "You don't give tiny pushes. You walk boys to the edges of cliffs and tell them to close their eyes before you shove them off."

"Not true!" I retort.

"So true," Katie says. She cups her hands to her mouth and mimes shouting into a canyon. "Watch . . . your . . . step!"

"Whatever," I say. "Let's go look at that shirt."

"In," says Cooper.

Katie makes another face, but she tags along, and five minutes later we're all critically scanning Cooper's image in the clothing store's mirror. He's still in his boy-next-door trousers, but over them he's now wearing the shirt from the shop window, and he's jammed a scarlet fedora onto his head.

"See, there's the Cooper I know," I tell him. "You're glorious."

"This is true," he returns. "Am I pulling off the hat?"

"You should *take off* the hat," Katie says, and then laughs at her own wit.

Cooper and I roll our eyes at her. "You should get it," I tell him.

He removes it to check the price tag, and when he does, his hair flies up with it. I think it's adorable, but Cooper is horrified. He tosses me the hat so he can paw at his head, but—thanks to what must be an immense amount of product—his hair remains sticking straight up, a dark frizzy halo hovering above him. "I need lubricant," he says.

"Gross," Katie says.

"I mean water."

As Cooper keeps messing with his hair, a familiar figure appears in the mirror behind us. I spin around to greet Glen Jackson with a squeal and a hug, which turns into a bit of a roller-coaster ride when he lifts me off the ground and spins around before setting me back down. When I catch my breath, I give him a playful slap on his giant biceps. "Glen! I didn't know you work at the mall."

"Pays better than the ice-cream place," he says, grinning down at me with his beautiful wide mouth.

It's been several years since I've kissed that mouth. We met at YMCA day camp over the summer between eighth and ninth grades. I noticed him for two reasons: (1) He brought decks of cards and taught everyone to play Spades, Hearts, and Nertz. (2) When he smiled at me from across the picnic table, his teeth were bright white against his soft brown skin, and I immediately wanted to kiss him. Since I was new to kissing at the time, it took me a while to get up the gumption to do it, but eventually I did. We were joined at the face for the rest of the summer, during which the counselors did everything they could to dissuade us campers from hooking up, but to very little avail. We practiced kissing behind the bathrooms, behind the playground structure, and even behind a dumpster. Glen was no less perfect as the end of summer approached, and since I had no perfection of my own, I knew exactly where this had to be heading: Rejection City.

I knew it for sure when we were all sitting on a quilt in the grass during lunch. Someone had brought a big bag of licorice and set it in the middle of the quilt for all of us to share. I was only a month out of braces, so I planted my hands on my knees, giving my fingers a place to tap out a pattern so I wouldn't be tempted to reach for the sticky candy. Glen noticed and gave me a weird look. "What are you doing?"

"Nothing," I said. Except that I *had* been doing something. Something that calmed and soothed me. Something that no one knew about. I grabbed the licorice and took a big handful. As I'd suspected from the beginning, Glen was too perfect to be with a girl like me.

Later that day I led Glen to believe that I was going to join every extracurricular activity at my high school. I was suddenly extremely enthusiastic about the debate team and student government and field hockey. Since Glen would be attending a different Burbank school, this would leave no time for our make-out sessions. He broke up with me on the bus as we were coming back from our last camp field trip: a tour of the natural history museum. It seemed like a day of symbolism, the season and the relationship relegated to the annals of my personal history on the same day.

It's been two and a half years since then, and I don't run into Glen very often, but it's never awkward between us. In fact, he's always supernice to me. Who knows, maybe it's his way of making up for dumping me on that bus.

"Do you have an employees' bathroom my friend can use?" I ask.

Glen's eyes dart to Cooper's hair. "Yeah, just be fast." He gestures to the side of the dressing room, where there's a closed door sporting an EMPLOYEES ONLY sign. As Cooper disappears and Katie wanders off to flip through a rack of sundresses, Glen turns back to me. "So how are you, Lark? Do you know where you're going to college?"

"I'm doing two years locally before I transfer to start an architecture degree," I tell him. What I *don't* tell him is that I wish I were starting at a four-year college right away, but it's a money thing. "How's Allie?"

"She's great. We're applying to the same places, so fingers crossed. . . ." He trails off with a shrug and a bright white grin, implying that he and his girlfriend will be together forever.

When Cooper returns, his hair is slicked down, but he looks somewhat worse for the wear, with water still dripping from his left ear.

"Gross," says Katie.

"Your sink pressure's too high," Cooper tells Glen.

"I should have warned you." Glen pulls us in so he can

whisper. "If you guys want to buy anything, I can score you fifteen percent off. Employee discount."

"You rock," I tell him. Yup, he's definitely still feeling guilty.

"I know," he says. And it's all perfectly normal and delightful until Cooper and Katie and I head back out into the mall, Cooper's new scarlet fedora perched on my head, to protect his hair. Once we're away from the clothing store, Cooper pulls me to a stop. "Okay, *enough* already!"

"What?"

"Lark." He sets his hands on my shoulders and looks into my eyes. "Sweet baby Lark. You have *got* to stop. Were you even paying attention to that hot boy offering deep discounts for alternative clothing?"

"Fifteen percent is hardly a deep discount," I protest. "It's shallow at best."

"He *is* beautiful," Katie says. "It's a shame you guys didn't work out."

"Have you met Lark?" Cooper asks her. "Do you know why it never went anywhere with her and Glen?"

"Yes, and duh," Katie says. "Because they were basically fetuses at the time."

"Lark is standing right here," I tell everyone. No one listens.

"Agreed," Cooper says to Katie, totally ignoring me. "But that's how it always goes with Lark. She gets out of things at the speed of light because she never actually gets *in*."

"Sex?" I ask him. "Are you talking about sex?"

"No," Cooper tells me. "Sex is the easy part."

"Gross," Katie says.

"Since when do you have sex?" I ask Cooper.

He ignores the question. "I'm talking about the full relationship experience. All the colors of the rainbow."

"That is the gayest thing I've ever heard," Katie says.

"Thank you," Cooper says.

"Relationships are rainbows?" she asks.

This time Cooper ignores her instead of me. "On the ROY-G-BIV scale, you're living in the tiny slice between dusky peach and light yellow," he tells me. "You're missing green. And blue. And *purple*." He gives a dramatic sigh. "Purple is *so good*."

I'm genuinely confused. "Purple is sex?"

"Nothing is sex!" Cooper explodes. "I'm saying you need to try something new."

"I agree with that," Katie says.

Since when do they agree on anything?

"You need to pick different kinds of guys," she continues.

"Wrong," Cooper says.

That's more like it.

"Try someone who's not popular, who isn't a team captain or an honor roll student. And then you need to end it like a human," Katie finishes.

"How about we stop referring to me as less than a human?" I try to make a joke out of it.

"See, *that*." Cooper points at me. "See what she does, joking about something serious instead of being real. This is what she does with the boys. She kisses them in shadowy corners where no one can see. She pulls away before anything gets real, and she does it in a way that makes *them* the bad guys. She weasels out like a thief in the night."

"I'm really not loving this," I tell them both, wishing we were anywhere but standing in the middle of a mall, doing anything but having this conversation. They don't even look at me. I try again. "Hello? You both just saw me have an extremely healthy interaction with an ex-boyfriend. Isn't that supposed to be the point? To have fun and get out without anyone getting hurt?"

"No," Katie tells me.

"Yeah, the only reason you get shopping discounts is because you never had anything real with Glen in the first place," Cooper says.

Okay now, that's just rude. But before I can say it, he and Katie are back to negotiating.

"I'm with you on her breakups," Katie tells Cooper. "I haven't known Lark or any of her boys to shed a tear when things end. Not one."

"It's not normal," Cooper says.

"On top of that," Katie argues, "Lark is only ever with externally perfect guys who are jocks or scholars or both. I'm saying try a goth. Take a hipster for a spin. Give a band geek a whirl. You know what they say about brass players and how they kiss. . . ."

Cooper's eyes light up. "Ooh, I hooked up with Omar Taylor in tenth grade. Second-chair trombone. It's all true."

"See," Katie says, tugging at the edge of her scoop neck T-shirt so the lace strap of her lavender bra is visible.

"I do not see," I tell her. "You want me to—what? Go hang out at marching-band practice?"

"Yes," Katie says.

"No," Cooper says.

"You *said* you liked the trombone boy," Katie points out.

"Fine, pick up a brass," Cooper tells me. "Or a woodwind. They're good with their hands, all those little keys. Whatever, stay in it long enough to know what it's about. Don't get him to dump you two weeks in, when no one gives a crap yet. Stay in longer."

"And then dump him louder," Katie says.

I open my mouth, but Cooper railroads right over me. "We're in agreement, then," he says to Katie.

"Yes," she answers.

"I'm not," I say. "I don't even know what I'm supposed to be agreeing to."

"I'll break it down," Katie says. "Find a boy. Someone different from your usual cookie-cutter boys. Start with kissing him, like you always do."

"Approved," Cooper says. "And then give him a chance. Make him love you. Make it last."

"But then break his heart." Katie shrugs. "Or fall in love and get married and have babies, whatever. But no getting *him* to dump *you*. If you want it to be over, you have to get out by having an awful, awkward breakup conversation, like the rest of us."

"Because *that* should be the goal," I tell them both.

"No," Cooper says. "The goal is proving you can have a re-lationship where *someone* gives a crap about the other person."

God, do they think I'm a monster or something?

"What if the guy I want doesn't want me back?" I ask.

"Cross that bridge when you come to it," Cooper says.

"Reeling them in is not where you have trouble," Katie says.

I guess they're right. Then again, convincing a horny teen-aged boy to kiss me is hardly a difficult act.

"Tell you what," says Cooper. "If we agree on a boy and you can't get him to kiss you, the deal's off. Game over."

So now it's a game. Wonderful.

"You really think I need this?" I ask, and am immediately met by fervent nods from both of them.

"Without a doubt," says Katie.

"One hundred percent," says Cooper. He turns to Katie. "How much do you like me?"

"Not even a little."

"The feeling is mutual." He turns back to me. "If we're agreeing on this, you know we're right."

Who am I to argue with logic like that? Besides, I hate arguments.

"Fine," I agree.

"Good girl." Katie gives me a triumphant smile. "Come up with some names. Cooper and I will do the same, and we'll talk tomorrow. I'm late for a manicure."

"She has to sharpen her claws," Cooper says. Apparently, their goodwill toward each other only exists when they're ganging up on me.

"Whatever." Katie blows me a kiss, throws Cooper a snarky look, and sails off.

I watch her go, wondering what I've gotten myself into, and then turn to glare at Cooper. He's still gazing after Katie. "She wears colored contacts, right? No one has eyes that color."

I ignore the question, as I have always ignored the question, because—yes—Katie's eyes are really light brown, but she swore me to secrecy in ninth grade.

Cooper turns to me and, in one motion, grabs my hand and pulls me into a hug. "You know I love you, Larks."

I drop my head onto his shoulder, allowing him to hold me. "I love you, too, Coops."

He strokes my hair and I relax into him, thinking of the as-yet-unnamed boy in my near future and how he has no idea what's in store for him:

Reel him in.

Make him love me.

Break his heart.

CHAPTER TWO

I find an empty space in the Wheelz parking lot and swing out of my car. It's a used powder-blue Chrysler Sebring that my parents helped me buy last year with every cent I'd scraped and squeezed over the span of my entire life. It has dents and the radio doesn't work, but I love it.

I push through the double doors and into the familiar sensory overload of my family's business: an indoor go-karting establishment. Rock music blares over the speakers, competing with the sounds of karts zooming around the high-speed track and occasionally banging into walls or each other.

The vehicles are electric, so there's no odor of gasoline, but plenty of other scents fill the air: popcorn, sticky-sweet slushies, burgers frying in the back, burning rubber, and the faintest hint of sweat.

The business caters to parents throwing birthday parties, corporations hosting employee bonding events, and local teens who want to hang out and drive fast. It's a lot of work. My parents have several business partners, but they're mostly unseen on the actual premises. My dad is the boots on the ground.

I find my brother, Leo, in the party room, cleaning up after what appears to have been a very raucous Sunday-afternoon birthday party. "I thought you'd be ready to go," I say, swiping a handful of discarded napkins off a table and throwing them into the trash. Might as well help him finish. The sooner I can get him home, the sooner I can meet up with my friends.

"This party ran late," Leo says. "And another group just called to come in. Dad's in the back."

"I'm supposed to meet Cooper and Katie in ten minutes."

Leo looks surprised. He runs a hand through his light brown hair, a shade darker than mine but almost the exact same color as Mom's. "Both of them? Together?"

"They've found some common ground lately," I tell him. What I *don't* say is that their common ground is almost entirely centered around what's wrong with me.

"So no chance you can ditch them and help Dad out here instead?"

Guilt and frustration war within me. They both win. I glare at Leo. "Seriously? Where's Mano?"

"He got a gig to play a kid's birthday party in Sylmar, so we're down a person."

"Can't you stay?" I ask.

"Nope." Leo looks worried. "I've already worked the max hours. Child labor laws."

Crap. If Dad's only assistant manager, Mano, isn't here, that means Dad will have to stick around to help out with the incoming group. Leo and I both know that's not going to end well.

"Fine," I tell him. "I'll run you home, and I'll come back to help."

"Thank you," he says.

"You're welcome," I answer, wishing everything could be different.

» » « «

Half an hour later Leo has been deposited at home and I'm back at Wheelz, this time behind the glass-encased redemption counter. Katie is perched beside me on a stool, and Cooper is slumped over the end of the counter with his head buried in his arms. We're all waiting for the eight-year-old kid before us to make a decision.

"Virtual-reality glasses?" he asks.

"You don't have quite enough tickets for that," I say. What I don't say is that he'd need, like, a thousand more.

"Stuffed frog?"

"Look at the bottom shelf," I tell him. "You can afford something there."

"Whoopie cushion?"

"That's on the second shelf." Beside me, Katie stifles a giggle.

"Monster teeth?"

"Third shelf." At the end of the counter, Cooper doesn't look up, but he squeezes his hand into a fist and gently strikes it against the glass. *Thump.*

The kid drops to his knees and presses his forehead against the front of the counter. Then he pulls back and looks at where his breath fogged up the glass. He pokes his finger at it, drawing two eyes and a smile.

"Have you decided?" I ask him.

"Can I have *two* bouncy balls?"

"You only have enough tickets for one," I tell him. From Cooper's end of the counter, there's another *thump*.

"Are these real rabbit feet?"

"Probably not."

Thump-thump. This time Katie doesn't stifle her giggle. And this time it's more of a snort.

"What's so funny?" asks the kid.

"Nothing," I tell him. "And I just remembered that actually you *can* have two bouncy balls." I scoop two balls from the bin and, for good measure, grab a third. I shove them all into the kid's hands and swipe his meager stack of tickets off the counter. "And there's a bonus one, too."

"Wow, thanks!" He beams at me, and I have to smile back because he looks so happy and his lips are stained with blue slushie. We watch him scamper off.

"Finally," Katie says. "We've got business to attend to. Who's Lark going to fall madly in love with?"

"Rasheem Woodward?" Cooper suggests. "Honor roll, cool shoes."

"She's already been there," Katie says. "Freshman year."

"His shoes *were* cool," I agree.

"Right. Weston Howard?"

"He's cute," I tell them. "But I think he's dating Amelia Grant."

"Plus, he's basically a carbon copy of every other guy Lark's ever kissed," Katie says. "How about Christopher Connor? He's different."

"The guy with the neck tattoo?" I ask.

Kate shrugs. "I'd date him."

"I don't think he's my type."

"That's the problem." Katie sounds frustrated. "We're trying to go outside of the box here."

"Think of someone interesting," Cooper says.

"Someone who you don't know but you *could* get to know," Katie chimes in.

The image of Ardy Tate zips into my brain.

"What?" Cooper pokes me. "What was that?"

"Nothing," I lie.

But Cooper sees right through it. "Who did you think of?"

I don't want to tell him. Ardy isn't my usual type: easy to reel in, easy to push away. He seems more . . . *substantial* than the guys I normally kiss beneath the bleachers. Plus, I'm pretty sure we've already determined that he's not that into me.

"Come *on*." Cooper pokes me again. "Give me a name."

"Yeah," says Katie. "I saw that, too. Who is it?"

"Hold on," I say. "I need a second." I lower my right hand behind the counter so that they can't see me twitching my fingers in a rhythmic pattern while I consider Ardy Tate. He seems self-aware. Intriguing. Maybe artistic. He doesn't seem like the type who would easily fall for my charm, for the way I go into Flirt Mode. Ardy could actually be a beautiful path to a win-win. If I *can't* get him interested—which I sincerely suspect will be the case—then the game's over. I mean, isn't he supposed to be Undateable? And if he *is* into me, well . . . there are worse things in the world.

For all I know, the Undateable may be the best person to date.

I blurt it out. "Ardy Tate."

Their eyes widen.

"Seriously?" says Katie.

"*Ardy?*" Cooper says.

"I said someone different," Katie reminds me. "Not a weirdo."

"He's not weird," I protest. "He's nice."

"I've talked to him a couple of times," Cooper says. "He was coherent. Articulate. Nice teeth. But he's also . . ." He trails off.

"A weirdo." Katie seems very sure of herself. "Who transfers for their senior year? I bet he got kicked out of his last school."

"I've heard that," Cooper says. "I also heard he got someone pregnant."

Katie nods. "That makes sense. I think Cici Belle is the one who told me to stay away from him. I've heard he's Undateable."

"Ditto," Cooper says. "But to be fair—he's not hard on the eyes. I mean, if you like the offbeat thing."

"That's worse," Katie says. "It's not that he's not attractive. It's that he's *not normal.*" She pauses, considering. "But he's definitely not Lark's usual, so . . . approved."

"What?" Despite the fact that I broached the subject in the first place, misgivings suddenly rise up inside me. "Okay, hold on. I only said his name because I ran into him yesterday—"

"Seconded," Cooper tells Katie. "Ardy Tate it is."

"Agreed." Katie holds out a hand and they shake on it. "Game on."

"Game on," I mumble. Secretly terrified . . . and also excited.

» » « «

After Cooper and Katie leave, I wipe down the front of the prize counter and clean the soda machines. There are only a few customers still driving the track, and our car operator, Dustin, is supervising them, so I push open the doors to the back hallway and wander down to Dad's office. It's a mess, as usual: piles of paper everywhere, crates of soda stacked in a corner. He waves from behind his desk, where he's tapping at a computer. "Hey, honey. Thanks for sticking around."

"No problem." I decide not to mention the grease stain on his shirt or the fact that his Dodgers cap is skewed. "It's almost seven. You should go."

"Actually, you can take off. I'll come up front."

For the second time today, my heart sinks. "You don't have to do that," I tell him. "My homework's finished. I don't need to get home."

"I'm swamped." He points to a stack of papers. "I have to schedule next month's maintenance, approve timesheets, and start on deductions."

"I thought you were going to hire a new manager." We've had managers before, but no one seems to last very long. When they bail, he's back to working crazy hours.

"I met with a couple of people this week," he says. "So we'll see."

I give one last push. "Maybe you could come in early tomorrow to finish up your work? So you could have dinner at home tonight?"

"Sorry, sweetie. Love you." He goes back to his work, and I head out, every fiber in my body drooping because I know tonight is going to be very, very bad.

» » « «

I'm in my room by nine-thirty, but I'm still awake when Dad comes home after eleven. I tried to defuse the bomb at dinner, but it didn't work. It's a bomb that can't be defused, that is never defused. No matter how many funny anecdotes I told about the weekend—the annoying kid at the prize counter, Cooper's hair after he tried on the scarlet fedora—and no matter what questions Leo asked about the new sous vide cooker Mom had used to make the chicken, she only gave short answers, after which her lips returned to a thin, tight line. Leo and I shared a look as we helped clean up the dishes. Mom was not happy that Dad hadn't come home for dinner.

Now I hope Leo is doing the same thing as me: trying to avoid the flying shrapnel that makes up our home life. I wonder if I should offer to switch bedrooms with him. From down here on the first floor, I can only make out a few particularly loud words and phrases—"just like every other damn time," "get off my ass," and my personal favorite, "shut up, the kids will hear you" (they both say that one)—but I know the whole thing must be crystal clear in Leo's room on the second floor. Hopefully, he's either asleep or playing video games with his headset on.

I have to believe my parents liked each other at some point. They must have had fun and wild passion and glorious moments, right? I know they had at least *one* moment of glory—apparently, that's how I was conceived. It's why they named me Lark. Because it's how I came to be and how they got married: "on a lark." Back when they were wildly in love. Back when it was good.

Whereas if I were to be born right now, they'd probably name me something more like Oh, Crap.

CHAPTER THREE

As usual, I drive Leo to REACH High. It affords me the opportunity to remind him what a great sister I am and how lucky he is to have me. Not all freshmen get to hang out with seniors. "I know, I know," he grumbles as he gets out of my car. "You're an angel."

"And a saint," I tell him, and we head toward our school.

I was there for REACH's inaugural year, when I was in ninth grade. The name stands for Raising Ethical Americans Charter High, and it's already taking the world by storm. At least that's what the administration likes to tell us. In reality, we might only be taking small swatches of the San Fernando Valley by storm. Or maybe by a gentle breeze.

That said, I have to admit it's fun to be a trailblazer. In that first year, everyone was constantly saying things like, "This is the First-Ever Basketball Game played on this court," "This is the First-Ever Yoga Retreat held in this gym," and "This is the First-Ever Meditation Assembly in the auditorium."

When you live in Southern California, you get yoga and meditation. It's a thing here.

My classmates and I basically made history every time we took a step. In May we'll all be making history again when we're the First-Ever Graduating Class.

Leo and I split off from each other, and I go in the direction of my locker, passing the usual array of posters and announcements on the walls: science fair applications, extracurricular aura cleansing, nominations for the Spring Fling Thing, which is our school's answer to the classic prom.

I also pass Peter Talbot, who waves at me. I hold up my hand in the classic "Live long and prosper" sign. As always, Peter grins and rolls his eyes. It's become a joke between us. In ninth grade he and I ended up making out in the back row during a class field trip to see an anniversary screening of *Star Wars*. It turned out that Peter was a rabid fan, which made it very easy later to make him say we couldn't kiss anymore—all I had to do was wax poetic about *Star Trek*. Now it's funny. Back then it was deadly serious.

I'm almost to my homeroom hallway when Katie catches up with me. "We need to get Cooper to play along, too," she says.

I'm lost. "Play along with what?"

"The game. He needs to promise not to *marry* Ian right away, the way he always does."

"Why do you care?" I ask her. "You don't even like Cooper."

"I care about the world," Katie answers, flouncing her hair back.

We round the corner, and I immediately spot Ardy down the hall, spinning his locker combination. He's wearing a plaid shirt over a white tee, and he's got a slouchy beanie on his head.

It's very messy, very hipster in a way that Cooper and I some-times mock, but . . . it's also very cute.

"There's your man," Katie says. I shush her and she laughs. "Go get him."

She peels off for her own locker, leaving me trying to roll the dice for a game I'm not sure how to play. Especially because I'm not sure how to talk to Ardy Tate. The "reel him in" part of the plan isn't as obvious as it usually is. When someone is really interesting, what would make them interested in *me*? My road to romance usually starts with a touch on the arm at a party or a flirty look across the room during math class. Not with any-thing real.

As I approach Ardy's locker, he glances up and makes eye contact. I start to shake my hair out to get his attention but then stop myself midway through because I suddenly think maybe it's not the kind of thing that will attract Ardy. It results in a very strange head movement, like I'm twerking with my neck. Luckily, Ardy doesn't notice, because of course he's engrossed in whatever stupid locker thing he's doing. I'm several yards past him when I decide this is ridiculous and I need to just go for it. I spin and walk back, head held high, landing right next to him. *"Hi."* The word comes out way more aggressively than I'd intended.

He looks at me for a moment before responding. "Hi." Then he waits, peering down at me. He doesn't seem uncom-fortable or awkward. He just . . . seems to be waiting. If our conversation thus far is any indicator, reeling Ardy in is never going to happen. "What'd you do this weekend?" I finally ask.

"Got lost at IKEA." His mouth tenses the tiniest bit at the edges, the beginning of a smile.

"You don't say."

"How was the mall?"

"Fascinating." Okay, I can do this. I can . . . talk. "I hung out with Cooper and Katie, and then I got a Coke in the food court. Where, apparently, you should never go on a Saturday morning, because it was overrun with middle school kids. They were all pretending to vape with Dragon's Breath."

Ardy's dark brown eyes blink. "With *what*?"

"It's a kind of candy. When you chew it, it looks like you're breathing smoke." Now Ardy is looking at me like I'm crazy. "I'm serious, it's a thing."

"Oh, I believe you. It's just not something either of us was doing in middle school."

"Hey, we hadn't met in middle school. For all you know, I was a daily Dragon's Breath breather."

"That would surprise me." Ardy cocks his head, sizing me up. "Too weird for you."

There's something in the way he says it that is almost offensive. It takes me a second to figure out why—it's because of the way he says *weird*. Almost like what he really means is *interesting*. Before I can respond, though, Hope Burkett appears by his side.

Of course she does.

"Good morning," she chirps, because Hope Burkett is the type of person who chirps. She's also the type of person who everyone—like, *everyone*—adores. She's beloved to a degree that I find bewildering . . . and kind of annoying. I'm sure people would give lip service to the love being about her general niceness, but it can't hurt that she's also extraordinarily pretty and stylish. She has a thick fringe of dark chestnut bangs sweeping above an angel's face, and, in a nod to her Chinese ancestry, she always wears a gold necklace of Han characters that I think spell her name.

Ardy gives Hope the same nod he gave me, which makes me feel better. Maybe it's his morning nod.

Hope beams at me. "Think we'll get our papers back?"

Right. All three of us are in English class together, under the not-so-watchful eyes of Ms. Shelton, who is notoriously late in the grading department. "There's a first for everything, right?" I say. My response inexplicably makes Hope laugh, and her laughter is clear and perfect, like a bell ringing in crisp winter air.

The Worst.

"See you guys later," I say, and make my escape.

I don't know where Hope's *actual* boyfriend, Evan McConnell, is, but clearly she's more interested in hanging out with Ardy than with him. Even though Hope and Evan are such the high school supercouple that they have a ship name. Which is—wait for it—Heaven.

Like I said—*the Worst.*

Everyone knows that Ardy and Hope are friends. Good friends. Possibly best friends. But they're together all the time, which I have to assume means they're *fake* friends. The kind of friendship where one person is genuinely interested in the relationship as it's presented to the world, but the other one is faking it because he or she is *actually* in love with the other. In this particular case, I have to assume that the one who's faking it is Ardy. Hope has a significant other, so if she was truly in love with Ardy, she could dump Evan and go for it. But she didn't . . . and she doesn't . . . so I assume she has no interest.

It definitely puts an extra wrinkle in the plan to get Ardy interested in me. And no matter how absurd the plan is, now that we've come up with it, I'm determined to make it happen. After all, Ardy might not be like the boys I usually date, but . . . I don't know how to say this . . . there was something about the way he almost smiled at me. That tiny tension around the corners of his mouth did something to me. To my insides. It's like I got tense, too.

But in a good way.

A way that's unfamiliar.

New.

What am I going to do with this?

» » « «

Cooper and Katie swoop up to me before lunch—mine, because they both have second lunch—and each grabs an elbow. They pull me to the edge of the crowded corridor. "We need to get some things straight," Katie says.

"*She* does," Cooper says. "Straight is not my forte, Sugar Blossom."

"Cute," I say. "And what are you talking about?"

"The game," Katie says.

"The *lifestyle*," Cooper says.

"*Shhh!*" I say to them both.

"We were discussing the rules in Trig," Cooper says.

"Please tell me you were quiet," I implore him.

"The soul of discretion," he promises. "We agreed that if you start dating"—Cooper stops, looks around, and then lowers his voice to a stage whisper—"*him . . .*"

"Oh God, just tell her," Katie says. "If he breaks up with you legitimately, it's a wash."

"But no lying," Cooper continues. "No faking your way out of it."

"Yeah," says Katie. "No impromptu strange hobbies."

"Or abrupt strict curfews," Cooper adds.

"Or like that time you pretended to join a cult to get Wade Collins to cut you loose," Katie says.

I heave a dramatic sigh. "Those are my signature moves."

"We know," Cooper says. "But the point is for you not to use them. Also, we couldn't remember—what's the longest you've dated anyone?"

"We're using the word *date* loosely," Katie clarifies. "From the first kiss to the last, how long?"

I already know the answer is five weeks, and that was only because Deondray Enos had the flu for the middle week but I pretend to think about it for a moment. Then, because I want to seem less pathetic than I actually am, I stretch it out. "About a month and a half," I tell them.

They exchange glances. "Perfect," says Cooper.

"Three months," says Katie. "We think you need to hang in there with—"

"Please don't say his name," I hiss.

"Fine," she says. "With You-Know-Who for twice as long as you've ever hung in there before. Can you do it?"

Honestly, I don't know if I can get Ardy to even look at me in the first place. The length of time I'm going to date him may very well not be the issue. "Sure," I tell them. "But I have another question. What about you guys? What are *you* going to do? Or am I the only one with any sort of flaw here?"

Katie looks at Cooper. "I did get a promise out of that one," she says. "As long as you're with He-Who-Shall-Not-Be-Named, Cooper will not get all married-like with Ian."

That's at least a bonus. Generally speaking, Cooper is my exact opposite. He is a serial monogamist who jumps in with both feet and falls in love superhard. His heart gets broken all the time, and I can't count the number of times I've listened to his tales of romantic woe. This could be a good thing for him.

If it works, I guess it could be a good thing for both of us.

"What about you?" I ask Katie.

"Please." She gives me a wide smile. "I'm flawless."

» » « «

I leave the line with my tray and glance around the buzzing cafeteria. I know this moment is stressful for some people, but my stress is reserved for other areas of my life. The nice thing about being me is that I'm welcome anywhere: the gamer table, the cheerleader hangout on the bleachers, the outdoor hallway where the band kids sit in the shade. I'm not a threat to anyone. Everyone is friendly and reasonably happy to see me.

What's less nice is . . . it's not like anyone's *asking*. I'm alone in a crowd. No one hails me over. No one misses me if I don't show up. No one *expects* me. My two best friends are the only ones who really know me, and they're in second lunch period.

Which is why it's shocking when someone *does* wave to me, and that someone is Hope. At first I pretend not to see her, but then I realize she's sitting at a table with Ardy. I walk over.

"How'd you do?" she asks, scooting her chair to the side and patting a spot beside her at the table.

"Fine." I sit, mustering up an awkward smile for Ardy, who looks like he's trying to do the same for me. "Garden burgers, hard to screw up."

"You'd be surprised," Ardy says, pointing to the half-eaten garden burger on his own tray. "I think one of the main ingredients is glue."

Hope shakes her head. "I meant the calc test."

"A-minus," I tell her.

"B-plus," she says, nudging her water bottle against mine in a toast. For some reason, her grade annoys me. It's like Hope is *so* perfect that her imperfections only add to the overall picture. It would be annoying if she got all A's all the time, but instead she gets the occasional B just to make her even more perfect.

If that makes any sense at all.

I take a big bite of my burger so I can get this lunch over with. Sadly, Ardy is right about the recipe. I look at him, and he immediately wrinkles his nose. It makes me realize I'm doing the same thing in reaction to my glue-burger. It also makes me smile. Which makes him smile.

"What?" says Hope.

I don't know why Ardy doesn't answer, but I don't because I seem to have lost control of my face. My smile is too wide to allow me to make words, and suddenly I'm worried I might have food in my teeth. I grab a napkin and wipe my mouth, abruptly rising to my feet. "I just remembered I have to make up a test," I say from behind the napkin.

Hope gives me a quizzical look, and I glance at Ardy. He swipes another napkin and holds it to his face. "Okay," he says from behind it.

I want to laugh, but I'm too busy fleeing.

» » « «

After the final bell rings, I'm heading out to find Leo when I run into Dax Santos in the stairwell. He stops on the landing, catching my arm. "Hey, Lark, are we good?"

I blink at him for a moment because the fact that he ended our non-relationship had already escaped my mind. I quickly adopt a look of nostalgia and nod regretfully.

"Cool." He leans over and gives me a quick peck on the head. "It was fun, huh?"

"While it lasted," I say with as much sorrow as I can muster. Dax nods, giving me a final smile before leaving, and I continue on my way, hiding my own smile about how easy it had been. All I had to do was tell beef-loving Dax that I was going vegan, and he was out.

I head to where Leo and I always meet, which happens to be where everyone else meets, too: the flagpoles in front of the school. There are two—the American flag and the school flag.

The school one is turquoise with a big bright yellow sun in the middle. Those are the colors of REACH: yellow for sunshine and turquoise for the ocean. So California.

It takes me a minute to find Leo in the crowd, but I do. Right after I grab him, Hope grabs me. "Hey," she says, sounding flustered. "Lark, you're perfect."

"Thank you?"

"No, I mean—are you leaving? In your car?"

It's a weird question, but . . . "Yes. What's up?"

"I carpooled with Ardy," she tells me. "But I remembered I have a French meeting that's going to last awhile. I don't want to make him wait for me. Do you think you could drop him off?"

It's like the fates are conspiring against my composure. Sure, I agreed to this thing with Cooper and Katie, but it's supposed to be on *my* terms.

"That's fine," I say just as Ardy arrives with his leather satchel slung across his body. He looks from me to Leo to Hope.

"Lark's offered to take you home," Hope says as an explanation. "I've got *le français.*"

Which, for some reason, makes Ardy's eyebrows dart together. "You don't have to do that," he tells me.

"I don't mind." It's true. Unless Ardy hates the idea of being with me, in which case I mind *a lot.*

"I can wait." Ardy looks super awkward. "Or get a ride with someone else."

He does mind. Fantastic.

"She's right here," Hope says. "She's going now. And I'm late."

She scurries off, leaving us standing there with Leo. "I'm parked on Oak," I say.

"Cool," says Ardy.

"Come on," I tell them both.

» » « «

Leo grumbles about being relegated to the back so that Ardy can sit up front in my car, but I tell him that seniority wins out. Leo says that *family* should win out, and Ardy says he doesn't mind sitting in the back, but the hell if I'm going to have Ardy behind me, staring at my ponytail. This is already weird enough. Besides, I think Ardy would have a tough time folding his long legs into the tiny backseat.

As we pull away from the curb, Ardy motions to the left. "That way, like you're going to Magnolia."

Leo's hand snakes up to tap Ardy on the shoulder. "Is Ardy a family name?" he asks. "I've never heard it before."

"It's short for Gerard," Ardy answers him. "It started when I was little and it kind of . . . stuck."

He seems embarrassed by the explanation, but I can't help thinking it's cute. "Leo used to call me La-La," I say, hoping it will make Ardy feel more comfortable.

"That was dumb," Leo says from the backseat.

"Shut up," I tell him.

"Hope is the one who started calling me Ardy," Ardy says, and just like that, it's awkward again. I don't say anything, and the moment stretches until Ardy feels like he *has* to say something else, I guess. "We were little."

"Cool." My single syllable is an obvious lie.

Ardy's house is two miles from school. Two miles in which no one says much of anything. I'm hyperaware of Ardy sitting on the other side of the emergency brake, his long pale fingers resting against his dark jeans. I imagine how those fingers would feel sliding between mine, and then I quickly pull back from the thought. Nothing about this game is set in stone.

Yet.

His neighborhood isn't far from mine, and yet I've never been to it before. It's only a couple of blocks off Magnolia Boulevard, but it feels like a state away. The houses are cute and well kept, and as we drive, I count four people walking dogs and three pushing babies in strollers. Several of the houses are flying high school flags from their porches. "Your hood is adorable," I tell Ardy. "You moved here last year, right?"

"No, I was born here," he says. "Last year is just when I transferred to REACH—turn left." I do as he says, and then take one more left to land on Ardy's street. He points. "I'm past the one with the red door. That's Hope's house."

Of course it is.

But out loud, all I say is "Oh, you're actual neighbors. Like, side-by-side neighbors."

"Yeah, she and her dads moved in when we were toddlers."

So to be clear: Ardy is basically mute for the whole drive, and then when he talks, it's about Hope. Fantastic.

I pull to the curb in front of his house, and Ardy opens his door. "Thanks for the ride," he says, before swinging out of the car.

"No problem." I wait for him to pull the seat forward so Leo can dislodge himself from the back and reclaim the front.

Then all hell breaks loose.

From somewhere nearby, there's the sound of a screen door slamming, followed by a bunch of high-pitched squealing. Two dogs bolt across the lawn on the other side of Ardy's house and take off down the sidewalk. They're followed by a horde of shrieking kids.

"Dammit." Ardy sags for a moment before slinging his leather satchel onto the grass. "The Watson kids let the dogs out again." And he takes off after the horde. I crane my neck to watch him loping away. He spins around—catching me watching him—and yells back to me, "Thanks again!"

"Come on," I start to tell Leo . . . but he's busy grabbing Ardy's satchel and throwing it back into the car, onto the passenger seat.

"We should help," he says, before barreling down the street after Ardy and the kids and the dogs.

I'm a few minutes behind because I have to close the windows and turn off my car and lock it, but eventually I'm jogging down the sidewalk, too. It's not like I have something important to get to. Not to mention that it feels like a very strange, obvious metaphor for the new game in my life: me chasing after Ardy while he—totally oblivious—chases after something else.

» » « «

Later, after a very exciting sprint through the neighborhood, the Watson kids and the Watson dogs are all safely ensconced in their home and I'm sitting across from Leo at Ardy's family's retro table. The top is made out of white Formica, and the chairs are sky-blue vinyl with chrome legs. The furniture is only made more adorable by the fact that the rest of the kitchen also looks like it belongs in a 1950s soda shop: black-and-white-checkered floor, white-painted cabinets with blue interiors, sunshine-yellow tea towels. If my house were this cute and calm and peaceful, I would never want to leave it.

Ardy sets three cans of carbonated lemonade on the table and sits down with us. "Thanks for helping."

"Are your parents going to come home and be weirded out by us being here?" I ask him.

"No." Ardy gives me a strange look. "Why would parents be weirded out?"

Oh, right. It's *my* parents who are like that.

"Well, they don't know us or anything."

"It's fine." Ardy shrugs. "And I only have one parent. My mom."

"What happened to your dad?" Leo asks the question and then visibly flinches when I kick him under the table.

"It's okay," Ardy says. "He died when I was little."

"Sucks," says Leo as he rises to his feet. "Where's your bathroom?"

Ardy jerks a thumb to the hallway behind him. "Second door on the right."

"Sorry about him," I say once Leo is gone.

"It really is okay," says Ardy. "I was little. I don't remember him. I don't know much except that he rode a motorcycle, and I only know that because that's why he's dead." He takes a sip of his lemonade, and I do the same. "You know what ER docs call motorcyclists?"

I shake my head, not sure how to contribute to this conversation.

"Eyeball donors," Ardy says. "When they die in accidents, their bodies are so destroyed that their organs can't be donated. The only parts that can be used for other people are their eyeballs, because they're protected in the helmets. That's all that's left."

"So did he?" The question pops out before I can stop it, and once it's out there, I have to keep going. "Your mom, I mean. Did she donate his eyeballs?"

Ardy looks thoughtful. "I don't actually know that. I'll have to ask her."

I'm relieved when Leo comes back into the room. Even though he's as annoying as every other little brother in the world, I like having him here as a buffer. As it is now, we're three people hanging out. If it were only Ardy and me, the mood would be more charged. At least, it would be for me. Who knows about Ardy. He's unreadable, which I guess is partially why I've always found him intriguing.

"Where's your mom, then?" Leo asks as he drops into his seat, like the conversation never stopped.

"On set," Ardy answers. "She works in production."

"Oh." Leo and I grew up in Los Angeles; we understand about television jobs. "So you basically live alone during the week?"

"Basically," Ardy says.

Being in production means you work around the clock—unless you're between jobs or on hiatus. Ardy's mom probably leaves at sunrise and comes home at midnight. It's why we natives don't think Hollywood is as glamorous as the rest of the world does.

"Well, I like your neighborhood," Leo says. "You hang out with the people who live on both sides of you."

"And the ones across the street," says Ardy. "And behind us, and three doors down. We know everyone. I can't get away with anything."

We don't know any of our neighbors, so I can't imagine that sense of community. "Was it always like that?" I ask.

"Yeah, it's basically a street full of hippies," Ardy says. "All the parents had a babysitting co-op when we were kids. They would trade us back and forth like we were books at a library. We had playdates all the time. It was only when I got older that I realized that part of the reason I got to play with my friends so much was that our parents were all drinking wine together."

"It sounds like your parents were the ones having the play-dates."

"Exactly." It seems like fun, having a family that socializes with the world around them. I realize I'm jealous of Ardy's childhood. "Some of the kids moved away because their parents wanted bigger houses, but I'm an only child, and so is Hope—we didn't need more room."

Right. Hope. Ardy can't get through a conversation without mentioning her.

I don't say that out loud. Obviously.

CHAPTER FOUR

Leo is relegated to the backseat again so that I can bring Cooper home with us after school the next day. I'm planning to drop Leo at the house so Cooper and I can go hang, but my mom is out front when we arrive. Aunt Beth—who must have driven up from Venice for the day—is there, too, helping Mom pull weeds from the front flower bed. They wave when we arrive, which means we all have to get out of the car and greet them.

"It's fine," Cooper tells me. "I have to pee, anyway."

"You're taller," Aunt Beth says to Leo after hugging him. "You're going to catch up with your sister."

"Dare to dream," says Leo, and heads into the house.

"We're going to run in, too," I tell Mom. "And then we're going out."

I start to follow Cooper inside when Mom calls me back. "Lark, remember—" I return to her side, and she drops her voice. "Not in your bedroom."

"He's *gay*," I remind her.

"Beth was straight in high school," Mom tells me. "People can switch sides."

I cringe at her cluelessness as, behind her, Beth makes a face. "Different story," she says.

"I know," I tell her, before returning my attention to my mother. "By that logic I can't have *anyone* in my room, boys or girls."

"Everyone is a threat," Aunt Beth says dramatically, which makes me laugh.

My mother—predictably—does not laugh.

Twenty minutes later Cooper and I have wended our way along the road between golf courses in Griffith Park to a field scattered with picnic tables. We're sitting on one, our feet on the bench, two smoothies between us. "Spill," he says. "How's it going with Ardy?"

I take a sip of my citrus mango smoothie, trying to figure out how to explain the situation. "I don't think he's into me."

"Dude." Cooper gives me a gentle elbow to the ribs. "He doesn't know you yet."

"I don't know if he wants to." It hurts to say it, more than I thought it would. "I can't tell if he's only being nice because Hope is suddenly acting like my friend."

"But what about hashtag Heaven?" It's his favorite way of mentioning Hope and Evan. "He obviously knows they're together."

"Yeah, but if Ardy's all star-crossed about her, maybe he doesn't care. Maybe he figures it's high school and nothing lasts, so Heaven will crumble at some point. Maybe he thinks he'll be there to pick up the pieces."

"God, I wish I had that kind of optimism," Cooper says.

"Me too." I'm quiet while Cooper drains his strawberry smoothie and picks up mine. "Unless he's gay," I say. "What if Ardy is Hope's Cooper?"

"I don't think so," Cooper says. "I've never gotten that vibe from him, have you?"

"No. But, seriously—what do I know? I'm not getting any vibe from him at all."

"Well, just because I'm gay doesn't mean I'm the arbiter of everything gay everywhere. You know—"

"There's no such thing as gaydar." I say it with him as a reflex, and we both laugh. "I did try," I continue. "I thought I was obvious, but maybe I wasn't."

"Is he playing hard to get?"

"But why would he?" I'm frustrated by my inability to understand what's going on with Ardy. Usually boys are so *easy*. Cooper's right—reeling Ardy in wasn't supposed to be the challenging part of the puzzle. "I've never seen him with a girl-friend, have you? Do you think he's dating someone from his last school?"

Cooper pulls his leg up, crooking his knee onto the table between us so he's facing me. He reaches for my hands to still them from their tapping against the table edge. "I have a fascinating proposal."

"Bring it."

"It's an innovative approach. Do you think you can deal with that?"

"Yes." I'll try anything right about now.

"Okay—buckle up, because this is going to blow you away."

"I think I can handle it."

Cooper peers into my eyes. "Instead of worrying about if Ardy likes you, maybe take a second and figure out if *you* really like *him*."

I pull my hands away, placing them behind me and leaning back so I can look out over the grass. Why *am* I attracted to Ardy? I knew he was new this year. Our school isn't small, by any stretch of the imagination, but you're still vaguely aware of who's there, who's missing, who's arrived. You know when an unfamiliar face appears in the midst of it all. . . .

Especially if that someone is tall and lanky with dark brown eyes. Especially if you're at your locker and they're moving easily between the clumps of people in the hallway, walking right past you without the slightest notice. And if they're wearing a ragged screen-printed T-shirt under an open plaid button-up. And especially if their hair has some sort of product in it that makes it stand up messy in front.

Okay, let's be honest here: I knew the second Ardy arrived at REACH. I didn't do anything about it because he didn't give me the slightest indication that he would welcome any interest from me. I like boys who I can flirt into submission. Boys who aren't a risk.

So, yes, I noticed all the cuteness when Ardy transferred here, including the first day we actually spoke to each other. It was in English. Ms. Shelton had stepped out of the room, which meant everyone was talking or messing around on their phones. I was busy texting Rahim when I noticed the smell of blueberries. I ignored it until then I caught a whiff of grape—the chemical version. Like grape gum or those stickers the teachers used to give us in kindergarten. No one to the right or the left of me was doing anything suspicious, so I turned around, sniffing the air. Ardy, sitting behind me, raised his hand to show me what was in it: a purple marker. "Someone left a box of them on my desk," he said.

He uncapped the green one and waved it toward me. Its scent was unmistakable. "Apple."

"Fake apple," he clarified, and then touched the tip of the marker to his index finger, drawing a bright green line down to his palm.

"If you keep doing that, your hand is going to smell like a fake fruit salad," I told him.

"There are worse things." He pointed the marker toward my fingers. "Do you want a fake fruit salad hand, too?"

I shook my head, and then—I don't know why I did this—I reached into my hair and separated out a long strand. I twisted it a little and wiggled it toward him. "I don't mind fruit salad hair, though."

Ardy first looked startled, then pleased. He took the lock and, holding it in his fingers, drew the marker down the length of it. The color barely showed up faint green on my brown hair, but it was there. "Cool," he said. "I'm Ardy."

"I'm Lark."

"I know," he said.

We exchanged smiles, but then Ms. Shelton returned, so I faced the front of the classroom again. Still, as our teacher started to talk about *The Handmaid's Tale,* I shook my hair out in the most nonchalant manner I could muster.

Nothing happened.

So I leaned back farther and ran my hands through my hair, purposefully allowing the ends to trail onto Ardy's desk. There was a pause, and then I was rewarded by the slightest tug from behind. Also the faint scent of bananas.

Or, rather, fake bananas.

Later, in a hidden corner of the teachers' parking lot, Rahim noticed my markered hair. I told him it was an art project, and then we went back to what we were doing.

And although I still can't explain it, there was something I liked about all those little pastel tendrils.

"What are you thinking?" Cooper asks, and I realize I'm holding one of the empty smoothie cups and my right thumb has dug a hole through its top edge.

I pull my hand away and lick mango syrup off it.

"I think I'm kind of weird," I say.

"We all are." He doesn't sound flippant. "The key is finding someone whose weirdness matches your own, right?"

I scoot closer and lean my head against his shoulder. "*We* match," I tell him.

"Yeah." He leans his head against mine. It's nice because he's warm, and it's starting to get a little chilly. I mean, it's Southern California, so it's not *that* chilly, but we're spoiled here. The minute the sun ducks behind a cloud, everyone's all like, *Where's a sweater?*

"Why do you like Ian?" I ask him from my comfortable position. To be honest, I can't quite imagine it. Ian is so . . . boring. At least in comparison to Cooper, who is funny and loud and unabashed, which is why I hate to see him dimming his light for someone who doesn't deserve it, who doesn't deserve *him*.

"You know I met him at work," says Cooper.

Cooper works at the downtown Burbank movie theater. Not only does that afford him ample opportunity to meet people, but it also means that when Ian first laid eyes on him, he would have been wearing something similar to what Ian wears in regular life: a crisp white shirt under a red vest.

It's *so* dorky.

"He came in alone," says Cooper. "I don't know anyone else who goes to the movies alone."

Like a loser.

Cooper notices my expression. "Like a baller," he continues. "Ian walked right up and asked for my favorite combo on the hundred-flavor soda machine. I said something gross, just to mess with him. Like Pibb Zero–Vanilla Coke–Iced Tea or something. After his movie, he walked out—"

"Alone." I can't help myself.

"Right." Cooper ignores my subtext. "He asked if he could have a refund because his drink was so bad . . . or could I give him my phone number instead."

I nod. I've heard this story before. Besides, Ian's still a loser who goes to movies alone. I don't say it, but it's like Cooper reads my mind.

"Solo movies are actually great," he says. "You can be in the world on the screen. You can lose yourself." He takes my hand again and gives it a gentle squeeze. "You might give it a try sometime."

But why would I, since I have friends who will go with me?

» » « «

By the next morning I have decided that Cooper is right, that I need to figure out if I actually like Ardy. Which, I guess, means getting to know him.

This is new for me.

Usually I blow right past the getting-to-know-you phase and move straight into the making-out phase. Admittedly, it might be a flawed system. Once you've catapulted over that first piece of the relationship road map, you don't throw your car into reverse to check out the place you skipped. And that place is the scary place. It's where someone could notice that my house is a festival of fury and I'm so much weirder and messier than the self I present to the world.

So how does this work?

Ardy and I only have English together, and the teacher gave us a new seating chart. Now Ardy and Hope sit on the opposite side of the room, so it's not easy to make conversation there. I can always try lunchtime, but of course that comes with Hope as an audience member. Maybe I can catch Ardy after school, but I have to drive Leo home.

So, with very few options, I rely on my old standby: the white lie.

I take Leo home and run inside to spruce up. I swipe an extra layer of mascara around my light brown eyes—almost the exact same color as my more-tangled-than-curly hair—and add a dusting of peach to my cheekbones. I try on a tank top before going with a navy blue V-neck T-shirt. I'm about to leave when I rethink my needs and add an extra swipe of deodorant under each arm.

The neighborhood is quiet as I pull up in front of Ardy's house. Half a block down, a young father chases his toddler up and down the sidewalk, but there are no hordes of screaming kids or barking dogs.

I sit in the car for an extra half minute, trying to calm my nerves. I check my teeth in the mirror, slick on some pink lip gloss, and chew a mint before getting out and heading for Ardy's porch. I'm about to knock on the door when a ninja opens it.

I step backward, startled, and the ninja gazes at me. She has Ardy's pale skin—because, of course, this is Ardy's mom—and a sleek inky ponytail. She's wearing an army-green canvas vest over a tight black shirt and black jeans, with combat boots on her feet and a square leather messenger bag slung diagonally over her body. Ardy's ninja mom cocks her head. "Can I help you?"

"Um, hi. I'm Lark. I know Ardy from . . ." *The game. My daydreams.* "School."

"Lark?" She juts a hand at me, and I accept it gingerly, feeling like she could kill me with her pinkie if she wanted to. "Ellen."

She gives my hand a firm squeeze before letting go and stepping back to gesture me inside. "Ardy?" she calls into the depths of the house.

Ardy appears almost immediately. He looks back and forth between us, surprised, his eyebrows floating above the frames of his glasses. Before I can say anything, his mom—I mean, *Ellen*—smiles at him. "I have that location scout. I'll pick up dinner on the way home." She nods at me. "Nice to meet you." And then she's gone.

I turn back to Ardy, not sure how to proceed. I'm shocked that his mom left us here alone, but also shocked that I'm here in the first place. Finally I just blurt out the lie. "I think I left a hoodie here. Light blue. Have you seen it?"

"No." He stays very still for a moment, like he's not sure what to do with me. I don't say anything else, because I certainly don't know what to do with him, either. Especially when all he's giving me is a single syllable and a long, inscrutable dark brown stare. I'm about to garble out some version of *thank you* and leave, but he motions me farther inside. "We can look for it. To make sure."

Thus, I'm in Ardy Tate's house under utterly false pretenses, and I'm making a show of looking around for a nonexistent piece of outerwear. Not in the kitchen . . . not in the living room . . . did I take it into the bathroom? Nope, not there, either . . .

Finally we're back in the dining area, where we started. I'm standing by the chair nearest to the door, and he's on the other side of the retro table. I shrug. "I guess I must have left it somewhere else."

"Maybe it's in your car?" he says.

"I'll look," I say, though it's ridiculous to think that I wouldn't have looked there before driving over here. "I should go. Homework."

But Ardy doesn't move toward the door. Instead, he sets his hands on the back of a chair, leaning his tall frame over it. "Do you have a lot? Of homework, I mean?"

He's making conversation. That's nice. "No. Not that I have to turn in. But I have to study for a test tomorrow. Calculus."

I almost don't say it, because so few kids at REACH take calculus. There are two classes, both honors, and there are only a dozen students in each. Mentioning that I'm one of them always makes me feel like I'm either bragging or flying a nerd flag. But Ardy doesn't look surprised, like so many others do. The look he gives me is more like respect. At least I think so. It's hard to read his expressions. "Fifth period's got the same test," he says. "Do you want to study together?"

Huh. So Ardy's in the other calc class. That's interesting.

I nod, and by the time five minutes have passed, we're sitting across from each other at the table, our textbooks and papers spread out in front of us. Studying.

Or at least pretending to.

And by that I mean *I'm* pretending to.

Twenty minutes later we're in the exact same position. The only sounds have been paper rustling, bodies shifting, and the occasional throat clearing. Also, eight minutes ago, I broke a pencil lead and had to get a new one. It's been a whirlwind of activity. I'm not learning anything about Ardy, and the silence is making me nervous. This is new to me. I'm not usually silent with boys unless it's because we're busy kissing.

I don't notice that I'm Being Weird until he points it out. "What's that?"

"What?" And then I see where he's gesturing—my left hand—and realize I'm tapping my fingers against the surface of the table. Deliberately, in a pattern. "Sorry." Heat rises to my cheeks as I quiet my fingers. "I'll stop."

"You don't have to." He's looking at me, curious. "But what were you doing?"

I pause, staring at him. Not sure how to explain, or if I should. He tilts his head, waiting for an answer, and because I don't have another white lie on deck, I shrug. "It's this thing I do."

Despite my best efforts not to let it happen, my face flushes again. Even though Ardy's not looking at me like I'm a weirdo. He merely looks interested. "Oh yeah?"

Since I'm already admitting it, I continue. "Yeah, it's my pattern." I guess this is a trial run at letting him get to know me. "I've been doing it since I was a kid."

"The exact same pattern?" he asks, watching my fingers. Which, now that we're talking about it, are going again.

I force them to stop.

"I think it's from growing up with a sibling," I say. "We were always so obsessed with fairness. If Leo got a cookie, I got a cookie. If I got to pick a show to watch, he got to pick one. It was a thing."

"I can see that." Ardy has folded his arms and is resting his elbows on the table, hunching over it so he can look at me. Intense.

"It kind of bled over into life," I tell him. "That sense of justice. Of needing things to be fair. If I stepped over a sidewalk crack with my left foot, then I had to step over the next one with my right foot. To be fair."

"To be fair . . . to your *foot*."

I raise my chin. "It's not perfect logic."

Ardy smiles at that. It's a wider smile than I usually see on him. "I bet it made for some funny-looking walking."

"Probably." I smile in return. "At some point the fairness

thing changed, and it wasn't enough to be equitable only as far as *portions* went. I needed to be equal in chronology, too."

"Okay, now you've lost me."

"I'll demonstrate." I raise my left hand and waggle my fingers, then tap my hand against the table. Here we go.

"I get it." Ardy gestures to my right hand. "Now you have to do the same thing with your other one."

"Yeah." I tap with my right hand. "But now that was a pattern. One-two, left-right. Which you would think makes everything equal, right?"

A faint crease appears between Ardy's eyebrows, like he's trying to figure it out. Like he's trying to figure *me* out.

"So now in order to be equal—in order to be *fair*—I have to do that same pattern, but back in the other direction." I do it. Right, left. "Two-one."

"O-kay," says Ardy, and I know I'm losing him. That he thinks I'm totally weird, with a head full of strange things, *boring* things.

Except he's smiling again. Like he's in on a joke.

"What?" I ask.

"You did one-two, two-one, but now *that* was a pattern," he says. "And you started on the *one*."

"Exactly!" It bursts out in something akin to a shout, and Ardy jerks back in his seat because it's so abrupt and so loud. "Sorry," I say, embarrassed by my display.

But he's still smiling. And now bigger than before.

"I understand the dilemma," he says. "Now you have to do all *that* over. The whole thing, but start on the other side."

"Two-one, one-two," I tell him. "And then—"

"Hold on." He raises a hand, and I fall silent, watching him work it out in his head. "Then you have to go two-one, one-two, one-two, two-one. Right?"

"Be careful," I tell him. "You're catching on really fast. You might start doing it, too." My smile won't stop spreading across my face. There's something about telling Ardy this little piece of myself that feels *good*. If this is what it's like when people are honest, maybe honesty isn't the scariest thing after all. "It keeps going forever," I tell him. "Into infinity. Or at least until I lose my place in the pattern. Because no matter what I do—"

"The *one* always went first," he says.

"You get it!" I beam at him, forgetting for a moment that Hope is the one who beams.

"I get it," Ardy says, and then keeps looking at me. Smiling in a way that doesn't allow me to stop smiling. Smiling in a way that—out of nowhere—makes me want to reach over and press my fingertips to his mouth. To feel his smile for myself.

But, of course, I don't. Because that would be weird.

And because we're just studying calculus, right?

CHAPTER FIVE

The calculus test is hard. Really freaking hard. I'm still finishing the last problem when the bell rings, which is why—by the time I've dropped the test on Ms. Perkins's desk and packed up my stuff—I don't have a lot of time to get to World History. And *that* means when I rush out of the room and find Ardy lounging against the wall, arms folded, waiting for me, I definitely shouldn't stop to talk to him.

And yet I do.

"How bad is it?" He grins at me, and it might be the first time I've seen Ardy *grin*. I've seen him smile before, but this is lighter. More casual. More . . . *familiar.*

"I'm not at liberty to say," I tell him, because Ms. Perkins gave us very explicit instructions not to tell the fifth-period class what's on the test.

"I know you can't give details," Ardy says. "But what am I looking at here? Like, on a scale from *no bigs* to *drop out of school*?"

"Hmm." I pretend to consider the question. "I'd say somewhere between *ugh* and *sucks to be you.*"

Ardy also pretends to consider. "So . . . a seven, then?"

"Maybe an eight."

I realize I've stepped closer to him. Like I belong there, like it's easy, like I've already reeled him in.

Is it possible Ardy's the one who's doing the reeling?

» » « «

I grab a chicken wrap in the cafeteria before hightailing it to the school library. I don't even have to smuggle my food in, because Will Hartsook is on duty at the front desk, presumably for extra credit. Will—who once gave me a hickey in the sports equipment room—sees my lunch but waves me in anyway. I find an empty aisle in the history section and drop my jacket to the floor so I can sink onto it and eat in peace. Although a big part of me wants to go back to the cafeteria and sit with Ardy, I can't. He's making me feel flustered, and it's all new and unfamiliar and—truthfully—*scary*. I need a minute to figure it out, to get back in control. Here in the library it's peaceful. No boys, no drama, no one to bother me.

Until close to the end of my lunch period, that is.

My chicken wrap is nothing but a ball of aluminum foil and scraps of shredded arugula when I unfold myself to rise from my little self-made nest. I wend my way back through the aisles, taking my time, breathing in the scent of paper, old and new. I've gone all the way through literature and am in the fine-arts area when I hear my name. It's Hope's voice.

"Lark! *There* you are."

Hope is dressed in a white peasant blouse, faded jeans, and bright green peep-toe sandals with cork wedges. She's standing at the end of the aisle, her hand on her hip. She looks exasperated.

"I've been looking for you *all lunch period,*" Hope says. "Who eats *here?*"

"It's quiet," I tell her. "No one bothers me."

We both choose to ignore the irony of that last statement.

"Ardy says you're a calculus rock star," Hope informs me.

I don't know about that, because—truthfully—Ardy kinda killed it during our study time yesterday. He understood everything. If anyone is the calculus rock star, it's him.

Besides, Hope and I both know this is really her move to open a conversation. It's a way to slide in, to get information. Obviously, after I left yesterday, Ardy ran right over to Hope and told her everything about our afternoon.

Because he tells her everything.

Because to him she *is* everything.

It's the most important thing I need to remember.

"Do you want to hang out this weekend?" Hope asks in what, to me, is a shocking turn of events. Cooper and Katie ask me to hang out, but that's it. Other people smile at me in the hallways and make casual conversation when I end up at their lunch table, but they don't reach out. They don't make plans. They don't want to *know* me. Everyone's aware that I have Cooper, Katie, and the boy of the week. There's no room for more.

"I could use a manicure," Hope continues, fluttering perfect fingernails in my direction. "Or we could see a movie. What do you think?"

"Okay . . ." The word trails out of my mouth, like it's not sure where to land. Because I'm not sure where we are landing right now. Or what the playing field is made out of. Or what the rules are.

"Ooh, I know!" she says in a chipper voice. "We could get a group together and hang out on Friday night."

"A group?"

"Ask Cooper and Katie," she says. "I'll bring Evan and maybe one or two of his friends."

It's all very casual and surprising, which makes me wonder what's really going on. Surely it's no coincidence that Ardy's Hope is suddenly asking to hang out right as I'm trying to get to know Ardy. Does she actually want a friend, or is she trying to suss me out for Ardy, or is she trying to throw another guy in front of me?

What's her endgame?

» » « «

At first Cooper was like *hell no* when I begged him to come. "It's hashtag *Heaven*," I reminded him.

He glared at me. "Only if I can bring Ian."

I said no, but Cooper wouldn't budge, so I finally allowed it. Of course, when I mentioned that to Katie, she was not having it. "I'm out." She shook her head. "No way am I fifth wheel on your Night of Weird."

"*I'm* the fifth wheel," I reminded her. "You'd be the sixth. We'd be like little training wheels joined together."

"Nope." She tossed her hair. "I'm going to the theater party with Neeley Washington, anyway. You could blow off your stupid thing and come with us."

"I already said yes," I told her, which is why I'm at a random diner by the mall on Friday night. And as it turns out, I'm not the fifth wheel at all. Or if I am, the training wheel I'm joined with is . . . Ardy Tate.

So maybe Hope is on my side after all.

The six of us are squished into one booth, and somehow, even though this whole thing started because Hope wanted to hang out with me, I'm not sitting next to her. Instead, I'm making an Evan sandwich with Hope as the other slice of bread. Ardy's across from me, with Cooper next to him, and then Ian is on Cooper's other side. We've been here twenty minutes and already we've heard about Ian's little sister, who is in kindergarten and apparently hilarious, as well as Ian's childhood interest in dinosaurs. The story included a fascinating account of the fossilized *Diplodocus* dung he once received as a birthday present. It basically destroys everyone at the table, and I join along with the laughter because I don't want to seem like an asshat, but . . . *really?*

"You know what's the best thing about that story?" Cooper asks.

That it's over?

"That everyone else would think that's a terrible childhood memory, but to you"—Cooper grins at Ian—"it's like your glory days."

Ian nods. "True."

"Worst childhood memory," Hope says, leaning over Evan so she can poke me. "Go."

"What?" Hope couldn't possibly know it, but this is an

impossible question for me to answer. I'd rather go back to talking about dinosaur poo.

But, of course, I don't say that. I merely cock my head and look up at the ceiling tiles of the diner. Like I'm thinking really hard. "Give me a second." It means I don't have to meet Cooper's gaze, because I'm aware that he knows the real answer to the question. When you have parents who take every opportunity to throw verbal weaponry at each other, it's impossible to find the safe places between the fights. So you stop pretending they're there. And you start pretending about other things instead. "There was that time Elijah Ridley saw my panties on the jungle gym in second grade," I say.

There's a round of boos. Evan sticks his finger in his glass and flicks a drop of water at me. "Weak," he says. "We'll come back to you."

A temporary reprieve. I'll take it.

"I've got one," he says. "When I was nine, I walked in on my parents having sex."

I groan, Hope squeals, Ardy laughs, and Ian basically doesn't change expression. Cooper makes a face like a cartoon detective and leans across the table toward Evan. "What position?"

"Gross!" Hope flicks a piece of ice at him (a gesture she and Evan have in common). "Nobody wants to know that!"

Ardy nods, agreeing with her. "Parental sex was not mentioned in the invitation," he tells Evan.

Ah. That makes sense, then. Evan's the one who invited Ardy, which must mean he's onto Ardy and Hope. He's thrown by them, he's worried about their "friendship." Which means he'd *love* to get me together with Ardy because it would rip Ardy away from Evan's girlfriend. Hope's boyfriend is smart.

And, however screwed up it is, our interests align.

Our server shuffles over with a tray of milk shakes and fries and—kill me now—a salad for Hope. He wobbles away, and as Hope steals a couple of fries from Evan (thank goodness for that!), I look at Cooper. I happen to know that he has the world's best/worst/most hilarious childhood memory. It's about when he was in kindergarten and he had this horrible habit of licking things—water fountains, stair railings, and once the hinges on a public bathroom door. It caused his parents all kinds of angst and embarrassment until, thanks to a pushy friend, they had him tested by a doctor. It turned out he had a mineral deficiency. They started giving him supplements, and *voilà!* No more licking. At which point in the story, Cooper would normally give a sly look and say, "Until now . . ."

But he's not telling the story, and I know it's because it's way too interesting and *flamboyant* for stupid Ian to handle.

Ugh.

On the other side of Evan, Hope lets her fork clatter to her ceramic plate. "I French-kissed my dad once," she says casually.

Evan does a spit-take, Cooper squeals, and even Ian reacts by clapping his hands over his face. Ardy looks at me. *Wait for it,* he mouths across the table.

"We can never be intimate again," Evan proclaims.

"No, listen." Hope grins, giggling a little. "It was in ninth grade—"

"Oh God, that's worse!" Cooper says.

"Than what?" asks Evan. "What is that worse than?"

"Shh!" Hope taps his arm. "Let me preface by saying this: historically speaking, we are a lip-kissing family." She looks around the table. "Anyone else?"

Evan raises his hand. So does Ian. Ardy and Cooper and I do not.

"See, totally normal," Hope says. "Except this time, Dad and I were on the porch—"

"Wait, which Dad?" Evan asks.

"Daddly," she tells him.

"What?" I say.

"I call them both Dad," Hope explains. "But when I'm trying to differentiate, the one named Christopher is Daddipher and the one named Bradley is Daddly."

"That's so cute, it's painful," I tell her.

"I know, right?" Hope shines her high-wattage smile at me. "Anyway, I was waiting for carpool and I was trying to tell him something and he was trying to tell me something else and we were both talking over each other. The lady driving carpool pulled up in front of the house and honked her horn. I was trying to finish my sentence and Dad was trying to finish his sentence, too. I grabbed my backpack, turned to kiss him good-bye, and . . . we were both still talking. And our tongues were out."

We all erupt in "No!" and "Gross!" except for Ardy, who shakes his head, smiling. I zero in on him. "You've heard this story before?"

"A couple of times," he admits.

The admission drains the laughter out of me because of *course* Ardy has heard it before.

Ugh.

"Poor Daddly was appalled," Hope says. "He was way more embarrassed than I was. All the lip-kissing stopped after that."

"Good, it's not hygienic," Cooper says. "And family members should be kissed on cheeks only. The mouth should be reserved strictly for romance."

"Like this," Evan says, pulling Hope in for a kiss. I forget to check for Ardy's reaction because I'm busy watching Ian. Who, if I'm reading the situation correctly, is barely—just barely—leaning toward Cooper, grazing my friend's shoulder with his own. I watch Cooper's cheeks turn rosy red, and I know I'm not imagining it. Which makes me feel *slightly* better about Ian.

"Your turn," Evan says to Ardy, now that everyone's stopped whooping it up over Hope's comic genius, because of course, on top of everything else, the girl has a knack for storytelling! "Worst childhood memory."

"My dad died," Ardy says. "That sucked."

His words elicit shocked silence from four people at the table, and an audible squawk of laughter from one person: me. Which I immediately choke back when I realize I'm laughing into the void. Ardy is staring at me. No, I take that back. *Everyone* is staring at me.

Which is *awful.*

I'm mortified, I'm a terrible person, I'm the worst of everything in the world. I'm laughing at Ardy's father's *death.* Even Cooper looks reproachful.

Except then I realize that tiny lines have appeared at the outer corners of Ardy's eyes. His mouth is tensed, like he's trying to control himself . . .

. . . and he bursts out laughing, which only sets me off again. I wad up my napkin and throw it across the table at him. "Jackass!"

He ducks, still grinning, as the others try to catch up. Ian looks from Ardy to me. "Wait, your father *didn't* die?"

Ardy shakes his head. "Nope, he did."

"He super did," I say at the same time.

Which makes Ardy and me laugh all over again.

» » « «

Later we've meandered up Delaware Road and are headed down Third Street toward the recreation center. We've naturally split into pairs to accommodate the narrowness of the sidewalk, so I'm walking with Ardy. The other four are ahead of us, both couples seemingly engaged in sparkling dialogue, but Ardy and I are quiet. Usually I don't have a problem making conversation with boys. Usually I *excel* at it. But with Ardy I'm oddly shy, maybe because I feel more like myself. Like who I really am, way down deep. The girl who someday could have the courage to use her voice to express real opinions.

That's the girl I hope to be, who I *could* be someday. Ardy makes me want to be that girl right now.

I just don't know how.

Or why.

He nudges me as we walk along. "Hey, I forgot to ask—how'd you do on the calculus test?"

Finally. A topic.

"A-minus," I tell him. "How about you?"

"A-minus."

"Really?" Because I'm going to take that as the universe telling me that we're perfect for each other.

"No."

Stupid universe.

Ardy flashes me a sideways smile that is so distractingly cute it makes me want to hug him. "B-plus. But a really high B-plus."

"So, practically an A-minus?"

"Practically."

It's midautumn, so the days are still long. There's a little pink left in the sky when we reach the grassy edge of the rec center property and cut up the paved walkway winding through it. Crossing over the pavers by the phallic war memorial (sorry, but it is), we head toward the center of the park. The sky is darkening, but the streetlights are bright enough to shine our way to the playground.

I'm standing on the concrete at the edge of the sand, trying to decide if I want to take my shoes off, when hands descend on my shoulders. For the slightest second, I think it's Ardy—that he's weirdly choosing this moment to make a move—but then, from the corner of my eye, I see delicate fingertips. I smell orange blossom shampoo, and I know it's Hope. I spin to see her smiling up at me. "You're it," she says.

I blink at her. "What?"

"You're *it*." And then she's off and running. "Tag!" she yells back at me.

I turn to look at Cooper so I can roll my eyes because what

are we, *children,* except he's gone, too. All five of them have scattered over the sand like marbles dropped on a table. Even Ian is running, tripping and slipping his way in and out of the shadows.

And if Ian can play tag, then—for the love of all that is holy—I can play, too.

I kick off my Vans and charge into the fray. Ardy and Evan are climbing to the top of a pile of fake rocks, Hope appears to be trying to hide behind a small yellow spring rider shaped like a duck, and the last thing I want to do is catch Ian, so I sprint toward Cooper. He's attempting to scramble up one of the hard plastic slides when I reach him. He *should* abandon his plan and vault over the edge to relative safety, but he doesn't. Which means it's easy for me to leap up and tap him on the ankle. "Coop's it!" I yell to everyone else, before taking off across the sand.

The game goes like that for a while. Cooper tags Hope. Hope tags Ardy, who tags Ian. Ian tags Cooper. From where I'm standing, it looks like Coop threw the game to give Ian a break—or maybe for an excuse to get Ian's hands on him—but whatever. Cooper then darts after Evan, who immediately bolts off the sand and into the park. "Cheating!" Cooper yells, but no one pays attention. To be fair, it's not like we ever established boundaries.

Evan's move is a game changer, and now everyone's following his lead. I vault over the sidewalk and onto the park grass, remembering far too late that I'm barefoot. Hopefully, I won't step in something gross.

Speaking of gross, I myself have become somewhat gross.

I'm sweating and breathing hard as I circle a bank of tangled Brickell bushes, slowing to a walk to give myself a chance to recover from the exertion. I slide the ever-present elastic band off my wrist and reach up to wind my hair into a messy bun. I have no idea where the others are as I round a corner on the path, dart into the shadow of a tree, and slam straight into someone.

I jerk backward, opening my mouth to scream, when slender fingers catch around my arms and—"Whoa"—Ardy's voice floats, soft and soothing, from the darkness above.

The normal thing to do would be to step back, to push away, to return to the game . . . but I don't do any of that. Instead, I freeze.

Ardy's hands loosen on my arms as he gently turns me to face away from him. Behind me, his head dips down until it's hovering next to mine. We're looking in the same direction, and even though we're not touching, I can feel the warmth of his skin. "There," he whispers. I follow the stretch of his arm, pointing into the murkiness . . . to Evan.

Evan, who obviously didn't dress for a night game, is wearing a bright white soccer jersey, which makes him visible as he tiptoes down a path on the other side of the Brickell bushes. He's looking for either a person to tag or a place to hide. Neither of which I'm interested in providing him. "We should have designated a safe zone," I whisper back to Ardy. "Like a home base."

"We didn't exactly put a lot of forethought and planning into the finer points of the game." His mouth is very, very close to my ear, and I resist the sudden urge to rise up on my toes so I'll be in contact with him. He's not holding on to my arms anymore, but I wish he were. I wish we were touching somewhere, anywhere. I'm hyperaware of his body, behind me and so close to my own. And of the starlight. And the leaves rustling above us. Everything is suddenly romantic. Everything is suddenly charged.

It's not just a game.

Any of it: this game of tag or the one that Cooper and Katie made up.

I might like this boy.

I might *actually* like him.

Crap.

» » « «

We're walking back to the diner parking lot when Evan offers up a new game. "That man in the guidance office who always wears a bowtie, the guy who mops the gymnasium floor, and Kelli from the football team."

Yes, we have a girl on our football team. And, yes, she is awesome.

"I'll guess B," says Cooper. "People you secretly want to snuggle."

Hope and Ardy laugh, but the softness of Cooper's joke bothers me. If Ian hadn't been here, there's no way the final word of the sentence would have been *snuggle*.

"What are you talking about?" Ian asks Evan.

"Screw, Marry, Kill," Hope answers for him. "It's a game. And I'm not playing."

"Why not?" Evan drapes an arm over her shoulders. "It's fun. Don't you want to know more about our new friends?"

"I don't think finding out who they would hypothetically bone counts as 'knowing more.'" Ardy's tone is mild, but he's trying to back Hope up.

"I'll play," I tell Evan, because I have no interest in backing up Hope. "Plus, this one is obvious. I'll definitely marry the gym floor guy."

"Oh, because he'll keep the house clean," Ardy says.

"Exactly." See, Ardy gets me. "Kelli for the sex."

"Intriguing," Evan says.

"Not really." I shrug, since it's all hypothetical, anyway. "Bowtie Man counseled me into taking advanced biology, so I kind of already wanted to kill him."

"Okay, I get the rules," Ian says.

Yeah, because this is neurosurgery.

"You're a team player," Evan tells me. "Unlike my girl-friend."

"Fine, I'll play," Hope says. "But only the PG version."

Evan groans, and Cooper joins him but then stops abruptly midgroan. Because—of course—Ian.

"Why?" asks Evan.

Hope adopts a prim expression and voice. "Because my boyfriend is here."

"Your *boyfriend* is the one who came up with the game," Evan reminds her.

"Kiss, Date . . . Punch in the Face," she says. "That's my final offer."

"I'm in," Ardy says, because of course he *has* to agree with Hope.

Still, I sort of want to hear his answers, so I nod. "Me too."

"But *why?*" Evan asks Hope.

"Because if I name someone who I would have sex with, then that's what you're going to be thinking about that person next week at school."

"I'll still be thinking it even if you only want to make out with them," he says.

"Not the same," she tells him, and then pulls his head down to hers for a kiss.

The way she does it—so casual, so easy—and the way he goes along with it . . . in that moment, I get them. I understand why they're together. This freedom they have, this joking thing. Evan acknowledging—albeit in his slightly dickish Evan way—that he has a stab of jealousy about his girlfriend. I've never gotten to that part with a guy: the vulnerable part, the freedom part. Now, looking at these two—at #Heaven—I wonder if it could be this easy for me if I was with the right person.

Along those lines, another thought: If Ardy and I had a ship name, what would it be? #Lardy? #Ark?

Uh . . . no.

We play Kiss, Date, Punch all the way back to the diner, branching out to include celebrities and, sometimes, weird made-up categories: a person who only speaks sentences in reverse, a person who subsists wholly on dried seaweed, a person who never wears shoes. We learn that Ardy likes anyone who plays guitar (not great news for me) and that Cooper is willing to punch people who vape. Hope surprises everyone by expressing great interest in a make-out session with the French teacher ("because afterward he might talk with that cute accent"). Evan and Ian give only predictable answers.

When we reach the parking lot of the diner, Evan gives a generic wave. "See you on Monday." He nods toward Hope and Ardy, who are standing together. "Let's go."

Hope beams at me. "I'm glad you guys came. This was fun."

"Agreed," Cooper says as Ian nods.

I know I need to respond to Hope, but instead I'm looking at Ardy. It's impossible not to when he's looking right at me. Finally I manage a smile for both of them. "Bye."

We split apart, Evan and Hope and Ardy piling into Evan's car while Cooper and Ian get into Cooper's. I slide into my own, and as I pull out, I look in my rearview mirror. I can see Evan's car, still parked behind me, and Ardy in the backseat. He's staring out the window at me, watching me go. It's hard to tell if he can see me in the mirror, but it seems like our gazes lock. I raise my right hand and flutter my fingers. If you're Ardy, it could look like I'm waving to everyone in general, but I know it's just for him.

And right before I swing out into traffic, he raises a hand in return.

» » « «

I've traded jokes with Leo and endured the maternal gauntlet of "what did you do, where did you go," and now I'm in my bed, huddled under my comforter, with my phone propped on my pillow so I can play games before falling asleep. I'm in the middle of a word battle with a stranger when a text notification pops up on my screen. I slide to look at it . . . and it's two words, from an unknown number:

Not punch.

I send back a symbol—?—and receive a few more words:

I wouldn't punch you.

Warmth blazes up inside me, and I type back a quick response:

I assume you wouldn't punch anyone.

The return message comes fast:

You assume correctly.

And is followed up with a second:

Punching is rude.

I type the question, even though I already know the answer:

Who is this?

The letters come one at a time, spelling it out vertically on my screen:

A
R
D
Y

I stare at his name. Up and down, to be visually interesting. Obviously, I already assumed Ardy didn't have a hidden desire to punch me, but texting me like this clearly lets me know that what he *does* want is one of the two other options: date or kiss.

Why not both?

I take a screenshot and then open the photo in an app so I can use my finger to scribble words next to his name. I save the picture and send it back to him:

A
Really
Decent
guY

I get an immediate LOL in return.

I respond with: Thanks for not punching me.

He says: It's the least I could do.

I don't respond, because I want to know what he could do, what he will do. This feels like flirting, *actual* flirting, and I want to know if he's going to make a move. If he's going to do something real.

I realize I want him to. I'm *aching* for him to do something real.

I need something real.

Three dots appear, flickering at the bottom of my screen. He's writing something. I wait, and a moment later the words appear—one at a time, like how he spelled out his name before:

Lively
Astute
Refreshing
Kind

I'm smiling so hard, my face hurts. Ardy's sent my name, typed out in adjectives. Really sweet adjectives. I don't know how to respond, so I send back one word:

Thanks.

He replies:

See you Monday.

Our exchange is over, so I turn off my phone and snuggle down onto my pillow. I think I'm still smiling when I finally fall asleep.

CHAPTER SIX

Ardy isn't in the hall when I go to my locker on Monday morning. He's not in the cafeteria when I pick up a barbecue chicken salad. Hope's there, but she's huddled at a two-person table with Evan, so we merely exchange waves and smiles. Instead, I eat with the cheerleaders. After school I linger at the flagpoles, but I never see Ardy. I consider texting him but can't quite muster up the nerve. What would I say?

Wheelz is always dead on Monday nights, so we all know Mom is expecting Dad to make it home for dinner. I have the six o'clock shift, which isn't taxing. I help some parents fill out their kids' waiver forms, I make change for a dude who wants to get arcade tokens but "not, like, twenty dollars' worth," and I sell a couple of bottles of soda. Dad is conducting assistant manager interviews in his office, so other than directing Tall Goatee Dude and then Blue-Haired Ponytail Girl to the back, I'm left largely to my own devices. Which is a very typical Monday. Nothing out of the norm.

Until half an hour before closing, when Ardy walks in.

He lets the door close behind him and stands there a

moment, across the lobby from me, getting the lay of the land. I watch his gaze rove over the karts whizzing around the electric track, the arcade bay, the Skee-Ball prize counter . . . and come to rest on me. Where I'm standing. Watching him.

For a split second, I feel caught. But then I realize—Ardy is here to see me. It's the only thing that makes sense.

Except it doesn't make sense.

Or does it?

I raise my hand in a feeble wave, and he lopes toward me, running a hand through his hair. My own hand rises to my head as I suddenly remember that I've piled my hair into a giant messy bun thing. Even though we do have teen clientele, I don't think of work as a place I'll see kids from school.

Ardy arrives at the counter and offers me a half smile. "Hey."

"Hey." I half smile in return. At least, I think I do. My face feels a little frozen. So do my reaction times and my instincts. I'm not sure how to handle this boy.

This might not be a boy who can be *handled*.

"I've never been in here," Ardy says, which confirms—in case there was any doubt—that he's here for me. "It's huge."

If Cooper were here, he'd respond with the old reliable *That's what he said.* But he's not, so I only muster a weak smile and an even weaker "Yeah."

"I saw Leo this morning," Ardy tells me. "He said you were working tonight."

Privately, I decide to bring Leo home a treat from the snack counter as a reward. But to Ardy I say, "Do you want to drive a go-kart?"

"No." He cocks his head, considering. "Maybe. I've never done it. Do you offer driving lessons?"

Before I can answer, Dad and Blue-Haired Ponytail Girl come out of the back. She looks eager—excited, even—as she and my dad shake hands. "Thank you so much, Mr. Dayton."

"You're welcome," he says. "We'll make a decision by the end of the week."

She beams and then leaves, her blue ponytail swishing behind her. My dad turns to the two of us and shakes his head. "Train wreck," he whispers.

"Really?" It surprises me. She looked put together. "She seemed nice."

"She had two misspellings on her résumé," Dad says. "And a grammatical error."

How well does an assistant manager at a go-kart facility need to spell, anyway? But to Dad I say, "Okay." Then I gesture to Ardy. "Dad, this is Ardy. Ardy, my dad."

Dad engulfs Ardy's hand with a giant paw. "Larry Dayton."

Yes, my father's name is Larry. And Mom is Lisa. They named their children Lark and Leo. We're *that* family. At least that's how it looks from the outside.

"Your friend's here," Dad says to me. "You can go if you want."

"No, I'll stay." I avoid Ardy's eyes. "You said you had to finish those orders." If I leave, my father will stay out front behind the counter. Which means he won't finish the orders. Which means he won't be home until late. Which means Mom will lose her mind and I will lose sleep. So I'll stay. It'll make everything easier.

"I'll go," Ardy says. "I was just saying hi." He turns to leave, and I realize it must seem like I'm blowing him off.

"Wait," I call. He turns back, and we look at each other for an awkward moment because I don't actually know what I was going to say. The moment is interrupted by Dad.

"I'll be in the back," he says, and disappears. Leaving me, the sounds of karts skidding into walls, and Ardy.

Ardy cocks his head, regarding me from behind his dark-rimmed glasses. "Is it weird that I'm here?"

Okay, so that's blatant.

"Um, no," I tell him. "Unless . . . I mean, why *are* you here?"

Ardy sets his hands on the counter. "Do you want to go on an adventure?"

"Now?"

"No." He smiles, and his smile is absurdly warm and inviting. He's here *for me*. Ardy Tate is here *for me*. "Saturday."

"What kind of an adventure?"

"Hmm." He looks like he's considering. "I don't think I'm going to tell you."

"Why?"

"Because I don't want you to say no."

"Is it a *bad* adventure?" I suddenly realize I'm doing that wide-smiling thing again, where my face is starting to hurt. "Might we *die*?"

"Probably not." Ardy says it with a straight face, but his lips twitch like he's holding back laughter. "No one has died with me yet."

"Oh." It a little bit kills the mood for me. "How many people have you taken on this adventure?"

Ardy's mouth settles, becomes serious again. He leans over the counter toward me. For the tiniest second, I think he's about to kiss me and I'm about to let him. But instead he gazes at me with those dark brown eyes. He drops his voice and says, "You'll be the first."

My mood is immediately resurrected. "Sold," I tell him. "What time?"

"Morning. For the whole day."

"But you're not going to tell me what it is?"

"Still no."

"I need a hint." Because—come on—a girl needs to know what to wear. "Does it involve hard physical labor?"

"No." He grins at me. "It does, however, involve other sentient beings, possibly getting your shoes muddy, and a two-hour drive."

Okay, everything about that is intriguing, but especially the two-hour drive. Where is he taking me?

"One last question," I tell him, because if Hope is all up in this, I might scream. "Is anyone else coming?"

"Nope." He straightens, reaches across the counter, and brushes his hand against my left arm. It's a fast, gentle caress. "See you at school."

I nod and swallow, watching him turn and lope back toward the door, his messenger bag swaying at his side. My right hand floats up to my arm, to the spot where he touched me.

I'm sure it's my imagination, but it feels warm.

"The San Diego Zoo," Cooper guesses from my left as he, Katie, and I sit on the top row of the bleachers, watching the junior varsity soccer team run practice drills on the field below.

"I thought about that." I take a bite out of the coconut milk Popsicle we're all sharing and pass it to him. "He did say there are other sentient beings involved. But isn't San Diego more than two hours away?"

"Maybe." Cooper licks the Popsicle thoughtfully. "Santa Barbara? There's a zoo there."

"I have no reason to believe it's a zoo," I tell him. "Humans are sentient beings, too, you know."

"He's going to take you out to the desert to kill you so he can bury you in the sand," Katie says, reaching over me for the Popsicle. "Stop hogging."

"That's why I'm telling you, so if I go missing, you'll know what to tell the police."

Katie turns to stare at me with wide violet eyes. "Seriously?"

"No, dummy." I whap her in the arm. "But guess what?" I look back and forth between them. "I like him." I wait for a response, like I've dropped the world's greatest bomb. There is none, so I try again. "You guys, I *actually* like him."

The smile Cooper gives me is a tolerant one. "You always like them in the beginning."

"Yeah, no one's buying it," Katie says.

"This one's different," I protest.

"Prove it," Cooper says.

"How?"

"You know how." He makes a swipe over me for the Popsicle, but Katie holds it out of his reach.

"Reel him in," she says. "Wait three months, break his heart."

"I want him to give a crap about her," Cooper tells Katie.

"Whatever," she says.

"He might," I tell them both.

"I hope he does." Cooper gives me a patient look. "But I want you to give a crap about him, too."

"That's the part I don't get," Katie says. "There's a buffet bar of boys out there, and you make a beeline for the one who's Undateable?"

"Don't listen to Katie," Cooper tells me. "She doesn't like it when we're happy."

"I don't like it when you're a freak," Katie tells him. "Which in your case is every day."

"Back to me," I tell them. "I think I do like Ardy. I *might*." The logic of the bet is unspooling in my head. "And if I like him, and if he likes me . . . I mean, if we give a *crap* about each other"—I emphasize the word to sound like Cooper—"if that happens, there's no way for me to win the game. Because we won't want to break up."

"Wouldn't that be so nice?" Cooper says, making another swipe for the Popsicle. This time when Katie jerks it back, the last piece of frozen coconut milk falls off the stick and lands on my lap. "Well, damn."

"Well, damn."

Hope knows. Whatever Ardy's taking me to do on Saturday, Hope knows what it is. Maybe it shouldn't irk me, but it does. Especially when, at lunch on Thursday, she pulls me off to the side so she can whisper in my ear: "Bring an extra sweatshirt."

"What?"

"On Saturday," Hope says. "Make sure you have enough layers to stay warm."

I stare at her, wondering if Ardy's lied before we've even gotten started. "He's taken you to . . . whatever it is?"

Hope shakes her head. "No."

Okay, I feel better about that. Until she continues—

"He tried once, but it's not my thing." She smiles at me. "I think you'll like it, though. Wear something warm."

And then she's gone. Leaving me with my questions, my insecurity, and my jealousy.

It's not a great combination.

CHAPTER SEVEN

As promised in his Friday-evening text, Ardy is at my house at eight o'clock sharp Saturday morning. My mother looks shocked when I come out to answer the door, fully showered and dressed. "Is it the apocalypse?" she asks me.

"No."

"Prom?"

"We don't have a prom." I open the door to let Ardy in, which somehow surprises my mother even though I had a conversation about it with her last night.

"Hi," Ardy says to both of us. His smile slips when he sees the deep look of suspicion on my mother's face. He holds out a hand to her. "I'm Ardy Tate."

"Ms. Dayton." She shakes his hand, letting go quickly. "I didn't realize you were planning on leaving this early, Lark."

"I told you last night," I remind her.

"I thought there would be more information first," she says. "Where are you going?"

It's exactly what I didn't want to happen: Mom questioning me in front of Ardy. "I'm not sure," I tell her. "I'll have my phone with me."

"And you'll be with a boy I literally just met." Mom folds her arms, looking stern.

I'm horrified and about to make a plea for freedom—or maybe fake a fainting fit—when Ardy takes a step forward. "Could I please talk to you in another room, ma'am?" Mom and I both stare at him. "I'm trying to surprise your daughter," he explains.

"Interesting," Mom says while I contemplate dying on the spot. "And just what is the nature of your relationship with my daughter?"

"Mom!" It bursts out of me as a deep blush rises to my cheeks.

But Ardy doesn't miss a beat. "We're friends," he tells my mom, which makes my heart sink and my mother's face tighten in disbelief. Except then he continues. "However, if today goes well and she doesn't hate it, and if she turns out to really be as cool as I think she is, I might try to kiss her."

My mouth drops open. So does my mother's.

"But not until the very end of the day," Ardy goes on. "Maybe on the front porch. With the light on."

I can't move, I'm so . . . I don't know what. Shocked? Astounded?

Terrified?

Mom doesn't look any less startled than I feel. We all stand there for a long moment before she gestures toward the kitchen. "After you," she tells Ardy. He nods and heads in the direction she indicates. Before marching after him, Mom shoots me a look that I think I can safely interpret as *WTF?*

Since I have no idea what one is supposed to do while one's potential love interest is confiding in one's mother, I sink to the living room couch and shoot a group text to Cooper and Katie:

You will NOT believe what is happening up in here.

It's a full minute before anyone responds. Then it's Cooper:

Is it sleep? Because that's what's happening HERE.

Dude. Come *on*. I text back:

COOPER. It's about Ardy.

But apparently his beauty rest is more important because all I get from him is:

ZZZZZZZZZZ!

Katie doesn't reply at all. I'm about to text something rude when Mom returns, with Ardy trailing behind her. I shoot to my feet, expecting the worst, but she doesn't look mad. She nods at me. "Get a coat."

I look at Ardy, and my face flushes again. If he notices, he doesn't mention it. He only says, "She's right."

Without a word, I spin and head back to my room. But after a minute or two of ripping my closet apart, I can find nothing remotely resembling a reasonably warm piece of outerwear. I come back to the living room to find Ardy and my mom still standing there. God only knows what they're talking about, because what kind of conversation *can* someone have with the woman who birthed the person you've just announced you want to kiss.

Might want to kiss.

Which I'm trying not to think about right now because otherwise I will melt into a useless puddle right here in the living room.

"I can't find my coat," I tell my mom. "Do you know where it is?"

"Maybe the boxes above the garage?" she guesses.

"It's not going to be *that* cold," Ardy says. "A hoodie would be fine."

"You have that pink one," my mother contributes.

"It's dirty," I tell her.

"Another one, then," she says.

"I don't have another one," I say without thinking, and then suck in my breath because immediately—horrifyingly—I'm jolted by the memory of the lie I told Ardy when I went to his house that day: *I left my hoodie here. Light blue. Have you seen it?*

OhGodohGodohGod.

"I mean, I lost it," I say as fast as I can.

My mother snaps her fingers like she's remembering something. "We put the jackets in the TV room closet."

"Great," I say weakly, and make a move in that direction, but she holds up a hand to stop me.

"Let me. I think they're in the box behind the Christmas decorations."

She's gone before I can say anything else. I stand there like a statue, facing in the direction she's gone, because I can't bear to look at Ardy. I'm so mortified by everything that's been said in this room today.

As a reminder, this day is only, like, an hour old.

Beside me, Ardy clears his throat. "Lark."

"Ardy." I still can't bring myself to turn toward him.

"We can talk about it in the car," he says.

"I might be too busy dying of embarrassment in the car." It elicits a burst of laughter from Ardy, which—somehow—makes me feel better. This time I turn toward him, and even though my cheeks continue to burn, I raise my eyes to his. "Do you want to cancel?" I ask.

Ardy is gazing down at me, a half smile playing across his face. I'm not totally sure, but I think his cheeks might be a little flushed, too. "Definitely not."

We're still looking at each other when Mom returns with one of Leo's ratty sweatshirts, a pink beanie, ski gloves, and a huge purple scarf that my grandmother knit. "I couldn't find the jackets," she says.

"This is fine." I grab everything and escape with Ardy.

» » « «

As is apparently our tradition in cars, no one says anything for the first twenty minutes while Ardy pilots us through Burbank and onto the highway heading south. I search my mind for acceptable topics of conversation and finally land on something that seems safe. "I thought you didn't have a car."

"I share this one with my mom," he says. "It was hers first, lest you think I chose to drive a minivan."

Okay, that's fair.

"What did you say to my mom?" I ask. "To get her to let me go, I mean?"

"Not much. She called my mother."

"What?!" That's horrifying. "She made you give her your mom's number?"

"I offered it to her," Ardy says. "She also took a picture of my driver's license."

I guess I'm going to have a daylong blushing session. Awesome.

"That's the worst thing I've ever heard," I tell Ardy.

"Nah." He seems nonplussed. "She's just looking out for you." He waits another couple of minutes before asking, "Anything else you want to talk about?"

Here goes nothing.

I shift in my seat, turning to face him, folding my left leg beneath me so my knee is crooked up on the center console, very close to Ardy's body. He glances at me, then—as he should—returns his eyes to the road. "Yes?"

"I can't believe you said that to my mom."

"Which part?" I know he knows exactly which part I'm talking about, but I suspect he wants to torture me and make me say it out loud, too.

"The kissing part."

"I know, right?" He shakes his head. "Who does that? It was weird."

"I guess it wasn't any weirder than Hoodie-gate."

"Hoodie-gate." Ardy grins. "I like that." Another glance in my direction, then he takes his right hand off the wheel for a second so he can tap me on the knee. "I already knew about the hoodie. I knew when you showed up at my door that day."

"Really?" I stare at him. "How?"

"Careful. We might venture into weird territory again."

"I can take it," I tell him.

"Okay." He pauses and I see him swallow. "Dark jeans with the bottoms rolled up."

"Huh?" I'm not following.

"Some kind of sandals with a heel. White shirt with buttons. Dangly earrings."

Ah. Now I understand. "Fringe drops," I tell him.

"What?"

"The earrings. Cooper gave them to me last year on the first night of Hanukkah. They're called fringe drops." Although before this moment I didn't remember what I had been wearing on the day when Leo and I drove him home, apparently Ardy did.

"Yeah, that. It's what you were wearing when I met Hope at the flagpoles that day." He glances at me again. "It's a cute outfit."

"Thank you." Because what else would I say?

"But it did not include a light blue hoodie."

All these blatant statements. I don't know what to do with them.

"No, it didn't." I wiggle in my seat, so uncomfortable with all this truth we're throwing around. But if Ardy can say things honestly—including to my *mom*—then I should make an attempt to be at least half as brave. "I needed an excuse," I say in a small voice.

"I figured that out." Ardy isn't smiling anymore, but somehow there's a smile in his voice. "But if you hadn't done that, if you'd knocked on my door and asked if I wanted to hang out . . . that would have been cool, too."

"Well, I know that *now*," I tell him.

This time the smile reaches his face. "Good."

There are a few more moments of silence, during which I weigh how to go about the rest of this day. It's like we've skipped over all the usual superficialities and gone straight into Real Talk. Which should be an improvement, except that it's also an unknown language. At least, to me. Ardy appears to be shockingly proficient in it.

He clears his throat. "Don't take this as anything more than a question of interest, but . . . what do you know about the prom?"

I'm not sure if I should be mildly offended by the way he qualifies it. We haven't even kissed yet. "Having a prom would be bending to societal norms," I tell him. "There will be no prom."

Which is true. We're the first senior class at REACH. The plan is to not have a "prom" the way other schools have them. We buck the system and all that.

"But there will be a party or something instead, right?" Ardy asks.

"The Not-Prom is called the Spring Fling Thing," I tell him. "It's sometime in February. You're not supposed to have a date for it. And it's going to be an overnight lock-in, with either roller-skating, bowling, or go-karting at Wheelz. I think we're going to vote on it next week. Because, you know, democracy."

"Which will you vote for?"

"I'm not sure." I don't tell him what's really going through my head: a pro for Wheelz is obviously more money coming in for our business. A con is that it'll mean a ton of extra work for Dad, which always leads to yet more fights on the home front. "I have concerns about the bowling alley smelling like feet."

"I have similar concerns about the roller-skating rink." Ardy considers. "If we're going to sleep on the floor somewhere, we should probably pick the place that is most olfactorily pleasant."

I have a sudden mental image of the two of us on the Wheelz party room floor, curled up together in a sleeping bag. I go warm everywhere, like I'm blushing on the *inside.* Not that any faculty member—even at our nontraditional school—would allow two students to cuddle up and sleep together, but *still.* The possibility exists. Of course, I don't say any of this. What I say is "Wheelz usually smells like buttered popcorn and burning brakes."

"Better than feet."

"Absolutely." I pick at the frayed hem of Leo's sweatshirt on my lap. "The teachers all talk about it like they're reinventing the wheel. Like, because we won't have corsages or a prom king and queen, it's something totally new and different."

"And *better*," Ardy agrees. "What I've noticed is that everyone is very smug about it." He puts on a terrible British accent. "Muffy, thank the Lord that we won't be putting on a *prom* like those common guttersnipes at the regular public school."

"Oh, heavens," I reply in my own horrible accent, the one that drives Cooper up the wall. "That would be simply awful . . . Aloysius."

Ardy raises an eyebrow. "Aloysius?"

I lean forward so I'm in his peripheral vision. "You said *Muffy*."

"Fair enough." Ardy laughs and switches back to his regular voice. "Trust me, the Not-Prom will end up being traditional. No matter what they do, it's still going to be the big event of our senior year. People will go together or in groups."

"There will be multiple conversations about what everyone will wear," I chime in. "And someone will get drunk enough to throw up."

"Exactly. Someone will get drunk enough to break up."

"Someone will lose their virginity. . . ." I trail off, suddenly appalled by what I've said. By the fact that the word *virginity* has come out of my mouth in the presence of Ardy. Because now the subject of sex has been broached. It was one thing when there was a group of us having a hypothetical conversation about killing or marrying (or punching or kissing), but this is entirely different. It's different because it's suddenly more personal. More present.

More *possible*.

I have to wonder—has Ardy had sex?

More importantly, if he posed the question to me—*Are you a virgin?*—how would I answer? The truth is that I don't really *have* an answer.

Sometime in the middle of junior year, I ended up fooling around with this guy named Elliot, who I met at the bookstore. He was in community college, and things moved fast. *Really* fast. Only a couple of weeks in, there was a moment when we almost did it. Like, *truly* almost did it. It wasn't even that I was so turned on in the moment, but three things combined in a perfect storm to make it almost happen: (1) Katie had recently lost her virginity and told me how it great it was and said she didn't know what I was waiting around for; (2) Elliot clearly wanted to—I mean, *really* wanted to; and (3) I was curious. Sex is supposed to be such a huge deal, and I wanted to know why.

But.

In that moment, when I was skin to sweaty skin with Elliot in the backseat of his car, none of that was *enough*. I wasn't ready.

I told Elliot that my period had started. For me, that excuse was way better than the truth: that although I had initially been on board, it was no longer the case. Looking back with a little distance, I should have been honest. There's nothing wrong with changing your mind at any point along the way.

Unfortunately, Elliot didn't agree. He was not thrilled about stopping. Not at all. Which clarified that I shouldn't have considered having sex with him in the first place. One thing I *do* know is this: if a guy tries to pressure you into doing it, get rid of him. Fast.

We broke up that night.

After Elliot, there was one other guy I came close to doing the Deed with. His name was Kai, and I met him in the frozen-yogurt place downtown. He was . . . there's no subtle way to say this . . .

So.

Freaking.

Hot.

It was at the beginning of last summer, right after Katie had sex for the second time, with Bo Garrison from the Catholic school. She would not shut up about how you need to figure it out in high school so you don't seem inexperienced when you get to college. Even Cooper started talking about doing it. It made me determined to get my virginity out of the way.

So Kai and I went out a few times. And by *went out,* I mean he met me at the field gate after football games and we found a place to park in his car. To be fair, we *did* go to see one movie, but even then we spent the whole time kissing in the back row. The last time we were together, however, was in his parents' basement. Things went in that direction—the *sex* direction—and this time I was determined to go through with it. I had two of Katie's condoms in my purse.

I. Was. Ready.

And I thought Kai was, too. I mean, he made it *seem* like he was. He *said* he was. But when it came down to Doing It, something didn't go quite right. We kind of started—at least I think we started, because by all definitions from middle school health class, the right things were beginning to move into the right places—but then he stopped and it was over. He seemed embarrassed, and I'm still not clear on what went wrong, but the whole thing was awkward and . . . to this day, I'm not sure whether I'm a virgin. The dictionary definition is a little blurry on this one.

We kind of stopped talking after that. It was a perfect mutual ghosting. Probably my easiest breakup ever.

"What?" Ardy says, which brings me back to *this* boy, to *this* car. I look at Ardy's profile—at the pale ski slope of his nose, the high expanse of his cheekbones, the brown swoop of his hair—and I come out with it: "You said you might want to kiss me."

"I did." Ardy nods, so matter-of-fact. "You'll have to decide if you want to kiss me, too."

"I . . . think I might want to." The honesty feels good. It feels *refreshing*.

"You don't know," Ardy says. "There's a whole day ahead of us. I could still scare you away."

"True," I return, and he laughs. Once again Ardy's laugh is so nice. Contagious. He lifts his right hand from the wheel and, without taking his eyes off the road, reaches over to where my hands are resting on my lap. His hand hovers above them and, after the tiniest hesitation, descends. He slides his fingers over mine.

"Maybe let's start here," he says. "Like this."

His fingers are warm and dry. They feel amazing. Maybe even perfect.

"Okay," I tell him.

"Cool," he says.

"Cool."

» » « «

We stop for food on the way—and then for gas, and then for
me to pee—which means we don't get to La Jolla until close
to noon. I, of course, am just excited to know the name of the
place where we're going.

La Jolla is on the Pacific coast, close to San Diego. For a
while on the drive, I thought maybe we *were* going to the zoo
after all, but then Ardy pulled off the highway and into a high-
end suburban neighborhood, so I knew that wasn't right.

My phone buzzes and I check it. A text from Cooper:

WHAT IS THE ADVENTURE?

I decide to ignore him. Not only because I don't know the
answer yet, but also because he blew me off earlier when I was
trying to tell him about the morning shenanigans. You can wait
for it, Cooper!

But still I tell Ardy: "Coop wants to know what the adventure is."

"You're about to find out." He turns onto a smaller road.
We wind past a sprawling resort, two gated communities, and a
public park until we find ourselves bumping over dirt. I know
we must be near the ocean, because sea air is coming through
the windows, but I don't know *how* close until we round a
bend. There it is, past a parking lot and beyond a grassy hill:
the Pacific Ocean.

We grind over the parking lot gravel and into a spot among the scattered pickup trucks and sedans and luxury vehicles. There doesn't seem to be any one specific type of person who does . . . whatever this adventure is.

Ardy gets out and swings around to my side of the minivan. At first I think he's going to open my door, which seems very adult and gentleman-like of him, but instead he slides open the side door behind me. I hop out, tying Leo's sweatshirt around my waist, and watch Ardy tug a cardboard box across the bench seat. "What's that?" I ask.

"Here." He rips a strip of packing tape off the box's seam and steps to the side. "Take a look."

I fold back the box flaps, revealing a dozen pairs of gloves. They're not like any gloves I've seen before. These are made from thick, stiff leather. The cuffs are long—they would reach halfway up my arms—and there's a metal ring on the inside wrist of each one. "Um, are we gardening? Trimming rosebushes?"

"Keep looking—there should be something else in there."

I dig beneath the gloves and find . . . well, I'm not sure what they are. There are six of them, each a narrow length of leather, maybe as long as one of my legs. They're like straps, except I don't know what they're for. At the end of each is a stainless steel shackle that is clearly meant to attach to something.

It's not a sex thing, is it?

The confusion must be evident on my face, because when I look back at Ardy, he's grinning. "It's not a sex thing," he says, and then laughs when I make a sighing noise of relief. "Come on."

He hefts the box into his arms, and I slam the scratched and dented minivan door. We trot across the gravel and to the top of a slope. Over the grass to our left are several small buildings, and way off to the right is the edge of a forest. Before us is the ocean—blue and choppy and going on forever. Above it is a throng of paragliders, their sails bright patches of color in the sunlight. I stare at them: humans floating high above dark water in a way their bodies were not born to move. It's beautiful and unnerving at the same time.

"Amazing." I say it under my breath, but not so quietly that Ardy can't hear me.

"Indeed." The timbre of his voice   serious, not laughing at all—makes me turn to him. He's facing me, with the box in his arms, not looking at the ocean at all.

Heat rises again. My heart swells, and I shine a smile right at Ardy. He blinks, and then he smiles back—sort of confused-looking. In that moment, I absolutely, 100 percent want to kiss him, no question about it. I can't wait for my porch.

But I'm going to have to.

I follow him to a patio near the buildings. Ardy *thunk*s the box onto one of the picnic tables. "I volunteer here." He looks mischievous, knowing he still hasn't given me an explanation. "The people who own it ordered these supplies from a store in the city, and I picked them up to save shipping charges." Ardy shoots me a grin. "Back in a minute."

What have I gotten myself into?

He disappears into a building, and a minute later he's back. A leather bag is slung diagonally across his body, and he's hold-ing . . . something. The something is square, and it looks heavy, because he's holding it with both hands, low and away from his body, like he doesn't want to bang it against his legs. His fingers are wrapped around the handle on top, and there's a leather covering over the entire item.

Is it a cage?

It might be a cage.

"Let's put an end to the suspense," Ardy says. I follow him back up the slope we came down, toward the place where it overlooks the ocean. "I guess I could wait for the great unveiling," he says. "But I'm going to cut to the chase. It's a bird of prey."

I don't know what I expected, but it definitely wasn't that. "Like an eagle?"

"It's called a Harris's hawk," Ardy says. "I'm in a falconry apprenticeship program."

He pauses, watching me. Waiting for my reaction. I'm confused, since as far as I'm concerned, he could have said he's learning to be a taxidermist or a lunar scientist or a trapeze artist, for all the understanding I have about what he's just said. "A *what?*"

"Falconry." His voice sounds very patient, like it isn't the first time he's had to explain this to someone. "This place teaches people about birds and the environment. I started off by taking lessons about how to fly the hawks."

Which begs the question . . .

"Am I about to get a lesson in falconry?"

Ardy lets one hand loose from the handle long enough to push his glasses up on his nose. "Unless you don't want one."

"I think I want one," I tell him. "At least, I don't *not* want one."

"As a warning, you'll have to touch something you've never touched before."

I mentally run through a list of things I've never touched—a Bentley, caviar, the moon—and end on something that I more and more *want* to touch: Ardy Tate's mouth.

"A dismembered quail foot," Ardy says.

WHAT.

But before I can respond, we've reached the crest of the slope and we're overlooking the rainbow cloud of paragliders. And three minutes after that, I'm wearing a pair of the new leather gloves, and Ardy is standing several yards away with a bird tied to his wrist.

The bird has red and brown feathers, a sharp yellow beak, and black beady eyes that, Ardy informs me, can see for miles. "See those paragliders? If this bird was where they are, and if you held up a book, he could read it."

"Are you telling me that bird can read?" I ask.

"I don't actually know," he says, and I laugh.

The bird's name is Torch. It's an incredibly cool name for an incredibly cool creature. In fact, everything here is so much cooler than I would ever aspire to be. Than I ever *could* be.

Over the next hour, Ardy teaches me how to convince Torch to fly to me. Ardy starts by holding his arm outstretched so that the bird can perch on it. From where I'm standing, Torch doesn't seem very happy about the situation. He keeps making a loud squawking sound. And his face—I mean, I don't know much about bird faces or what one looks like when they *are* happy, but I can safely say that Torch doesn't look happy at all. Torch looks *pissed*.

Ardy tells me to hold my leather-clad hand high in the air while I call for Torch. It takes me several tries to be loud enough and convincing enough, but eventually Torch leaps off Ardy's glove and sails across the distance between us. He glides low and slow over the grass, arcing up to land on my glove. Even though he's not very heavy—less than three pounds, Ardy says—I'm shaky with the responsibility of it.

Ardy and I fly Torch back and forth between us a bunch of times, and by the end of it, I feel like I'm sailing with him. When he dives off my hand, I can almost feel the air under my own wings. I hold my breath when he leaps, and suck in oxygen again when he lands.

It's exhilarating.

Then Ardy clips one of the leather straps to the tiny band around Torch's ankle. He reaches into the bag, taking out a quail foot. Yes, it's a dismembered body part from another bird. Ardy throws the foot to Torch. Torch sails after it, doing a midair flip along the way, and catches the foot before it hits the ground. He doesn't take time to savor the snack. He basically inhales it.

Ardy looks at me. "Do you want to try?"

I hesitate for a moment—because *quail foot!*—but then I nod. After all, when am I going to have this chance again?

I shove down the part of me thinking that if I play my cards right, if Ardy and I end up as a thing—a real thing—maybe I will have the chance again. Maybe I'll have many chances.

"Okay, hold it far away from your body," Ardy tells me. "Torch isn't big, but his claws can grip with two hundred pounds of pressure per square inch."

"So this bird could basically rip me to shreds?"

"That's a little overdramatic," Ardy says. "But definitely don't drop the quail foot on your *own* foot—"

"Because Torch would swoop down with his talons and beak and eff me up," I finish for him.

"Again—not to be overdramatic . . ." Yet he grins at me.

Ardy and I fly Torch back and forth for almost an hour, until Ardy says Torch is probably tired. Ardy carries Torch over so I can look him in the eye. "It was nice to meet you." Torch averts his eyes and makes a disgusted sound. "I don't think he likes me," I tell Ardy as he tucks the bird back into his covered cage.

"It's not that," he assures me. "Training the hawks takes a lot of time. You have to establish the relationship."

Which, obviously, is not something I'm awesome at.

"They don't trust easily." Ardy straightens up from the cage. "It's not in their nature."

The way he's looking at me, it's like he's giving me a message. Is Ardy like that, too? Or does he think I am?

Ardy takes Torch back into the building, and then we return to the crest of the hill to watch the paragliders. The air smells salty and clean, but it's cold as it ruffles through our hair and presses our clothing against us. I wrap my arms around myself, trying to ward off the chill, when suddenly I'm enveloped by warmth. Ardy has stepped behind me and opened his jacket, wrapping it around me as far as it will go. Pulling me into his body, protecting me from the wind. "Is this okay?"

"Yes." It comes out in a whisper.

He rests his chin on the top of my head, and I lean back the tiniest bit. Pushing my shoulders into his chest and settling in, breathing the clean-laundry scent of him. His arms tighten around me, and we stand there, looking out over the water. At all those rainbow sails.

"You're shivering," he says, and I don't correct him, although it's not the cold anymore but *him* that's the cause. It's less a shiver than an ongoing tremble, an electric current just below the surface of my skin. Vibrating everywhere, everything. Like I'm more alive than I ever have been, like I'm powered by his nearness.

I move, turning within the circle of his embrace, feeling him lift his chin from my head so he can tilt his face to look down at mine. He is half smiling, which I think I'm doing, too.

I almost always kiss the boy first. It's how I stay out of awkward territory. Otherwise—well, I can't stand the thing where you're in some hidden location with a guy and you're making small talk, waiting for him to make the move: to kiss you or *not* to kiss you. That's why—even if I'm not sure I like him yet—I do it. It's easier. I grab, I pull him toward me, I kiss him—good and long and hard—and I move away. It's better than *waiting*. It's better than *talking*.

But in this moment, as I'm standing on a hill overlooking the Pacific Ocean and encircled by Ardy's long, thin arms, it's not about getting something over with. It's not about breezing through to escape the awkwardness. Right now, kissing Ardy Tate would only be about . . . kissing Ardy Tate.

I tilt my head a little to the right, beginning to rise up on my toes, locking my eyes on his. I feel his hands flatten on my lower back, moving higher, sliding up to my shoulders . . .

Where they press down, ever so slightly, rooting me to the ground. He pulls me in close. All the way to his chest, the wrong position for our mouths to meet.

It's a hug.

I got ready to kiss him, and Ardy turned it into a hug.

Confused, I slip my arms around his waist because it seems to be what's being asked for, and also because I'm embarrassed. Am I misreading the situation?

I turn my head and rest it against his chest. It's rising and falling, but beneath the regularity of his breath, his heart is beating fast and hard. It makes me feel better about my own uneven fluttering.

We stand like that for a long moment, and then he pulls away and clears his throat. "Ready to head back?"

The loss of him—his warmth, his touch—is palpable. I spin back to the water, closing my eyes, not wanting to forget the rough texture of his sweater against my cheek. Not understanding what moves this boy, what drives him, what he wants.

But all I say is "Sure."

Things are quiet between us after that. The only time we really talk is shortly after we leave the gravel parking lot. Trying to make conversation, I ask Ardy why he switched schools last year. He shoots me a look across the minivan console. "Why?"

It seems like an obvious question to me.

"I mean, was there something wrong at the public school? Did they not have enough yoga classes or something?"

"No." There's an odd look on Ardy's face as he gazes straight ahead of him at the road. He doesn't elaborate, so I try again.

"Why didn't you start at REACH in ninth grade? Especially since Hope's family and yours are such good friends. It seems like you would have gone to the same school from the start."

"Mom wanted me to have the most normal life possible." He seems to relax a little. "Since I don't have a father and her job is so busy, she wanted me at a school that seemed to be really regular."

Seems reasonable. But then . . .

"So why'd you switch?"

"Needed a change." Ardy shrugs, which does nothing to illuminate the question for me. I wonder if he moved schools to be with Hope. In fact, I'm wondering a lot of things about Ardy Tate.

Our day was strange and fun and interesting, but now I can't tell how he feels about me. I gave him the clearest sign that I was open for kissing, and he not only didn't do it but pushed me away.

It's so confusing.

We finally get back to Burbank. There's no talk of continuing to hang out—like coffee or a movie or *anything*—so I'm not surprised when Ardy pulls to the curb in front of my house. He puts the minivan in park and turns to face me, but he doesn't move closer and he doesn't unbuckle his seat belt. He smiles, but it's very friendly. Too friendly. *Friend*-friendly.

Did I do something wrong? Is the kiss on the porch off the table?

"I'm glad you were up for an adventure," he says. "I've only helped my mom teach a class. I've never taught the whole lesson by myself. Thank you."

My mouth almost drops open. Was I his student? His *practice* student?

"I don't know what to say." At least *that's* honest.

"Say 'You're welcome.'" Ardy nods at me. Like I'm a business associate or something.

What. The. Heck.

"You're welcome." I mutter it through stiff lips before grabbing the beanie, ski gloves, and scarf that I never even took from the car. I hop out, turning back to say "See you on Monday" before slamming the door.

He waves and takes off down the street.

And that's it.

I don't know what to do with any of it.

CHAPTER EIGHT

Mom is in the kitchen when I come in. She points to a pile of produce. "Wanna help chop?"

I wash my hands and pull up a stool at the counter between the kitchen and the living room. She slides a cutting board and a knife to me, and I get to work on a carton of mushrooms. The board is one Mom gave me when I was little. My name is burnt into the wood, and now, as I slice the mushrooms, I try to line them up in the corner of the *L* before each cut.

I can feel Mom's curious eyes, but I'm not going to be the first one to talk about today, especially since I don't know what happened. I make it through the mushrooms, two shallots, and an onion before she can't stand it anymore.

"How was the falcon?"

"It was a hawk." I grab the next item in line—a bulb of garlic—and start peeling off its papery skin. "His name was Torch, and I thought it was really cool even though he hated me."

"How was Ardy?"

"Fine." I'm not sure how I'd answer the question if it came from Cooper or Katie, much less from my mother. I set a garlic clove on my board, concentrating on slicing it into thin disks.

"How was the"—there's a smile in my mom's voice— "porch?"

Before I can answer, the front door bangs open, and we hear my father's voice. "Who wants pizza?"

Crap.

He swings into the kitchen and sets a big flat box on the counter next to me. I don't have to look at my mother to know there's a line deepening between her eyebrows. "I told you I was making dinner," she says.

"Did you?" Dad asks.

Mom picks up a head of lettuce and slams it against the counter to loosen the core. Except the way she hits it, I'm not sure there's any core left. "I said I found a recipe online that I wanted to try."

"So try it tomorrow," Dad says. "It'll still be there."

"We've already cut everything up," she says, her voice growing louder.

I grab another clove and hunch over my board with it.

"Then the pizza can be an appetizer," Dad says. "Or dessert. Or we can throw it out, whatever."

"I don't *care* about the pizza," Mom says. "I care about you *listening* to me."

"I listen." Now he's getting loud, too. "It doesn't mean I always have to agree with everything you say. I wanted pizza, so I got pizza. What's the big deal?"

"It's fine," she says, starting to chop the lettuce. Since it's obviously *not* fine, I push my garlic-covered board into the center of the counter and slide off my stool. No one notices.

"I'm going to my room," I tell them. Neither one answers.

Our house is old and bizarre and seems like pieces of three or four houses that someone smooshed together in no particular order. Apparently, my parents bought it like this because, as long as I can remember, they've been saying they're going to renovate it. Occasionally they even get so far as to print out a bunch of floor plans and spread them over the breakfast table, but nothing ever happens.

The front door opens into what we call the sitting room, I guess because it's long and narrow and doesn't seem to have any other purpose than to sit in it. There's only a handful of mismatched armchairs and a loveseat. It's where Mom prefers I entertain guests. At least it's where I'm supposed to entertain Cooper. Katie's allowed in my bedroom.

Straight past the sitting room is our teeny-tiny kitchen that, inexplicably, overlooks an enormous living room with a giant rock-wall fireplace. There's no obvious place for a dining table, so we have a small round one shoved in the corner. It's big enough for the four of us to cram around, but more often we sit on stools at the counter between the kitchen and the living room.

My bedroom is the only one on the ground floor. It's small, but it has two closets, one of which is very deep and opens into the TV room. When we were little, it was one of Leo's and my favorite hiding spots during hide-and-seek because if someone came looking for you in one of the rooms, you could always sneak out into the other one. If the room you snuck into was the TV room, you could then make it all the way into the backyard without being seen.

After leaving my parents with their root vegetables and rage, I must be tired from the day of sea air and confusing feelings, because I immediately fall asleep. I don't even get under the covers; I just sprawl onto the quilt and I'm out. I only wake up when Leo is sent in to wake me, which he does by kicking the foot of my bed.

"Quit it," I mumble, wiping drool off my chin. I sit up and yawn, realizing I'm breathing in the scent of something delicious. "What is that?"

"Dinner," Leo says. "Come on."

Dinner turns out to be a baked fish, flavored with all the things I chopped. The pizza box is gone and so is Dad, which means my mother's lips are pressed in a tight line. Luckily, Leo is able to get her laughing with a story about a kid in his science class who blew up a burner. Usually that's *my* job—distracting the parents from how mad they are at each other—but tonight I'm glad Leo is taking over.

After dinner I put away a load of laundry in my room before opening my computer. I don't have a ton of homework this weekend, but I'd rather not wait until the last minute. Besides, it's better than obsessing about Ardy.

I guess my parents aren't the only ones who need to be occasionally distracted.

I finish calculus and get a head start on some reading for World History class before succumbing to temptation and going online. I can't resist finding Ardy on social media. He doesn't post very often, but then—as I'm staring at the screen—a new photo pops up.

It's me. Or, more specifically, my arm, which is stretched toward the sky. The slightly blurry photo captures a moment when my new frenemy Torch descended onto my hand, his wings outspread. I stare at the picture, which Ardy captioned *Spent the day with a couple of birds.* I decide to "like" the photo first thing in the morning. I spent the day driving almost all the way to San Diego and back with him, he taught me how to fly a bird, and we sort of held hands. It should really be a no-brainer, but I also don't want to jump on it too fast.

It's worth a deeper dive into Ardy's online persona, so I start clicking around. Most pictures are random—a blue rock on the ground, a cane leaning on a bench, a crushed soda can—but I do find a picture of him with his mom. There's also one of him and Hope. The picture is at least a couple of years old. They're sitting on her front porch, eating ice cream. It makes me wonder if he's ever kissed her.

Or if he wants to.

As I stare at the image of them, my phone buzzes. Text from Cooper.

Coffee and tell all?

I text back immediately:

Not now. Homework.

I think I need a second to figure out what happened with Ardy before I talk about it, but then I change my mind and call Cooper anyway. "I don't understand boys," I tell him.

"Welcome to the club," he says. "Did you kiss? Do your three months start now?"

"I wish."

"Ooh." I can picture Cooper sitting up straighter, wherever he is. "So now you *do* definitely want to kiss him?"

"Yeah, but I don't know if he's into me. He had the perfect opportunity, and he didn't take it. We were basically at the Pinterest page of ideal romantic settings, and nothing happened."

"Weird," says Cooper. "Did he say anything?"

"Yeah." I slump on my bed. "In the morning he said we'd kiss at the end of the day, but then he never did it."

"Huh." Cooper's trying to figure it out along with me. "Is that a straight-boy thing? To announce in advance?"

"No." The boys who kiss me don't tell me in advance. They don't even ask what I want. By the time the touching starts, they're usually aware of my interest level. Or they assume it, and I allow things to keep moving because I don't want to explain otherwise. I don't want to disappoint. I don't want conflict. "I guess Ardy's different."

"That's not a bad thing." I hear the chagrin in Cooper's voice. "Maybe stupid Katie is right."

"Stupid Katie has her moments," I agree, smiling to myself at Cooper's ever-present annoyance with my other BFF. We hang up, and I go back to trying to figure out Ardy by myself.

Maybe this is normal for him. Maybe strange and slow is how Ardy rolls.

I close my computer and head to the kitchen for a snack. Mom and Leo have gone upstairs, so there's no one to complain about me digging through every cabinet and then the freezer before moving to the fridge to select a string cheese.

I basically inhale it and am headed back to my room when there's a soft knock on the front door.

It's Ardy. He's standing on the porch in the same jeans and sweater he wore today, but now topped off with the slouchy beanie that is so cute on him. "Hey," he says.

I stare at him, completely befuddled, before finally managing to mumble out a "Hi." I glance toward the stairs—Mom must not have heard the knock, since she's not coming down—and I step outside, gently closing the door behind me. I don't know what the hell Ardy is doing here, but whatever it is, I don't want an audience for it. I look behind him—no sign of the minivan. "Where did you park?"

"Down the block. I didn't want to slam the door outside your house." It's dark out here, but not so dark that I can't see Ardy's teeth gleaming in a grin. "I have a question for you. Do you think I'm a freak?"

Katie does. Apparently, people at his last school do. Maybe Cooper still does, too. But me, I don't know anymore, so I shake my head because it seems like the thing to do. Especially because showing up like this is . . . a little freaky. I want to ask him why he's here, except the corners of my mouth are turning up. It might be because of the cute beanie but—whatever it is—I'm having a hard time forming coherent thoughts. Much less sentences.

"That's good news." Ardy moves closer, so he's looming over me, all tall and angular and adorable. He sets a hand on my left shoulder. It's warm through the thin fabric of my shirt, and without consciously deciding to, I arch my back the tiniest bit, pressing my shoulder up into it. Wanting to feel more of him. He pulls me slightly to him, reaching his other hand toward me . . .

And then *past* me, over my body.

To my front door.

Which he opens.

"What are you *doing*?" I whisper. "My mom doesn't know I'm out here."

"I'm doing this for your mom," he whispers back, reaching inside my house.

"I'm rethinking the *freak* thing," I tell him.

"Noted." His hand scrambles against the interior wall, and then the porch light flips on, nearly blinding us. Ardy squints against the bright glow as he oh-so-carefully pulls the front door closed again and then stands there, dropping both hands to his sides. His eyes—now that I can see them—are dark and serious behind his glasses. "I don't like your type of pretty," he says.

Offensive.

He must see it on my face, because he hastens to clarify. "I mean—shit, sorry. You're the kind of pretty that most people like—"

I am?

"—and I don't usually like what most people like."

This time I say it out loud. "Marginally less offensive."

"Starting over." Ardy clears his throat and runs his fingers through his hair. "What I mean is, I do think you are pretty."

I'm not sure if the statement warrants gratitude, so I don't thank him. I just keep looking at him. Trying to figure out if this is a romantic moment or an extremely bizarre break-up-before-romance-even-happens.

"But I also think you're funny," Ardy says. "You're smart, you have loyal, long-standing friendships, and you're not afraid to hold a dismembered quail leg."

Okay, it might be a romantic moment.

"You're not afraid to give a girl a dismembered quail leg," I tell him. "It's an unorthodox move."

"Some might say that I don't really understand how to do *moves.*" Ardy's mouth twitches up on one side, hinting at a grin. "I didn't get that memo in Boy School."

"It's the only thing I got in Girl School. . . ." I trail off at the end, suddenly realizing how it sounds. A rocket flare bursting over my disingenuous behavior, illuminating the most superficial parts of me. Ardy's brows tilt toward each other—he's trying to figure out how to react to that—and I decide to cop to my transgressions. "But it doesn't always work out so great. I'm interested in trying something new."

"Fair." Ardy edges closer. He touches my shoulder again, but this time only with the back of one finger, running it down the length of my arm to my hand. He dances his finger across my knuckles, and I open my hand, stretching it out and then closing it. Capturing his finger between my own. A warm ball of energy gathers in the pit of my stomach, making me want to fling myself into his arms, to get things started.

But this is different—Ardy is different—and I don't want to rush into my same old habits. To repeat the patterns. To do what I always do: reel them in, run away, hate myself.

And so I wait, fingers entwined with his. I watch him . . . watching me.

"What I'm trying to say is that I'm not *only* kissing you because I think you're pretty."

I raise an eyebrow and take a tiny step toward him. "You are aware that you're not kissing me at all, right?"

Because now it's just torture.

He nods. "Ready?"

I swallow, suddenly nervous. "Yes."

Keeping his eyes locked on mine, Ardy moves his hand—the one that's entwined in my own—up to his chest. He holds it there for a second, then unfolds my fingers, opening my hand. He pulls it up to his face and presses his mouth against my open palm. It sends a shiver through me—the warmth of his breath, the feeling of his lips. . . .

But then he twitches back, making a face that he quickly squelches. He tries to cover, pulling me toward him again, but I realize—

"Oh God, my hands smell like onions." I yank them away from him, burying them in my pockets.

"I would have guessed garlic." Ardy's amused, but I'm horrified.

"That too," I admit. "I washed them, I swear."

"It's pungent, for sure." Ardy is grinning now. A full grin, not the half one from before.

"I think you're supposed to use lemon, but we didn't have any, so I tried with hand soap, but I guess it didn't work." I am appalled. This is *not* how I do first kisses, all embarrassed and awkward and rambling like a fool. "You should know that I'm generally a very hygienic person and—"

"Lark." Ardy puts both hands on my shoulders. He's still smiling, and his eyes are shining, but they're also focused. Intense. "You are perfect."

Then in one motion he slides his hands down my back and pulls me in, dropping his head so he can kiss me solid on the mouth. I freeze for a moment—the slightest moment, when I'm simultaneously thrilled and terrified—and then I'm kissing him, too. And running my hands up his chest to slide behind his neck, sinking my fingers into his hair, moving him even closer to me. His hands tighten on my waist, anchoring around my hips as his mouth opens against mine. I allow it, doing the same, shifting so the entire length of my body is touching him. . . .

And then it's over. He pulls away and smiles down at me, his hair a little tousled, his eyes a little bright. "I did say end of the day, on the porch, light on."

I inhale, trying to steady my breathing. "Mission accomplished."

He flashes a grin at me. "See you at school." I watch him lope down the front path, away from the porch light, becoming a dark shape and then disappearing down the sidewalk.

Ardy Tate is so weird.

And I like him so, so much.

CHAPTER NINE

I change my outfit five times before school, finally going with something that will only have meaning to one other person. It's a pair of dark jeans with the bottoms rolled up, my tan suede sandals, and a white button-up shirt. And, of course, the fringe drop earrings.

As I hoped he would be, Ardy is at his locker when I turn the corner. I spot him immediately. He's wearing a leather jacket over a plaid shirt and slamming shut the door of his locker. I arrive as he's turning to leave, and when he sees me, he sets his bag down and leans back, one foot against the lower locker to brace himself. He folds his arms over his chest and looks at me. "Morning."

"Morning." Suddenly I don't know what to say. I didn't have a flirty greeting planned; I'm not sure how to launch into witty banter. "What'd you do yesterday?" I finally ask.

"Homework and laundry. Very glamorous."

"Indeed." I picture Ardy doing laundry, getting an armful of clothes and loading them into a machine. Detergent, fabric softener . . . why is it so easy to imagine him doing routine household chores? Maybe I've been *imagining* him a little too much lately.

"I have to go," he tells me. "I have to return a microscope to the biology lab before first period."

"Okay."

He leans down, grabs his bag, and heads away down the hall. Yes, that's our romantic, sparkling interaction upon first sight after the weekend kiss. I'm underwhelmed, to say the least.

Ardy stops walking and turns around. "Hey, Lark."

"Yeah?" Maybe he's paying attention after all.

"See you at lunch?"

A plan. I like it. So I nod, and Ardy breaks into a grin. It's everything I could have asked for, because his grin is wide and a little goofy, and it lights up the hall. I immediately smile back, and as we turn away from each other, going in opposite directions, I can't stop smiling.

In fact, when Cooper and Katie grab me outside of Calculus, I'm still smiling like that, all big and ridiculous. Which I don't realize until Cooper points it out. "What's wrong with you?"

"Nothing's wrong with me. What do you mean?"

"Your mouth is all weird. . . ."

"Oh *God,* it's the boy." Katie pulls a face. "Seriously, Ardy Tate is making your face do that?" She turns to Cooper. "You said nothing happened."

"That's what Lark told me." Cooper's looking at me. "Did something happen?"

I raise my chin high in the air and say in a prim voice, "I'm not going to kiss and tell." But then of course my face splits into the same wide grin I've been wearing, the one I can't control. "You guys, something totally happened."

"Three months," says Cooper. "Which makes it . . . let's say Valentine's Day."

"Ooh, a Valentine's dumping," Katie says. "That is awesome heartbreak."

"You're an asshole," I tell her, and she laughs. I give Cooper a stern look. "And you'd better start looking around at other guys."

"Please." Cooper jabs a hand into his hip. "I haven't ever stopped *looking*."

"Speaking of which"—Katie nudges me—"after the game on Friday, there's a party at Jonathan Lee's house. His parents are in the Bahamas. All the football players are going." Belatedly, she looks at Cooper. "Crabby Pants can come, too."

"Gee, thanks," he says, sarcastic as always.

"I'll let you know," I tell her. "I kinda want to see how the week goes."

Katie's perfectly arched brows dart down in a frown. "You're, like, a minute in, and you need permission to go to a party?"

"No." That's not it at all. I don't need Ardy's permission. It's more that . . . I don't know if I *want* to go to a party with Katie right now. She'll hook up with someone and expect me to do the same. "My three months just started," I tell her. "I'm off the market."

"Whatever." She looks from me to Cooper. "It's high school. No one said *marry* him. The bell's about to ring."

And then she's gone.

All through Calculus and World History and Art, I can't stop thinking about Ardy. I picture the way his eyes were serious when he first showed up on my porch. How he touched me with one finger. I even find myself replaying the angle at which he carries his bag, with the strap slung diagonally over his body. It's like the sun is shining brighter today, and if I were outside, I'm pretty sure I would hear birds singing just for me.

Yep, I've turned into a Disney princess.

Lunch can't get here soon enough.

» » « «

When I walk into the cafeteria, the very first person I see is Hope. She brought her lunch today, so she's already planted at the table where she and Ardy and Evan usually sit. She waves me over. "Eat with us," she says, which of course I was planning on doing anyway.

"Okay." I drop my backpack on the chair beside her and head to the lunch line. By the time I return with my turkey-and-arugula sandwich and bag of kale chips, Ardy and Evan are there, too. I bump my backpack to the ground and drop into the chair between Ardy and Hope. Everyone—including Ardy—gives me a halfhearted wave and then continues the discussion.

"No way the student body votes for bowling," Evan is saying. "Even if it's *not* a prom—"

"It's definitely not a prom," Hope says.

"—no one wants their commemorative senior-year activity to involve sticking their fingers in someone else's ball holes."

"Don't say *ball holes*," Ardy says.

"Agreed," I chime in. "With Ardy, I mean. I don't know how people will vote."

"How will *you* vote?" Evan asks me.

"Probably for go-karting."

"Oh, right." He makes a face. "Daddy's place."

"I agree with Lark," Ardy says. "It's the most pleasantly scented." He glances at me. "Like popcorn and burnt rubber."

"What?" Evan looks outraged. "What do you think roller-skating and bowling smell like?"

"Feet," Ardy and I say together, and then smile at each other.

"They're not wrong," Hope says. She's smiling, too.

"Whatever," Evan says. "The whole thing is bullshit. We should be having a normal prom like normal schools."

"Because you want to be crowned king," Hope teases him.

"You'd be a hot queen." Evan leans over and kisses her on the mouth. Ordinarily, I would be revolted, but now I find myself wishing Ardy would do the same thing to me.

Hope pulls back from the make-out session and glances at me, then at Ardy. It makes me wonder what she knows.

Unless it's nothing because, against all odds, Ardy *didn't* tell Hope. And if that's the case, why not? *Does* he have feelings for her, as I have suspected all along? Am I merely a means to an end, a way to make her jealous? Sure, it was romantic when he showed up on my porch, but what if that's all it was? Fifteen minutes of romance and then . . . nothing.

I have no idea. All I know is that while I have certainly been into a new boy before, it's never felt like this.

Ardy stretches in his seat, and his knee brushes against mine. It's like an electric shock, jolting me into awareness. At first I jerk away, but then I wonder whether he did it on purpose. I allow my left knee to drift back, very slowly, until it's resting against his, just barely, under the table. So, so lightly, like it's hardly there. Ardy might not notice it, it's so faint. In fact, it's possible that I'm only flirting with his slim-fit denims right now, because although Ardy doesn't pull away, he doesn't make a move toward me, either.

Ardy and I stay in that position—our knees kind of touching, neither of us budging—while the four of us talk about homework and Evan's upcoming soccer game. But even as I'm making casual conversation, I'm tingling. Every fiber of me is focused on that one spot—the very outer edge of my left knee—that is resting against Ardy.

If only I could know for sure that he's feeling the same way.

Or that he knows it's happening.

» » « «

After English, although I don't see Ardy for the rest of the day, I spend the remaining classes thinking about him, wondering if this is going somewhere, if I even know how to *get* somewhere with another person. He's not in my locker hallway (I go to my locker between all my classes, just in case), and I don't run into him anywhere else, either. I'm resigned to spending my evening wondering WTF is going on.

School's over and I go out to the flagpoles to meet Leo . . .

And Ardy's waiting for me.

I stop a couple of feet in front of him, and we smile at each other. "Hey," I say.

"Hey," he says.

"Are we driving you home again?" says Leo, walking up.

"Leo." I might kill him.

"What?" My little brother clearly doesn't have a problem with being dead.

I shoot him a *don't be a jerk* glance, and then—when he shrugs—I dig my car keys out of my purse and toss them to him. "Wait in my car. I'll be there in a minute."

Leo walks away, and I turn toward Ardy. He's smiling, and it's that same smile from before. The sunshine one. The one that twists me upside down. "I like your outfit."

Just like that, I know he got my message, the one I was sending when I got dressed this morning. He's paying attention; he's *been* paying attention. So why . . .

Why.

WHY.

And this time, I don't give him a pass. In fact, I set my hands on his arms and give him a little shove. "Dude."

Which makes Ardy look *really* confused. "I . . . what?"

"Is this your *thing*?" I ask him, exasperated past all exasperation. "You're confusing for hours on end, and then you suddenly show up at the end of the day to be all dashing and romantic when I'm not expecting it?"

Ardy looks taken aback. "Is that what I'm doing?"

"Yes!" I explode at him. "Get a new move!"

Ardy folds his arms and seems to be considering. "That's

a fair assessment," he finally says. "It's just that it takes me a minute to sort through things."

"*Things?*" I'm at the end of my rope.

"What I'm feeling."

I wait, tapping my foot.

Yes, *literally* tapping my foot, the one that's encased in a tan suede sandal. Going from toe to heel in my pattern.

"I don't think we're supposed to move too quickly," Ardy says. "Like we shouldn't jump straight from quail leg to committed relationship . . . right?"

If Cooper were here, he would be like, *Why is* quail leg *a relationship step?* But he's not, so I ask a different question. "You're saying we should take it slow?"

"I guess so?" His brown eyes are pleading. "Let's be friends." Before I can answer—because I'm nearly choked by the instant pain bubbling up in me—he takes a step closer, setting his hands on my shoulders. "Not *just* friends. I'm not saying that. I mean . . . let's be that, too."

I relax a little. It's not a before-it-starts breakup. "You want to get to know each other?" I clarify.

"Yes." The pressure of his fingers on my shoulders increases. "A lot." His voice is so low and gentle that—somehow—it makes me *clench* inside.

"I want that, too," I whisper. Because it's true. Because I'm *dying* to know everything about him.

"How do we make that happen?" he asks.

"Tomorrow night," I say. "I'm working at Wheelz."

He cocks his head. "And . . . ?"

"Come by. I'll hook you up with a race and some popcorn."

"I'll be terrible," Ardy says. "I mean, not at the popcorn. I'm pretty good with popcorn."

"That's okay."

"Are you sure?" He's looking at me in a way that tells me he's not only talking about the racing. "I really might not be good at it. I might not know what I'm doing."

"We'll figure it out," I tell him, 100 percent meaning it.

"Okay." His smile shines all over me, warming even the most cynical of places. "Tomorrow, then."

» » « «

I glare at Cooper over our booth at Bob's Big Boy in Toluca Lake, then take a sip of my Oreo milk shake to try to cool off. It doesn't work, so I set it down and continue my glare.

"Do not," I tell Cooper. "Please do not make me feel bad about the stupid game right now. Not when I'm actually happy."

"How do you *know* you're happy?" Cooper rests his elbows on the table, leaning toward me. "You've been here before. Like, a lot."

"Can't you let me enjoy this?" I ask, frustrated. "Aren't you supposed to *want* me to have a decent relationship?"

"You're calling it a *relationship* now? Today—this actual day, like a few hours ago—you said you needed a minute."

"A minute to enjoy it!" A man in a checkered shirt across the aisle glances at me, and I lower my voice. "Cooper, I really like him. Let me have this. Please."

Cooper takes in my pleading and the anger behind it. Then

he reaches across the table and slides both his hands over both of mine. "I have to tell you something."

My heart sinks. "What?"

"You know Ian goes to the public school. Katie thought I should ask him about Ardy."

"Really, now you and Katie are on the same side?"

"Never," Cooper says. "But we did agree that Ian might know something about Ardy's reputation."

"Everyone has *some* sort of reputation." I frown, pulling away from him. "I have one, you have one. *What?*" Because Cooper is looking at me with something approximating sympathy.

"People there think he's weird."

"Weird? Is that the worst Ian can come up with? What does that even mean?"

"Ian says he's one of those guys who don't get invites to parties."

"Why?"

"He's different or something."

Well, that's just stupid. The reason I even like Ardy in the first place is *because* he's different. I glare at Cooper. "Isn't the *point* that I'm supposed to be with someone different? Isn't that what you wanted?"

"That's what Katie wanted," Cooper clarified. "I wanted you to like a boy you make out with."

"Mission accomplished," I tell him. "So stop bugging me about it."

"That's not all." Cooper looks more earnest than before. "They say that Ardy's breakups go . . . bad."

"What is that supposed to mean?" I cannot—*cannot*—believe that I'm getting this crap from Cooper right now. Now, when I'm at the very beginning of something that could be awesome.

"It's why they say he's Undateable," Cooper says. "It's not about being with him—it's about breaking up with him. He's like the opposite of you. Ian said that, in good conscience, he needed to tell me about it."

It makes me hate Ian even more. Not only is he the most boring boyfriend who's ever existed, but also he apparently lives to ruin other people's happiness.

"Except you're not telling me anything. You're giving me a stupid adjective—*Undateable.* Like that means anything. From what you and Katie say, people should be calling *me* Undateable."

"I don't know anything else," Cooper says. "Ian didn't have details. But he says everyone knows it at his school. It's one of those things that's spoken about in hushed tones. Like, he leaves dead squirrels on his exes' porches. Or sets fire to their cars or something."

"*What?*"

"It's bad," Cooper says. "Like, cops-are-involved bad. But you can't Google it because of juvenile privacy laws."

I'm so angry and resentful and worried that I don't know what to say. Cooper can obviously see it all over my face, because he sighs. "I don't know a lot of details, and neither did Ian. But—seriously—it's a *thing* there. Everyone knows it." He follows it up with, "Don't shoot the messenger."

Screw the messenger. I'd rather go straight to the source.

"You'd better get me some names," I tell Cooper. "Ian had better have solid freaking data if he's going to throw crap like that around."

"Larks." Cooper looks at me beseechingly. "I wasn't going to say anything, but then you started talking about actually liking him. I don't want you to get mixed up in something that's going to end up really bad."

"You started a game that's all about how I *can't* end things badly!" My voice scales up, and once again Checkered Shirt Guy glances over. This time he scowls. I scowl right back, and he returns his eyes to his newspaper. "You *want* someone to be heartbroken!"

"I didn't," Cooper assures me. "And I don't. I'm only letting you know what Ian said."

God, Ian sucks.

"I'll get names," Cooper says. "Maybe it's nothing. Maybe they're just rumors. I'll ask Ian."

"You'd better."

I grab my milk shake and start drinking it again, two thoughts racing through my head. The first: I loathe Ian to the core of my being. And the second . . .

Oh shit.

CHAPTER TEN

I'm in first period when the morning announcements tell us to vote for the Not-Prom location. We all use the phones we're supposedly not supposed to have in class to vote on the school website. At least the people who care about the Not-Prom do. As I look around after casting my vote for Wheelz, I realize there are plenty of kids ignoring the summons to perform their civic duty.

See, this is what's wrong with America.

I take different hallways to get to my classes so I can avoid Cooper and Katie. I just need a few hours without being judged and watched by them. At lunchtime, I grab a poor excuse for a meal from a vending machine—cucumber-infused water, Marcona almonds, kale chips—and head for the first-floor stairwell. To my chagrin, Wade Collins is already here with Keeshana Pierce. They're doing exactly the same thing *I* did the last time I was here with Wade: making out against the wall. "Oops, sorry," I say when I round the corner and almost run right into them.

"Oh, hey." Keeshana brushes a dreadlock away from her face and grins at me. "I hope go-karts win, don't you?"

"Duh," Wade says. "Her parents own the place."

"Really?" Keeshana's eyes get big. "You can race whenever you want?"

"Pretty much." I back away, not wanting to intrude. "Come by when I'm working sometime. I'll give you a discount."

"Cool!" they say simultaneously as I make my escape.

Luckily, one of my other romance spots is empty: the storage closet on the third floor. I close the door behind me and sink to the floor between two computer carts to eat my vending-machine lunch.

Given last night's revelation—or potential revelation—I'm not ready to see Ardy. Not quite yet.

» » « «

I come into English as the bell's ringing, so all I have to do is flash Ardy a quick smile over the desks before sitting down. I register his quizzical look but then keep my eyes forward for the rest of class. I pack up my things well before the end of the lesson so that when it's over I can bolt from the room with only a quick wave first.

Votes are announced while I'm sitting in sixth-period Advanced Biology. Ms. Wilkins comes on the loudspeaker to let us all know that the Spring Fling Thing will be held at . . . Wheelz. I accept a handful of thumbs-ups and high fives before holding my phone under my lab desk so I can text congratulations to my dad.

Then I go back to trying to pay attention to the workings of the nervous system.

It's difficult when my own nervous system is in overdrive.

Even though everyone here has their own reusable water bottle—and I mean they're literally handed out on the first day of the school year—I dork around in the hallway by the French classroom, pretending to get a drink from the fountain. Hope finally comes out, and she all but tackles me as I conspicuously wipe water from my mouth. "Lark! Where were you at lunch?"

Okay, I've shared a cafeteria table with her, like, five times. We have not leveled up to forever-lunch-buddy status.

"Around," I tell her. I'm here to see if she wants to hang out, to try to wiggle my way into her confidence so maybe she'll drop secret information about Ardy.

What's wrong with me?

Luckily, I'm saved by Hope herself. "I was going to text you anyway." She twirls one of her shiny black pigtails between her fingers. "Do you want to spend the night this weekend? Maybe Friday?"

I was not expecting that.

"Okay," I tell her.

"Cool!" Hope tugs her hot-pink backpack farther up on her shoulders. "I have a glee club rehearsal. See you tomorrow!" And she's off, waving to at least half a dozen people before rounding the corner and disappearing.

» » « «

I don't normally put a lot of thought into what I look like at work, but tonight I do. Inspired by Hope, I braid my hair into two long, messy ropes and secure them with silver elastic bands.

I pull on a long denim shirt over black leggings and shove my feet into the cowboy boots I scored from one of the vintage shops on Magnolia, topping the whole thing off with a thin white pullover sweater. The tiniest bit of extra mascara to pop my brown eyes, and I'm ready to go.

Here's my plan:

1. See if Ardy actually comes in tonight, like he said he would.
2. Watch out for red flags.
3. Go with the flow.

It seems reasonable. I need to hang out with Ardy in a place where I'm comfortable. Not his car on a mystery road trip. Not holding a hawk on a bluff over the Pacific Ocean. Just my normal work life, my normal world. Like people do. Then I can decide what to do about the rumors from his last school.

There's an early wave of go-karters, so Dad and Mano are very happy when I arrive. Only the three of us are working tonight, and for once Dad has plans to leave a little early. Now that we found out about the Not-Prom being held here, Mom is all hopped up about him coming home at a reasonable time this one night, because she knows it's going to be nothing but chaos for the next couple of months.

By eight-thirty, the early go-karters have cleared out, the place is practically empty, and I am debating whether or not to text Ardy to see if he's still coming. I've decided against it (for the tenth time) when I look up from the soda machine to see him coming through the double doors. I immediately spill the cup I'm refilling for the frat boy waiting for it. "Sorry," I tell him, hurrying to wipe the stickiness away and pour him a new soda. By the time I've rung him up and sent him on his way, Ardy is at the counter. He hovers there, seemingly not sure what to do with his hands—he keeps taking them in and out of his pockets in a way that melts all my misgivings. It's like he's gotten more adorable in the last twenty-four hours. More so when he finally takes his hands out and plants them on the counter so he can lean over it toward me. "Hello, miss. Can you assist me in renting one of your fine vehicles?"

"Why, certainly," I tell him. "I can put you into a kart for the fine price of zero dollars."

"I have cash." Ardy drops the act. "I mean, I'll take a discount, but it doesn't have to be *zero* dollars."

"Well, it is. Benefit of knowing the go-kart girl."

He opens his mouth like he's going to say something, but then he closes it again.

"What?" I ask.

"I wanted to make sure you still wanted me to come by," he says. "I didn't see you at lunch, and you left English so fast."

"Yes," I tell him. "Sorry. I had stuff to do." *Like try to figure out what to think about you.* I smile up at him. "I'm glad you're here."

"Okay."

Ardy trails me to the driver station, where I tag out Mano. I get Ardy set up with a name (surprisingly, he goes with *Ardy*) for the digital wall board and explain how the controls work.

Then I help him choose a helmet before handing him one of the head bandannas that you wear underneath it. "For hygiene," I tell him. "It's like a little head condom."

And then I'm blushing.

Ardy tugs it over his hair. "I must really like you if I'm willing to look like this," he says, pulling on his helmet.

I reach up to help him buckle it under his chin, trying to ignore how I tingle at his words. Or maybe it's his warm skin against my fingers that is making me feel like this. Whatever it is, it's all new.

And it's all good.

A few minutes later, Ardy and two guys who chose their driver names from *Star Wars* are racing around the track in the electric cars. And Ardy was right: he really sucks at it. He doesn't hit the brakes before the curves or understand how to pump the gas when he comes out of them. He seems to be having a difficult time manhandling the car around the turns, and Womp Rat and Wookie have already lapped him. As I watch him spin out for the sixth time, all I can do is hope he'll make it through unharmed. After all, I think a big part of what I like about him is his brain. I'd really prefer if he could manage to not injure it.

Ardy only does one full ride before turning in his helmet. "I don't think this is going to be my new hobby," he tells me. "But I'm happy to help make popcorn or something."

"You can play basketball." I point out the token-fed arcade game in the corner. It's where Leo and I learned to shoot hoops. "Or there's pool."

Ardy considers for a moment, then lopes off to the basketball game. I watch before heading back to the snack counter to relieve Mano.

Dad comes out from the back. "You guys can lock up," he says. "If it stays dead, feel free to call it early."

"Will do," Mano says, adjusting his LA Lakers cap over his forehead, almost like he's giving my dad a military salute.

Dad leaves without noticing that Ardy is here. Which is perfectly fine with me. No reason to raise any red flags.

The minute Dad is out the door, Mano turns to me. "I have this event in Arcadia," he says. "With my band. A gig, kind of. I mean, it's at this dude's house, so it's not like a pro thing or anything—"

"You can totally go," I assure him.

"Thanks." Mano peers down at me. "But, like, I don't love the idea of leaving you here alone at night. So maybe you could text me when you're in your car or something?"

I roll my eyes even as I smile at his protective behavior. Mano has been working here for almost a year. He came over from Hawaii to try to jump-start his music career, and so far he's been in four different bands. I set my hands up on his broad shoulders and give him a gentle push, turning him in the direction of Ardy. "See that guy?" Mano nods, and I allow him to face me again. "He is going to walk me to my car."

Mano takes a second look at Ardy, who is sinking . . . not much at all. "He's got no b-ball game."

"Yeah, he sucks at driving, too," I tell him.

"Good thing he's cute." Mano and I grin at each other. "I mean, if you like that kind of thing."

"Yeah." I allow my gaze to drift back to Ardy. "I think I like that kind of thing."

Mano takes off, and maybe half an hour later, our last customer does, too. It's 9:15, and the place is empty except for me and Ardy. This late, no one is going to come by to start a night of go-karting, which means I can close up.

It also means that I am utterly alone with Ardy in this huge, empty place. As I flick off lights in the party room and Ardy gets up from where he's been dorking around on his phone at the snack tables, I have a moment of hesitation. Is this a bad idea? Not because Ardy is dangerous or scary (even though stupid Ian said that stupid thing), but because—despite our conversation where we admitted to desiring otherwise—I don't *know* him that well.

To be fair, it's not exactly like I've let him get to know me, either.

I should do something about that.

Tonight.

I step out of the party room, meeting Ardy in the middle by the wall of arcade games, and walk right past him. "Come on." I don't look back, but I know he's following as instructed. I know because my entire body has gone into hyperalert. I can *feel* him behind me as I lead him along the narrow path on the edge of the pit.

We walk past the length of the track and around the curve to where light shines from between the doors at the back. I open them and head inside to a big open space. Ardy moves to my side and looks around at the mechanical lift, the two parked go-karts, the walls of equipment, and the defunct Ms. Pac-Man game that my father keeps saying he's going to get repaired. "What is this?"

"Crash pad. Look." I walk him to the go-karts and point to the big dent in the side of one. "We have a mechanic who comes every couple of days to fix any karts that have been damaged by people driving recklessly. She's always appalled by how often we manage to mess them up."

"Moving too fast can be fun, but it can also screw things up." Ardy gives me a look that is half serious and half overly dramatic.

"You're so deep," I tell him.

"Anyway, I'm sure I contributed to your mechanic's work-load this week." Ardy grimaces. "You should apologize to her for me. I wasn't very good out there."

"You did warn me. Besides, I've seen worse." It's only half a lie. "Sometimes we have a glow-in-the-dark race night. The next day this room is filled with effed-up cars."

"Okay, maybe that makes me feel better. A little."

"You can't be good at everything." I say it in my school-marm voice, which I immediately wish I hadn't used, because it's about the nerdiest thing I do. But it makes Ardy laugh.

"Thank you, Miss Dayton."

"That's *Ms.* Dayton." I say it mock-sternly and then head over to the switches so I can turn off a bank of lights. "We're going to do a lot of this before we leave," I warn him.

"Allow me, please." Ardy bounds to my side and starts flip-ping switches. "I need to do something to restore my masculinity."

Privately I think that shouldn't be a problem for Ardy. Sure, he's not, like, the sports buffs at school, or one of the actor guys who's constantly going on auditions, but he's cute in his own way.

It's a way that I really like.

Once the switches have been flipped, we leave the crash pad and return to the giant main room, where the overheads are now off. We make our way back along the path, with only the dim track lights to show us to the lobby.

One more piece of the Wheelz puzzle to go.

"Please note the snack counter," I tell him as we walk past it. "On nights when we're superslow, I've been known to clean the display windows six times."

"They're spotless," Ardy assures me.

We cruise past the soda machines and popcorn maker to the back hallway, where I sign Mano and me out before continuing all the way to my dad's office. There, I lock his door and then flick off the hallway lights.

Which puts us in absolute darkness.

"Damn," I hear Ardy say from somewhere nearby.

"Sorry. I should have warned you." I take a step toward him, hand outstretched, and accidentally poke him in the ribs hard enough to make him jump. "The front switch doesn't work." It's all very innocent, but suddenly I'm ultra-aware that we're alone and standing in the dark. And my hand, which I'd originally yanked back, is now floating to Ardy. My fingers find the edge of his trench and wrap around it. "Come on." I don't think my voice is shaky, but I can't be sure.

I hold on to his jacket until I've shuffled past him, and then his hand slides up to my own. My fingers loosen of their own accord, allowing his to wrap around them. "This is spooky." Ardy doesn't reference the fact that we're now holding hands. "Do you usually do this alone?"

"Totally." I start to muddle us back toward the front of the building, past the other office doors, pulling Ardy along with me as I shuffle through the darkness. "We've owned this place as long as I can remember. It was a point of pride when my dad started trusting me to work here, and then when I could help lock up. I don't usually get to be here by myself, and when I am, it's . . ."

I don't know how to explain it.

"A little magical?" Ardy suggests, scuffling along behind me.

"Kind of." I shift our path to the right for the slight bend in the hallway that I know is there. "It's more like I'm a boss. In control. Or that I'm in on some sort of secret."

"I like that," Ardy says. "The secret of your family's business."

"Yeah, and I know it *should* be scary, but instead all the shadows and smells . . . they're like history."

"That seems really—" Ardy starts to say, but then, "OW, DAMN!"

His hand jerks away from mine, and I immediately know what happened. He ran right into the thing that I avoided on instinct: a stack of soda cartons shoved haphazardly near the corner.

"Are you okay?" I turn and stretch my hands out, taking

careful steps toward him. "I should have warned you that was there—"

But then I stop. Because my palms are flat against the canvas of his jacket.

Which is flat against his chest.

Which is moving up and down with his breathing.

"Sorry." It comes out as a whisper, because apparently that's what sometimes happens to my voice when I'm with him.

"It's okay," he whispers back, his hands sliding up to cover my own. They're warm and narrow and smooth, and they make me lose all willpower. I take a step toward him, allowing my hands to part and slide around his rib cage under the edges of his jacket, following his bones until I can no longer discern where they begin and end, linking my hands together behind him. Ardy follows my lead, wrapping his arms around me and pulling me to him. I turn my head so my cheek is against his chest in the darkness.

And then we stand like that for a long time.

Quiet.

Breathing.

Until, even though I'm dying to kiss him, it's been roughly a thousand years and he's made no move in that direction, so I step back, turning away from him. His hands descend to my hips as I face the front of Wheelz and—without a word—start walking slowly.

Very slowly.

Pulling him with me.

Frankly, I don't *want* to reach the end, where we'll be lit by the dim running lights under the snack counter. Where we'll be able to see the front door and the world beyond this moment. Where it could look like an escape, an ending, an inevitability.

We move that way for another half minute—Ardy's hands on my hips, my feet shuffling ahead of his—and then he takes a larger step, catching up with me, holding me fast where I am. I pause, letting it happen. Allowing his arms to slide back around my waist, his head to dip to the side of my own. Ardy's face is rough—the tiniest bit of stubble—against mine. I can see the glimmering light of the Wheelz entrance ahead of us, but now we're paused.

Stopped.

Frozen.

And this time, like it's the most natural thing in the world, like I've done it every day of my life, I turn to face Ardy. One of his hands runs up into my hair and gently guides me until our foreheads are touching. "Is this okay?" he whispers.

I answer by tilting my head and pressing my mouth to his. And we're kissing. This time I'm more sure of myself. Or maybe he is. I don't know, but either way—oh my God, it's working. My fingers are in his hair, traveling down his back, holding tight to his jacket. His hands are on my waist, my neck, my face.

It lasts and lasts and lasts until I almost can't breathe anymore. . . .

And then Ardy pulls away. I can't see him because it's too dark, but as he again sets his forehead against my own, I can feel and hear his breath. It's calm and steady, and I don't know how he's managing to sound that way, because calm and steady are the *last* things I'm feeling right now.

But I regulate my breath to meet his, in tandem with him. Inhaling the feeling and the scent of his body. And finally—

Finally—

Ardy says, "I like you."

It's so blatant—so bald—that it takes me a minute to register. To be able to say, "I like you, too."

"Yeah?" I can't see his smile, but I can feel it in the darkness. There's a pause before he says, "Hey, Lark, do you want to be my girlfriend?"

"Hmm." I try to say the syllable in a way so that he can feel my smile right back at him. "I guess that depends on if you want to be my boyfriend."

"I think that might be cool."

"I think so, too," I tell him.

We stay there, leaning into each other.

Cooper's warning flits through my mind, but I brush it away.

Because screw Cooper.

And screw Katie.

And screw Ian.

And more than anything else, screw the game.

CHAPTER ELEVEN

It turns out that before now, I only *thought* I knew about kissing at school. Sure, I used to have my favorite locations to get busy, but Ardy and I are taking it to a whole new level. With the other boys, it was about sneaking around, doing it in private. With Ardy, everything's right out there in the open. *We* are in the open. Like he's proud of what we're doing. Like he's proud of me. Of us.

It starts at my locker. I've taken a little extra time on my appearance this morning. Actually, that is a lie. I've taken a *lot* of extra time. But every minute spent straightening hair and highlighting brow arches and blending a dot of white shimmer into the center of my lower lip to make it look more pleasing and luscious was all done with the intention of seeming like I'd done nothing at all.

Even Katie notices when she passes by me. "You look glowy," she says. "You're not pregnant, are you?"

"Shut up," I hiss, and she laughs as she saunters away.

I'm pulling out a textbook when Ardy lands beside me, leaning against the locker by mine. I look up, and for a second the fluorescents hit him at just the right angle for me to see my own image reflected in the lenses of his dark-rimmed glasses. I look eager and hopeful and excited, all of which makes me pull into myself, shrinking away, concentrating on shoving my textbook into my backpack. It's a lot to see myself looking so . . . open.

I focus on making my book fit until I hear his voice.

"Heads up," Ardy says. "I might not be very good at this."

I finish zipping my book away, straightening to my full height. "Which part?" I ask him, making a valiant attempt to channel the Ghost of Lark Past. The one who doesn't get nervous about a boy. "Lockers? Mornings? Calculus?"

"This." Ardy makes a gesture that seems to indicate our whole situation. He accompanies it with a look I believe is meant to be pleading. "Showing up at your locker," he continues. "Or not showing up. I don't know the rules."

Ah.

"I think we get to make the rules," I tell him.

"That's so much responsibility."

"I know, right?" I smile up at him, because that's what you do when the boy you like is so close and so adorable. "I could meet you after second period, in the first-floor east stairwell."

Ardy cocks his head to the side. "Why there?"

I open my mouth and then snap it closed.

For making out.

But of course I don't say that. I only stare up at him, flummoxed by what to say. Finally, when neither of us has moved for at least a full minute, I come up with something. "I don't know if you've dated anyone at this school—"

"I haven't."

All right, then.

"It's one of the places where people go." Aaaaand now it's awkward. "When they want to be, like, alone."

Ardy nods, getting it. "I have a different idea," he tells me.

"Okay . . . ?"

Although I don't have any expectations about what he's going to say, what I definitely don't expect is for him to take a step toward me and drop his mouth onto my own. I also don't expect him to run one hand into my hair and the other around my waist, pulling me into him. But what's *most* surprising is what I do in return.

I kiss him right back, totally ignoring everyone in the hall who may be watching. Like we're a legit couple. Like this means something.

When we break apart and I open my eyes, he's smiling down at me. "I don't have anything to hide," he tells me.

I stretch up to give him a final peck. "Me either."

Except for how we got here in the first place.

» » « «

I briefly consider not going to the cafeteria at lunch, just to make Ardy wonder where I am, but then I remember what he said about not knowing what the rules are. Hiding out would be a deliberate attempt to confuse him, to keep him on his toes, and I don't want that. It all began with that stupid game, but now that I'm in it, I don't want to play games.

Besides, if I didn't go to the cafeteria, I wouldn't see Ardy.

And all I want is to see Ardy.

As usual when I arrive, Ardy and #Heaven are already seated. I plop down and everyone smiles at me, but Ardy doesn't make any extra movement in my direction. It again makes me wonder what Hope knows about us. I mean, if he's willing to be so open with all the public displays of affection in the hallway, surely that means Hope's got a clue, right? But as we engage in our traditional griping about the food, she doesn't give me any sort of nudge-nudge or wink-wink.

"By the way, congratulations," Evan says to me. "On hosting the Not-Prom. Your parents must be happy."

"I don't know if congratulations are in order, but thanks." I don't share the story about my parents' warfare this weekend. It started with the Not-Prom but somehow devolved into a screaming fight about something from when they started dating in high school.

So, y'know . . . relevant.

Next to me, Ardy sets his spinach wrap down and lowers his right hand beneath the table. It floats onto my leg, just above my knee, barely touching. Almost hovering. I take a mini-scoot toward him, letting him know that his touch is welcomed. The slight weight of his hand increases, and his thumb moves in tiny circles against the outer edge of my knee. He's very discreet, and what he's doing is not at all obvious to anyone else, but it drives every other thought out of my mind. Which becomes obvious when I hear Hope say my name and I suddenly realize it's not the first time.

"Lark? Hello?"

"Sorry." I shift my focus to her. Or at least I try to. "What?"

"Will everything be open at Wheelz? Unlimited driving and arcade games?"

"I don't know. Probably?"

"Hey, guys." It's Wade Collins, looming over our table. "You know why I'm here, right?"

Since my last interaction with Wade was yesterday, when I interrupted him and Keeshana under the stairwell, I have no idea.

"Doing my team duty," Wade continues. "Encouraging you all to come to the soccer game on Friday." Oh, right. That. The sportsball players are constantly trying to drum up support for their teams. "We're playing Verdugo High," he says. "It's a big one for us."

Hope looks at me—"Do you want to go?"—and I remember that I'm supposed to spend the night with her on Friday. If we go to the game first, maybe Ardy will come, too.

"Okay." I look at Wade. "We can do that."

"Thanks, Lark." He beams down at me. "You always were cool." He points to Ardy. "You should come. Isn't that your old school?"

Ardy nods, chewing, and Wade heads off for another group of people. Hope addresses our table. "Boys? Come with?"

"Not me." Ardy shrugs. "I don't like soccer."

So much for thinking he would want to go because of me.

I realize Evan is looking at me. "Didn't you used to have a thing with Wade?"

Why is he asking me this?

"Barely." I immediately feel Ardy's hand coming away from my knee. He brings it up above the table and resumes eating his spinach wrap. I don't know if it's coincidence or if he doesn't want to touch me while discussing my past romances.

"It's nice that you guys are still friendly."

"Life's too short not to be, right?" I say it as casually as I can, but I'm overly aware of Ardy sitting beside me. Eating his spinach wrap and not saying a word.

» » « «

Cooper is waiting on the hood of my car when Leo and I arrive. As we reach him, my phone shivers, and Cooper waves his own phone. "That's me," he says. "Three names."

"Names of what?" Leo asks.

"Songs," I tell him. "Cooper and I are making a playlist."

"Worst." Leo gets into the passenger side and slams the door. I turn back to Cooper, lowering my voice.

"Three girls?"

"Yeah, from Verdugo High. See what you can find out."

I look at Cooper for a long time. "How's Ian?" I finally ask.

"Fine." Cooper's gaze drops to the ground. "We're going to Buffalo Wild Wings on Friday to watch college basketball."

"You hate basketball."

"I know."

"*He* should know," I say scathingly, and watch Cooper wince.

Whatever.

» » « «

I wait until I'm home and in my room before reading the text from Cooper. Three names: Krista Willis. Elle Campbell. Trissa Jefferson. Three girls, purported to have had "bad" breakups with Ardy. I stare at the names, hating the possibility that there's a side to Ardy that I won't like.

I grab my laptop and hop onto my bed, scrunching my pillows up against the headboard so I can lean against them. Before I start investigating these girls, it seems like maybe I should find out a little more about Ardy himself.

I already know that Ardy doesn't have a huge presence on social media, which is fine. Not everyone's into that. I quickly look at what's out there but don't find anything of interest. I *do* spend some time staring at a picture of Ardy posing on a beach in swim trunks. In it, he's flexing one of his biceps, looking at the camera and laughing. He's clearly making fun of guys who pose on the beach in earnest, but I can't stop looking at his image. Even though it's a joke, he still looks amazing.

But then it crosses my mind to wonder who took the photo. Was it Hope?

I click away from the beach picture and go to Verdugo High School's website. It takes me a few minutes, but eventually I find an archive folder with links to old photographs from clubs and activities. I go back three years, to when Ardy was a freshman, and after scrolling through the art and ASL clubs, I find him in a small group of kids making funny faces and holding a banner that reads BOWLING CLUB. I make a mental note to tease him about it later, and I enlarge the photo so that I can see him better. Freshman Ardy is not quite as tall, and his hair is shorter and spikier. But he has the same dark eyes and gentle half smile, the same vintage style. My heart twists in my chest at how young and earnest he looks. He *can't* actually be Undateable.

Can he?

In ninth grade, Ardy was apparently also involved in the creative writing club, the National Honor Society, and student government. Busy guy. I click to the next year, discovering that although Ardy left bowling and student government behind as he aged, he picked up the paintball and game clubs. He also grew at least four inches.

I find eleventh grade—junior year, Ardy's last at Verdugo High—and start looking through the pictures. I scan down the entire page but don't see Ardy's face anywhere. I go back to the top, thinking maybe I scrolled too fast. But nope—no photos of him.

Except . . . I catch sight of his name under the creative writing club picture. *Not pictured: Ardy Tate.* I go to the honor society page, where I find the same notation. Paintball, too.

Huh. I wonder why he didn't get his picture taken for any of the clubs. Was he sick that day or something? I click back a year so I can look at his tenth-grade photos. He's wearing different clothes in every picture, so Verdugo High must not take all the club photos on the same day. Which means Ardy missed a bunch of days, not just one, in eleventh grade.

Weird.

I decide to move along to the internet at large to investigate his ex-girlfriends. It's easy to narrow down the hundreds of Krista Willises to the one who goes to Verdugo High. She's short and pretty, with thick jet-black bangs over darkly lined eyes. She looks very emo, very intense.

I find myself feeling jealous, even though that's ridiculous. This is a girl from a year ago. Surely she's not in his life now, and if she is, I don't have a leg to stand on. Not with my dozens of exes waving at me in the hall and inviting me to soccer games and giving me mall discounts. But that's not why I'm jealous of Krista. I'm jealous because she knows Ardy. She knows things about him that I don't, like who he was before he appeared at REACH. And I'm jealous because—presumably—she's tilted her head up to kiss him, the way I did this morning. And maybe he looked at her the way he looked at me, like she was something he'd never seen before.

I do some more online stalking, eventually finding references to Krista's after-school job at the used-book store downtown. It makes sense. Of *course* someone who looks emo and intense would spend their afternoons surrounded by literature. And of course Ardy would like that.

There's the jealousy again.

In good news, assuming she still works there, it ought to be easy to find Ardy's ex-girlfriend and see what she is willing to spill about him.

CHAPTER TWELVE

My plan is to pull away, to keep Ardy at arm's length until I can talk to Krista, but . . .

But *Ardy*.

I keep forgetting about the Krista thing because instead I'm paying attention to him, to us, to how in the first few days, people would turn, surprised, when we walked past holding hands . . . but then they stopped. Or maybe it was that I stopped noticing.

Or caring what they thought.

The only person who said something blatant was Cici Belle. She cornered me with a snarky look on the way into English. "Surely there are at least a couple of dateable options you haven't kissed under the bleachers yet."

I froze, feeling the anger boil up inside me. But I squashed it down, instead turning my high-beam smile on her, the one I'd learned from Hope. "I haven't kissed Ardy there yet, but now that you mention it, maybe we'll hit it up after school."

"No, what I meant was—"

"Unless you wanted to reserve it for you and Darren?" I

watched as redness crept up Cici's neck. Darren is her second cousin, and there was a rumor going around last year that they'd had sex. I'm sure it's not true, but neither is Ardy's Undateable quality.

So screw Cici.

I left her in the hallway and walked into class with my head held high.

Other than that moment, everything at school is perfect with Ardy. I'm hyperaware of the details that make up *him*. How he sketches animals on the front covers of his notebooks. And how he often gets songs stuck in his head, like he's living the soundtrack of his own life. And how that thing he was doing against my knee in the cafeteria the other day—moving his thumb in circles against my skin—it's something he does when he's touching me. It seems to be his way of letting me know that even when we're only holding hands in the hall, he's not checked out. He's aware of me beside him.

Also, it kind of makes me melt.

He's doing it in the middle of the week after school when we turn a corner and Hope nearly mows us down, she's moving so fast. She skids to a stop when she sees us, her eyes darting to our intertwined fingers, then back up to our faces. She smiles—and I *think* it's genuine, though I can't be sure—but all she says is "Sorry! Late to French club!" before taking off again.

I want to ask Ardy if he's already told Hope about us or if the sight of our linked hands was new information for her. But I don't, because he's pulling me in for a kiss.

"You are *very* friendly at school," I tell him when we come up for air.

"I'm friendly everywhere," he says. "What are you doing this weekend?"

"Soccer game and spending the night at Hope's on Friday," I remind him.

"I happen to live next door to Hope."

"I happen to know that." We grin at each other. "Maybe we'll run into each other."

Later, Christopher Connor is at the locker next to mine when I'm getting a textbook. He looks over at me. "You dating Ardy?"

"Yeah."

"Cool." Christopher closes his locker and spins the dial to lock it. "See you later."

See, the word's gotten around . . . and it's fine.

» » « «

I'm on the schedule to help out at Wheelz more than usual this week, so it's Thursday afternoon before I'm able to go to the bookstore. I planned to drop Leo at home first, but when I stupidly tell him where I'm going, he wants to come along. I can't think of an excuse to say no, so I allow it.

Other stores have come and gone, but BeBe's Books has been here as long as I can remember. The aisles are narrow, and the shelves are tall and packed with paperbacks. The smell reminds me of my grandparents' basement on the East Coast: a little musty, a little familiar.

I spot Krista Willis immediately. She's on a step stool in the romance aisle, cramming books onto an already full shelf. Leo wanders off to the fantasy and sci-fi section, and I make a bee-line to Krista. She looks down at me. "Can I help you?"

"I'm looking for a good romance." At least that's somewhat true.

"What kind?"

"Um . . ." I clearly haven't thought this all the way through. "Maybe something with pirates?"

Krista's eyes brighten. "Ooh, I just shelved a bunch of swashbucklers. Hold on." She finishes stocking the books and then descends to my level. "Do you like a lot of sex?" I stare at her and she laughs. "When you're reading, I mean. Or do you want it to be mostly implied?"

"Oh. Maybe split the difference?"

"I'm with you," she says, making her way down the aisle. "I like heat, but nothing too graphic."

Did you have heat with Ardy?

Obviously, I don't ask the question. Instead, I ask a different one as I follow her. "What high school do you go to?"

Krista turns around and gives me an overly dramatic look of disappointment. "What, you don't think I'm in college or something?"

I let my gaze travel over her heart-shaped face and upturned nose. "Don't take this the wrong way, but I would believe it if you said you were still in middle school."

"I get that a lot." Krista laughs. For an emo girl, she's very friendly. "I'm at Verdugo. How about you?"

"REACH."

"Do you know Will Hartsook? He used to be my boy-friend."

He used to be my not-boyfriend, but I don't tell Krista that. "Yeah, he's in my biology class." I figure it's a harmless piece of information to give out. "Do you know Ian . . ." *Crap, I can't remember his last name.*

"Ian Charnock?" Krista says. "That's the only Ian I know."

"Yeah, one of my friends . . ." *(stupidly dates him)* ". . . is friends with him."

"We're in English together," Krista says. "He's that guy who always knows the answer but doesn't raise his hand first because he doesn't want to be *that* guy."

And yet as far as I've seen, Ian is totally and absolutely *that* guy.

"Cool." The good news is that even if I didn't have a se-cret agenda here, this would be a totally normal conversation to have in Burbank. Everyone's interrelated in some way. I watch Krista look through pirate romances for a minute, and then—like it just occurred to me—I throw out another name. "Oh, Ardy Tate goes to my school. I think he used to go to Verdugo, right?"

Krista's hand falls away from the books. She turns to face me, dropping her voice. "Yeah, I know that guy."

"You do?" I should be in drama club—it comes out in such a tone of genuine surprise. "What's his story?"

"I used to date him, too," Krista says in a conspiratorial tone. I lean in, waiting. She drops her voice to a whisper. "I was an asshole. I cheated on him."

I wait, but that seems to be the end of the story, so I give what might be the correct response. "Oh, man."

"I know, right? It was with a waiter from Fuddruckers. He's, like, five years older than me and *so cute*. He's an actor. He's going to be in a Lifetime movie next month."

These are the moments when I hate Los Angeles.

But all I say to Krista is "That's cool."

"Yeah. Ardy was shockingly nice about it. I mean, I wouldn't have been. I would have lost my mind. But he was like, whatever."

It's also not at all the dramatic story I was expecting.

Krista shrugs. "Honestly, even if I hadn't gotten my Fudd rucked—"

She pauses, and I realize she's holding for laughter. I oblige with a forced giggle.

"—Ardy and I wouldn't have lasted. He's weird, and I didn't want to be up in that anymore. Do you know he races pigeons or some shit?"

"I did not," I tell her. Then I grab a pirate book, pay for it, and signal Leo to head for the door. "Thanks," I tell her as I leave.

I even mean it.

When I get home, I send Cooper a text:

> Ian's full of crap. Girl #1 has issues. Not Ardy. She cheated and he dealt with it.

He texts back right away:

> There's 2 others.

I ignore it, and a moment later he texts again:

Also—Ian is hot and awesome.

Ugh.

» » « «

We lose Friday's soccer game to Verdugo High, even though I imitate Hope's cheering and screaming every time one of our players steals the ball or makes a goal. But, sadly, our enthusiasm isn't enough to lead REACH to victory. When the game is over and our players are trudging back to the locker room, Katie sails up. "You can still change your mind about the party." She says it to me but a second later seems to realize she's being rude. "Oh, you can come, too," she tells Hope.

"Not this time," I say.

"On Monday I'll regale you with what you missed," Katie says before taking off.

Hope looks at me. "We can go if you want to."

I shrug. "I've been to a lot of parties."

On the way to Hope's house, I ask why Evan didn't come to the soccer game.

"He doesn't like sports." Hope glances at me from behind her steering wheel. "He's kinda like Ardy in that way."

She's trying to start a conversation about Ardy, but I'm not ready to go there. Not with her. Not yet.

I change the topic. "I didn't bring a sleeping bag or pillow. Should we run back to my house?"

"No. We have stuff. Hillary stays over all the time and she never remembers to bring a toothbrush. My dads started stocking extras for my friends, literally because of her."

It would never in a billion years occur to my parents to do that, but then they're not exactly trying to woo my friends into staying over. On the rare occasion I do an overnighter with Katie, it's almost always at her house. Neither of us is allowed to spend the night with Cooper, which always results in his feelings being hurt if we sleep over together.

I'm sure my mom would be even worse about it if she knew my first kiss was with Cooper.

We were in eighth grade when he asked me to go under the middle school bleachers with him. That's where Cooper kissed me for what was the first time for both of us. Cooper smelled like the grape Popsicle he'd eaten as we'd walked there, but our mouths didn't touch long enough for me to register whether he tasted like it, too. He pulled back immediately—like, *so* immediately—and beamed at me. "I'm gay," he said. I burst out laughing—because it was so weird and blunt and random—and he set a finger on my lips to shush me. "Don't be mad."

"How can I be mad? I'm laughing."

"I wanted to make sure," he continued. "Because I really like you, and if I can't get it up for *you*—"

"Gross!" I buried my face in my hands, but it didn't stop Cooper from talking.

"—then I know for sure that I can't get it up for any girl." I finally pulled my hands away from my face to find Cooper staring at me. Very serious. "Good news," he told me. "I'm going to be so much better for you than any boyfriend."

"How's that?"

"Guess you'll see." He grinned, and he was still wearing braces at the time, so his teeth flashed metal at me. "Wanna walk to the high school and watch the boys' track team run around?"

I grinned back at him. "Totally."

And so began our friendship. Now, sitting next to Hope as she pulls off the darkened street into her driveway, I wonder if that's how all friendships work . . . without the kissing part, of course. One person decides it's going to be a thing, and the other one accepts it.

Is that what's happening with Hope and me?

Hope's fathers greet us at the front door. They introduce themselves as Chris and Brad, and they both offer to get me a soda—which I decline—before asking me questions about myself. Chris, who has dark brown skin and a goatee and short hair twisted into a hundred tiny tufts, asks how I know Hope and what classes we share. Brad—possibly the blondest man I have ever met—wants to know how long I've lived in Burbank and what my parents do. I answer their questions until Hope finally pulls me away, telling them that we're *trying* to have girl night and can they *please stop.*

Hope drags me away into the kitchen and starts opening cabinets. "I'm so sorry," she says, pulling out a bag of gluten-free crackers.

"For what?" I honestly don't know what she's talking about.

"The dads are like that with new friends. . . . Sparkling or flat?" Hope opens the fridge, gesturing to an array of bottled waters with one hand while grabbing a bag of soy string cheese with the other.

"Sparkling."

"It's like they're trying to be best friends with my friends." Hope scoops out two bottles of sparkling water and hands them to me. "I hate it."

"They seem nice." I'm telling the truth. My parents have never made an effort to befriend my friends. I don't think they know how. Based on the limited circle of their *own* friends, maybe they've never known how.

"It's so annoying." Hope has finished assembling our snacks, and now she's heading toward the back of the house. "I'll show you."

I follow her, wondering if being embarrassed by your parents is universal. Maybe my parents aren't so awful after all. Maybe they're just one particular brand of awful.

Hope leads me out the back door and onto the covered patio. She tucks the snacks under an arm so she can pull out her phone and use the light to show me her yard. Like many California yards, it's encircled by tall cinder-block walls because good walls mean good neighbors, or something like that. Straight across the middle of the grass, there's a giant tree, and built lovingly into it is . . . a playhouse. If I were to design a yard for a home with children, this is the perfect example of what would go in it. Even with only the light from Hope's phone, I can see the big, beautiful fuchsia wooden house up in the tree.

A bright yellow ladder leads up to it. "Dads put it in when I was little," Hope says. "It used to be pastel pink, but they had it repainted last year to account for my maturity."

She says that last bit in a wry tone, which amuses me. Or maybe I'm not feeling amusement but rather . . . jealousy? Or am I impressed?

Something.

"Can we go in it?"

Hope nods, leading the way across the grass. She switches the snack bags to her right hand and, with practiced ease, uses her left to catch nimbly from rung to rung as she climbs up. She scrambles onto the little platform around the tree house and then calls down to me. "Throw me the waters."

I do, and—after a couple of tries—Hope catches the plastic bottles and shines her phone light down so I can use both of my hands to ascend. I clamber onto the platform and follow Hope, crouching to enter the dark tree house through the curtains covering the small door.

"Here." Hope turns her phone on and gives it to me so I can shine it at her hands. I can't totally see what she's doing, but a moment later lights glow to life around the perimeter of the ceiling, and I realize she's plugged in a string of white Christmas bulbs. They illuminate the inside of the tree house, which—despite Hope's embarrassment—is nearly unbearably awesome. There's a cozy turquoise rug spread over the rough wooden planks of the floor, and narrow shelves are built into the walls. I want to be a little girl again so I can fully enjoy it. It's better than any IKEA room I've ever been in.

"Bananas, right?" Hope takes her phone back from me and plops onto the rug. "Evan's ongoing joke is that this is where we're going to have sex for the first time."

I'm surprised as I sink beside her. Not that I've given it any thought, but if I *had,* I would have assumed that #Heaven had already done the Deed. They've been together forever, at least by high school's time line.

Apparently, my thoughts are clear on my face, because Hope shakes her head. "I want to be supersure, you know?"

I *do* know. At least, in theory I do. It's what I *should* want. Actually, ever since Ardy has come into my life, maybe it *is* what I want after all. I guess we'll see. But the only thing I say to Hope is "Yeah."

"Then when we do it, I want it to be perfect," she continues. "And so far, I haven't been sure, and it hasn't been perfect. So we haven't."

"But how can it ever be perfect?" I cock my head to the side, looking at her. "I mean, how can you *know?*"

Hope shrugs. "I hope I'll know when the time is right."

I'm not so sure I'm with her on that one, but I keep my mouth shut about it. "So you never have?" I ask her. "With anyone?"

"No. Have you?"

I consider how to answer that. And *why* I'm answering it. Are Hope and I becoming friends?

"Yes." Hope's eyebrows rise at my half-truth. She doesn't look like she's judgmental, only curious. "One time."

"What was it like?" Her question comes out hesitantly,

which is surprising given how Hope never seems to hesitate about anything. She marches straight ahead, assuming she'll be included, assuming she'll be wanted. At least that's what it seems like from where I'm standing. But maybe we're all insecure about something.

"I don't know," I tell her honestly, remembering Kai in his parents' wine cellar. "I didn't have a lot of time to figure out what we were doing, and then we stopped seeing each other."

"So it wasn't perfect."

"Not by a long shot."

"Yet here you are." Hope smiles at me. "You don't seem all regretful and broken."

"Is that why you're waiting—so you won't be regretful and broken?"

"I guess it freaks me out." Hope pulls her knees up to her chest, wrapping her arms around them. "We're in high school, right? So no matter how much we love the boys we're with, chances are not great that we'll stay together. But I can't imagine it, what would break us up."

Whereas the assumption I live under is that every time I'm with a guy, it's a short-term thing. It's easier to go into it that way. When you're standing at the beginning and already able to see the end, everything in the middle doesn't have to mean very much. You can skate right through it. But if Hope is the opposite, I can see why the middle part is so weighted with meaning.

I try to flash forward to the inevitable end with Ardy. How I'll wriggle out of it, what I'll say to make him leave me. But unlike my usual sense of relief at the possibility, the thought of it sets an ache gnawing inside me. This time I don't want to see the ending. This time I don't want to arrive there.

"You've been friends with Ardy since you were little, right?" Might as well cut to the chase. I'm on a fact-finding mission: What does Hope know about his ex-girlfriends, and how close are she and Ardy?

"Yay!" Hope does what looks like a jazz-hands thing. "I was hoping we were going to talk about him. Do you love him?"

I stare at her. "It's been, like, half a minute."

"I know, I'm kidding. I'm *mostly* kidding. You like him, right?" Hope beams her signature beam at me. "You know I didn't really have to ditch him for *le français* that day you drove him home, right?"

I stare at her, trying to figure out how to answer. If the thing I've suspected all along is true—that Ardy secretly, or even not so secretly, loves her—my being with him would help Hope maintain equilibrium. That is, if it's true that he wants her, she knows it, and she wants to stay friends with him. Everything becomes a lot easier if he has a girlfriend. Namely, me.

I have to answer her, so I finally say, "Yes. I really like him."

Which is true. Very true. Painfully true, and becoming more so with every minute I spend with him.

"Good." Hope is nodding. "I wouldn't want him to get hurt."

It makes me wonder how much she knows about what happened at Verdugo High, about Krista Willis and those other two girls. How can I get her to tell me, without obviously fishing for information? Without letting her know that I've already done some investigating of my own. I can't figure out a way in, so I go with a completely blatant question. "Have you and Ardy ever . . . been a thing?"

"No. Not even a little." Hope shakes her head almost violently. "We grew up together. It would be like kissing a cousin or something." I give her a stern look, and she bursts out laughing. "I know, I know . . . the thing with Daddly on the porch. I never should have told you all that."

"But we're so glad that you did."

Hope sobers. "Anyway, Ardy and I are BFFs. I don't think we could be if we had history between us. It would be weird."

I disagree with Hope but don't want to explain why. After all, I'm fine with all those boys I used to kiss. It doesn't have to be huge. It doesn't have to be *fraught*. People can move on and continue their lives. I do it all the time.

I'm about to change the subject when a soft *thump* comes from somewhere back behind the tree house, in the rear of the yard. I tilt my head to listen, immediately on edge. "Did you hear that?" I ask Hope. "Coyotes come down from the hills sometimes."

"Don't worry." Hope's eyes twinkle. "Coyotes can't climb ladders."

Down below, something bumps against the trunk of the tree. I jump, and this time Hope laughs out loud. "I'll protect you," she says, scrambling to her feet.

"Don't—" I say as she pulls the curtain open while down below there's the sound of movement on the ladder.

"Trust me," Hope says right as Evan's head pops over the edge of the platform.

Of course.

And how annoying that I didn't even think of that.

"Ladies," Evan says, pulling himself up. "Is Ardy coming?"

"Let's see." Hope pulls out her phone and starts texting. It sets a little fire of excitement inside me. I was already hoping I'd see him while I was here—like, maybe I'd run into him in the street outside. Now that he might come over on sort of a spontaneous double date, it's just about perfect. "Ugh," Hope says. "He doesn't want to get me in trouble for having boys over illicitly. I'm telling him that my dads are in for the night. They're watching movies in their room."

Evan looks at me. "Lark, you should text him."

"I'm telling him you're here," Hope says. "Anyway, I wouldn't get busted for him being up here—only for Evan."

"I'm the troublemaker," Evan admits. He climbs inside the tree house, which is starting to get crowded, and flops onto the rug. "I'm always trying to make trouble up here." He raises his eyebrows at Hope in a not-very-subtle way. Gross. "What's he saying?"

"Nothing," says Hope.

And then there's another soft *thump* from somewhere in the yard. The ladder starts shaking again. "That's for you," Evan tells me. "Close the curtain behind you."

I'm glad I already had the talk with Hope so I can be certain they're not going to have sex in there while I'm on the platform with Ardy. That would be awkward. And gross.

I duck through the curtains (making sure they swing shut behind me) and step out onto the platform, where I drop to my knees and crawl to the edge. Ardy looks up at me from the ladder below, starlight reflecting in his glasses. The sight of him makes me ridiculously happy until—"I'm not coming in," he says.

"Why?"

"I'm a rule follower." He climbs another rung. "I don't want to piss off Hope's dads. We kind of have a good thing going between us."

I choose to shove any thoughts about that away for the moment, glancing back at the curtain behind me. It's silent inside the tree house, which I assume means Evan and Hope are engaged in a slobberfest. And since they're occupied . . .

I lower to my stomach, wriggling to the edge of the platform. "You don't have to come all the way up," I tell Ardy. "Just come close enough."

"I can do that." He ascends until his hands are on the top rung. I prop myself up on my elbows, allowing my hands to rest on his shoulders. It's not the world's most comfortable position, but I don't care. I only care about one thing: kissing Ardy Tate. I think about kissing him so much—all the time, really—that I'm not going to let this opportunity get away.

Ardy stands there, holding on to the ladder, smiling into my eyes. "Is this close enough?"

"Let me check." I tilt forward so I can bring my mouth to his, kissing him like I've been wanting to kiss him all day.

Yes.

The kiss lasts and lasts, slow and gentle and perfect, like we've been doing this for years. He shifts, and a second later one of his hands is sliding into my hair. I pull away just far enough so I can whisper, "Don't fall." And then he's caressing the back of my neck, pulling me in farther so our mouths are pressed hard against each other. I don't know if his breathing has sped up, but mine has. Even more so when he takes his mouth off mine, dropping it to the side of my neck. A shiver runs through me, and I think I make a tiny gasping sound in my throat. I hear it a second after it's out, as he's pulling away, putting distance between us.

He pauses, then presses his forehead to mine. Holding me there in an embrace that doesn't allow for more kissing. "I'm rethinking my refusal to join you up there," he says.

"I'm rethinking my reasons for being up here in the first place."

We stay like that for a moment, and now I can tell that, yes, our breathing is slowing down, both of us returning to normal. "You should know," Ardy finally says, "that this is me exercising great self-control."

"Impressive." I dart forward to peck him on the lips, the thought flitting through my head: Has Ardy had sex?

» » « «

Later the boys are gone and Hope and I are in her room—her on her bed, and me on the trundle that pulls out from under it. I think she's asleep when I get a text. I pull out my phone.

    i Like
    A
    Really amazing
   LarK

It's my name again, like he wrote to me the night we played hide-and-seek. A smile leaps to my face as I stare at the screen, writing a message in my head before I thumb-type it out. It takes me a minute to lay it out right, but then I send it to him:

i **A**m wild about
eve**R**ything I know of this
Dude who makes me
happ**Y**

Then I turn off my phone and put my head down, letting thoughts of Ardy drift me off to sleep.

CHAPTER THIRTEEN

By the time I get home late Saturday morning, Katie has texted several selfies of her having a great time at last night's party. She writes:

> Don't text back. I need a nap.

I texted Cooper three times, and he still hasn't texted back. I haven't heard from Ardy, either. I hoped we'd see each other on the way from Hope's porch to her car, but there's no sign of him, and because we're still so new, I have no idea what his usual Saturday morning routine is. Does he sleep late? Get up and go jogging? Help his mother with housework?

No idea.

When Hope drops me off in front of my house, she grins at me. "More, please."

"Okay." I think I'm agreeing to more sleepovers, but I'm not totally sure. I haven't completely learned how to speak Hope's language yet. Maybe she means scheduling more times for us to make out with our boyfriends while adjacent to each other.

When it's early afternoon and I still haven't heard from Cooper, I resort to my old standby: online stalking. Cooper is checked into one of the frozen-yogurt places on San Fernando. He's also posted a photo of what he's eating, which the caption tells me is pistachio swirled with pomegranate acai, topped with chunks of lychee. More important than what Cooper's eating, however, is who he's eating it with. Across the table from his frozen-yogurt treat is the front of what *has* to be one of Ian's classic—and classically boring—blue shirts.

Enough. Seriously—enough, already.

I'm still in what's basically pajamas from my night at Hope's—leggings, a long-sleeved cotton T-shirt, sneakers—but I don't care. I throw a sweater over the whole thing, grab my keys, and head for the door. Looks like I could stand to eat some yogurt.

By the time I've driven the mile and a half, found a spot in one of downtown Burbank's parking structures, and hoofed it over to the yogurt place, Cooper and Ian are coming out of the store. As I cross the street toward them, at first I think they're holding hands, but then I clear a planter filled with greenery and I realize they're each holding someone *else's* hand. It's a young kid—a girl, maybe four or five years old—who walks unsteadily between them. There's a telltale smear of (probably chocolate) yogurt around her mouth and a set of hard plastic braces around her legs. Since Cooper doesn't have a sibling, I have to assume this one belongs to Ian. I'm about to retreat because the last thing I want is to have weirdness in front of Ian and whoever this kid is, except that Ian sees me and waves.

Cooper looks surprised, but the two of them lead the girl toward me.

"Hi!" My tone is falsely bright, which I know Cooper won't buy for a second, but Ian probably will because subtleties are lost on him. I smile down at the young kid. "Who's this?"

Ian gives her a nudge. "Want to tell her your name?"

The girl nods, looking up at me with light blue eyes that are strikingly similar to Ian's. When she speaks, her voice is low and slow and deliberate, like she's thinking carefully about how to say each word. "I'm Claire. I'm six."

Older than I thought. I give her a solemn nod. "I'm Lark. I'm eighteen."

"That's a funny name." Her comment elicits a snicker from Cooper.

"You are not wrong," I tell her before looking back at the boys. "What are you up to?"

"Yogurt," Cooper says, giving me a deeply suspicious look. "And sunshine. What are *you* up to?"

"The same." I know I'll have to answer to him at some point, but that point isn't now. Besides, he'll have to answer to me later, too.

Claire speaks again. "Do you go to school with my brother?"

"No." I gesture toward Cooper. "I go to school with that guy."

"Oh, he's funny," Claire says. "He knows how to make paper airplanes."

"He's cool like that," I tell her.

"Do you want to go to the park with us?"

I glance at Cooper, who gives me the tiniest headshake—
don't. "No thank you," I tell Claire. "I have a lot of homework."

"My brother always has homework, too," she says. "High school is stupid."

"Sometimes," I agree with her, then exchange a round of waves with everyone before darting away and into the store. Might as well make that part of what I said true.

I'm back in my room with a cup of mango frozen yogurt when I get a text from Cooper:

I got more info.

I send him a fast return text:

From your secret boyfriend, you mean?

Cooper:

He says Ardy keyed a girl's car and slashed her tires.

Okay, so that gives me pause. I stare at Cooper's text for a long time before typing back:

Whatever.

It's not much of an answer, but . . . whatever. It can't possibly be true. I pout in my room for a while until I (finally) hear from Ardy. It's a text:

What are you doing tonight?

After what Cooper said, I know I need to get to the bottom of this. But I don't want to put Ardy on hold while I do it.

Seeing you? I get off work at 8.

Ardy:

I'll pick you up.

I drop my phone on the bed and reach for my laptop. There's some more investigating in order.

» » « «

Elle Campbell doesn't have a job. Or at least not one that she talks about online. But what she *does* seem to have is an insatiable need to post her every single move. Today alone, Elle Campbell has been to Starbucks, the public library, five stores in the mall, and now—get this—Starbucks again. She's still there when I roll in. I get in line for a latte, keeping an eye on her.

Elle has long dangly earrings and short, spiky blond hair with fire-red tips. She's wearing leggings like mine, but hers are paired with a Verdugo High jersey under a camouflage tunic, and combat boots. Her lipstick is dark blue, her biceps are clearly defined, and she's angry-typing on her laptop.

Elle Campbell looks like she could kick my ass.

Nevertheless, I receive my latte and plop down at the table next to hers. She glances at me, and I nod at her. She turns her gaze back to her computer. I clear my throat. She looks up again, and I give her a tentative smile.

"What?" she says.

Real pleasant girlfriend, Ardy.

I decide I have nothing to lose, so I gesture to her jersey. "I know a guy who went there," I tell her.

"So?"

Sheesh.

"Ardy Tate." I wait for a sign of recognition. There is none, so I forge ahead. "I heard about the car."

This time Elle's facial expression shifts . . . to one of guilt. She runs a hand through her blond-and-red hair. "Yeah, I shouldn't have done that. I was really pissed."

Um. "You . . . keyed his car?" I ask in a small voice.

"It's an ugly minivan," Elle tells me. "But I slashed one of his tires, too. He broke up with me right in the middle of marching-band rehearsal. I was pissed."

I stare at her, trying to make sense of the puzzle pieces. This rumor floating around: it's about the wrong person. Ardy's not the violent one, or the cheater. He's the person who had bad things happen *to* him. Yet another reminder that the Burbank rumor mill is a maddening source of misinformation.

"What?" Elle says, and I realize I'm still staring at her.

"Uh . . . what instrument do you play? In marching band?" It's a way to make conversation before I can extricate myself from this awkward situation.

"Piccolo," she tells me.

"I like piccolos," I tell her. And then I grab my latte and flee. *What the ever-loving hell?*

» » « «

Normally I wear something like jeans and a sweatshirt to work, but today I choose a short flowered skirt with a white tank top and a cropped pink jacket. I pull my hair into a high ponytail and slide my feet into tennis shoes, both of which are intended to make me look like I didn't dress up *that* much.

I ask Mom if she can give Leo and me a ride to Wheelz because Ardy is going to pick me up there at the end of my shift, so I don't want to have my car. Her lips go tight and she presses them together before replying. "And where are you and Ardy planning to go after work?"

"Maybe the mall or something?"

"The mall closes at eight," she informs me.

"I don't know, Mom. We don't have plans yet. We might end up at Hope's house."

"Will Hope's parents be home?" Mom asks.

"Yes." Although, truthfully, I have no idea if they'll be home or if Ardy has any thoughts about going over there. We haven't talked much about tonight, just shared links to various movie trailers. "Maybe we'll see a movie."

"He seems like a nice boy." Mom levels a gaze at me over our kitchen counter. "But he's still a boy. Don't get yourself into a situation with him."

I sigh. "What are you talking about? Don't get pregnant?"

"You're a pretty girl," she tells me. "All the boys want one thing from you. Don't give it to them."

"I won't." It's the only way someone could possibly answer that statement. But what is that supposed to mean? That I should *never* have sex? That the *only* reason a boy would want me is for sex?

Ardy told me he doesn't usually go for my type of pretty. It appears true, as evidenced by Krista and Elle, who are both so different from me. And although Ardy enumerated a list of reasons why he *is* interested in me . . . if what my mom says is true, it could all be a lie.

But still—what about what *I* want? My body is programmed to want sex, too, just like any boy's . . . isn't it? Why does everyone talk so much about what boys want and so extraordinarily little about what *girls* want?

I don't have an answer at the moment, so I escape to my room to get ready for work.

But really to get ready for Ardy.

» » « «

Wheelz is hopping during my four-hour shift, which is par for the course on a Saturday night. I work the front register while Leo wipes tables and restocks snacks. Dad is out front for a while, but eventually he makes his way to the back. He's still there at eight o'clock, when Ardy walks in the front doors.

And also at 8:01, when my mom arrives.

She comes up to my workstation, where Ardy is waiting for a burger. His mom is in La Jolla, and as it turns out, Ardy does not actually know how to cook much. I'm preparing to count the money in the cash register before turning it over to Mano. Mom gives Ardy a curt nod. "Ardy."

"Hi, Ms. Dayton."

She gives me a meaningful look—*home by midnight*—before heading into the back.

"Will she wait up for you?" Ardy asks me.

"No. We have a system. I have to turn off the lights in the stairwell when I come in. So if my parents wake up in the night and the lights are still on, they know I'm not home yet." I start counting twenties. "One sec."

Ardy doesn't say anything, but he leans over the counter to kiss me on the cheek. It completely disrupts my concentration, and I have to start counting again. "Sorry," he says, but when I glance up at him, he doesn't look sorry at all.

"No distractions," I tell him in my sternest voice.

That's when the screaming starts.

CHAPTER FOURTEEN

I'm silent on the passenger side of the minivan as Ardy pilots us away from Wheelz. I keep my gaze firmly fixed out the window and feel rather than see his multiple glances over at me. After several blocks, he clears his throat.

"It's okay," he says.

I only shake my head, because it's actually *not* okay. It's bad enough that my parents can't keep their shit together when our family is alone at our house. But to have one of their battles out in public, at their place of business, in full earshot of their employees, their customers . . . and Ardy. It's mortifying.

What does he think of them? What does he think of *me*?

I keep my mouth shut as Ardy drives us toward downtown and then through and past it, crossing Glenoaks and going up into a neighborhood with bigger houses and nicer palm trees. There, he winds up and down, one block at a time, moving across the Burbank foothills.

Finally he sets his hand on my bare knee. Without meaning to, I jerk my leg away.

"Lark." His voice is so, so gentle. "Do you want me to take you home?"

"No." It's not his fault that his girlfriend and her family are a mess. I move my leg back to where it was, shifting my body so I'm facing him, watching his slim silhouette as it comes to life and fades away with each streetlight we drive under. I reach out and touch his arm, giving it a gentle tug. He releases the steering wheel and allows me to move his hand back to where he tried to put it. Back on my knee. Back where it belongs.

We drive for another few blocks before he speaks. "I left out something when I told you about my dad. His motorcycle accident." He stops, swallows, keeps going. "It wasn't an accident. He left a note."

My fingers contract around his as my heart does the same within me. Ardy's pain must be so much bigger than mine. I'm an idiot for being worried about how it looks when my parents have their stupid fights. "I'm sorry," I say, because it's the only thing worth saying.

"Last week I asked Mom if she donated his eyeballs. She said no."

It seems like such an awful and tragic waste, everything about it. What should have been a life. "Did she say why?"

"She said . . ." He pauses, and I sense how hard this is for him. Even if he doesn't remember his father, it's difficult. Even if you have never known what it's like to have all the missing pieces of your life, you can still feel the jagged places where they've broken away, where you're broken apart. "She said she agreed to donate everything but those. . . . She always would have been wondering. She would have looked for him in every stranger she passed, trying to find his eyes in someone else's face. Even though it doesn't make sense—medically, I mean—that's what she would have done."

It's the saddest thing I've ever heard. Ardy's father dying at his own hand, Ardy's mom dealing with the aftermath, someone else missing their chance at sight because she couldn't see out from behind her own pain.

"I'm sorry," I tell him again.

"If she'd done it, at least she would be looking at people's faces."

The way he says it, so raw and open and sad, I realize the depth of the pain and shame he's feeling. Maybe every family has something that hurts.

Ardy pulls to the side of the road and puts the minivan into park so he can turn and look at me. "What do you want to do?"

"What are my options?"

"Have you ever been to the Ridge restaurant?" I shake my head. "It's at the top of the hill. There's a big outdoor deck where you can see the lights of the city. We could get coffee and dessert." He grins at me. "That is merely one option out of many."

"What are the other options?"

Instead of answering, Ardy leans over the emergency brake to kiss me. I kiss him back, feeling a light prickliness around his mouth. I pull away so I can reach a finger up to trace the edges of his lips. "You're scratchy."

"I'm considering growing a goatee," Ardy says. "But only if you approve."

I run my finger down to his chin. Yep, the scratchiness is

there, too, just a little. "As long as it doesn't interfere with this."
I press my mouth to his again—a fast, fast kiss—and then settle
into my seat. "I'm still waiting for the other options."

"Okay. We could walk around downtown and see one of
those movies we were looking at. We could go to the outdoor
mall in Glendale. Or . . ." He pauses, glancing down at my hand
and then lifting it, sliding his fingers between my own. "Or I
could take you home, like I said before. It's okay if that's what
you want."

I gaze at him, not wanting that at all. My mother's words of
warning flash through my mind.

Don't get yourself into a situation.

Boys want one thing.

Don't give it to them.

And then those words are competing with others, also in
her voice:

I never should have married you.

Go screw yourself.

I hate you.

It's what she says to my father—and what he says back to
her—when they're in one of their screaming matches. It's some
of what Ardy heard as I frantically counted cash register bills
and he moved away from the counter to be respectful.

I make a decision.

I squeeze Ardy's fingers, pulling his hand up to my mouth
and nibbling along his knuckles. "Let's go to your house," I tell
him, knowing his mother won't be there.

He swallows. "Okay."

CHAPTER FIFTEEN

Ardy's house is dark when he unlocks the front door and leads me inside. He immediately turns on an overhead light. "Do you want something to drink? We have sodas."

"I'm okay."

"All right. Um . . ." Ardy looks around like he's not sure how to orchestrate any of this. "Come on."

I trail him into the living room, where he flips on a lamp with a pale blue glass base. The room is cute—coral walls, steamer trunk for a coffee table, a large clock shaped like the sun. I bet that during the day it's cheery and bright and open, but right now it feels small and cozy and warm.

And maybe romantic.

Ardy moves two green throw pillows from one side of the couch to the center. Then he moves them back. He sits where the pillows briefly were and looks up at me. "I don't know a graceful way to invite you over here."

"That's okay." I remember the other times I thought I was going to have sex, first with Elliot and then with Kai. If I'd really thought them through, how would I have gone about it?

I reach up to my hair, still in a ponytail from work, and slowly pull out the elastic band, shaking my head so my tangled hair tumbles down around my shoulders. I kick off my tennis shoes and wiggle out of my jacket, letting it fall to the floor by my feet. I reach behind to unhook my bra but then think better of it. I might be wearing the tank top in front of him, but unleashing the girls right out in the light like this would be . . . a lot to look at. I'm already trying to make peace with the idea that, in a minute, he's going to be front and center for all of it. I drop my arms to my sides and, trying to project confidence and security and readiness, level my gaze at Ardy.

Ardy looks like he's in a trance, his lips ever so slightly apart, as I walk to the couch and sink down next to him. I reach up to his face and gently remove his glasses, setting them on the steamer trunk. I stay there, waiting, while his eyes rove over my face, darting down to my body for a second and then back up again. "I want you to know . . . ," he whispers.

"What?" I whisper in return.

He doesn't finish the sentence, because suddenly his mouth is on mine and the whole world is on fire.

It's everything I had wanted on Hope's tree house platform: my hands running up and down the tight muscles of his back. His hands sliding around my rib cage. Easing under the edge of my tank top, tugging me closer, pulling me along as he leans against the couch cushions. Sinking farther down, reclining all the way, taking me with him. We kiss and kiss and kiss—I have no sense of how long it lasts—while our bodies move against each other. Suddenly he lifts his hips, pushing me up and over, moving his body to the outer edge of the couch. Before I can figure out what he's doing, or maybe ask him with actual words, he's rolling me onto my back, rolling on top of me. He takes his lips away from my own and nuzzles his nose against mine. "Is this okay?" he asks.

"Yes," I whisper, and then I gasp because his mouth is on the side of my neck, and the sound comes out before I know I'm going to make it. It's an automatic response to Ardy's touch, all my nerves tingling at the feel of him. His whole body is lean and hard, pulsing against mine, and now one of his hands is sliding back down my ribs, over my hips, plucking at the bottom edge of my skirt, dragging it upward. . . .

And I freeze.

I panic.

Because—and this is awful because I already said yes—I don't want to do it.

Although my body is responding to every movement Ardy makes, another part of me is not. I can't tell if it's my heart or my brain or my soul, but I know that *some* part of me is not ready. Not yet. Not this soon.

Yet here we are, alone in Ardy's house, halfway to Naked Town.

A zillion excuses run through my head: my period, a foot cramp, a science project I remembered I have to do. . . .

But this isn't Kai. This isn't Elliot. This isn't a dozen other boys I have kissed and quit. This is Ardy, and he deserves the truth. So when he realizes I've stopped moving and he asks if I'm all right, I tell the truth.

"I don't know."

And *because* he's Ardy, he rolls off me, landing on his side between my body and the back of the couch. He props his head up on his right hand, leaving his left on my abdomen, and takes a deep breath. "We can stop."

I move his hand to my shoulder and then slide my own to his face. "Are you sure?"

"God, yes. I mean, I might need a minute." Ardy drops his head to plant a firm kiss on my mouth before pulling away again. "I'm not ready to be seen in public at this exact moment, so let's not run right outside. . . ."

It makes me laugh, and then I *stop* laughing, because his eyes are so gentle and his pupils are so huge and his mouth is so beautiful. I stroke the side of his face with my thumb, a giant *I love you* bubbling up inside me. Which I don't say—obviously—because it's way, way too soon.

But if that's the case, why did I think it wasn't too soon for sex?

"I'm sorry," I tell him.

"No." Ardy's eyes go superserious, and he touches my lips with a finger. "You don't apologize for this, ever. You're ready when you're ready. Besides"—he gives me a giant grin—"I was just about to stop anyway."

"Shut up." I whap him on the chest. "You were not."

"I totally was." He's still grinning. "You beat me to it, that's all."

I grab the front of his shirt and yank him down so I can kiss him, hard. It lasts a full minute, and when we finally stop, both of us breaking apart at the same moment, Ardy slides his arms all the way around me, pulling me onto my side so we can lie there, pressed against each other. I run my hand into his hair, teasing it between my fingers, while I work up the nerve to ask my question. "Have you done it before?"

Ardy becomes very, very still, and finally he answers in a whisper. "Yes."

It's not that my heart sinks, exactly. It's more like a hot molten fire of jealousy volcanoes all over it. Which is not at all fair, and I recognize that, but I can't help wondering who it was: Krista? Elle? Trissa? Someone else?

"Have you done it a *lot*?" I ask him. What I don't ask is this: *If and when we do actually do it, am I going to be the only amateur in the room?*

"No." He buries his face in my neck like he's embarrassed. "Only twice. And it was a little blurry both times."

I feel much, much better. Maybe I shouldn't, but I do.

Ardy doesn't ask me the question, but since I know he has to be wondering, I go ahead and answer. "It was blurry the one time I did it, too."

He pulls his face out of my neck, raising his head to look at me. "Let's not be blurry," he says. "I mean, if we ever do it. I don't want to be even a little bit blurry with you."

"Me either," I assure him. And then we kiss some more.

Later, after he's driven me home to arrive in my driveway five minutes before midnight, Ardy turns to me and says, "This might sound weird, but this was a perfect night."

"For me, too."

CHAPTER SIXTEEN

I see all the important people in my life before the bell rings on Monday. Ardy swings into step beside me as I'm walking through the front doors. He slings an arm around my shoulders and pulls me to the side, planting a kiss on my forehead. "I wanted to check in." He looks down at me, his eyes sincere. "Are we good?"

"Yes." I beam at him, trying to channel Hope's exuberance into my smile. "*Really* good. But I have questions for you."

"Questions?"

"Yes, all kinds of them."

"What questions?"

"Things like *What's your favorite color?* and *Do you have any allergies?*" I tell him.

"Gray and no," Ardy says. "Also, you're weird."

"*You're* weird," I tell him. "Because gray isn't even a color. It's more of a shade. And anyway, those aren't *really* the questions, but I'm going to come up with some. You should, too."

"Getting-to-know-you questions?"

"You're catching on. I want to know everything about you."

"I like it," Ardy says. "No secrets."

Except one.

I rise to my tiptoes for a fast kiss. "See you at lunch."

I leave him there and run to catch up with Cooper and Katie, who are walking past. "Look at you two hanging out together." I smile at them. "It's like you're friends or something."

But as we turn the corner, Cooper gives me a dirty look. "Yeah, and it's like you're consorting with the enemy."

"Now Ardy's the enemy? Seriously?"

"We don't *know*," Katie says. "He might be."

"Whatever." I train my eyes on Katie. "You're mad because I wouldn't go to your party with you." I look at Cooper. "And you're mad because I busted you in a love nest with He-Who-Shall-Not-Be-Named."

"Ooh, let's hear about that!" Katie exclaims.

"It wasn't a love nest—it was yogurt," Cooper says. "And we had a chaperone."

"His sister? She's five!"

"Six!"

"You went on a babysitting date?" Katie asks. "You're actually the worst."

"Who cares, she's a kid," I argue. "Why are you hanging out with Ian, anyway? As long as I'm with Ardy, you're supposed to be keeping it casual."

"She's not wrong," Katie says.

"Why do you care?" Cooper says to her. "Yogurt is the most casual of the afternoon treats. And Lark's the one who shouldn't be with Ardy. Not if he's the degenerate that Ian says he is."

"It's already been established that Ian knows *nothing*." If I were someone who needed to worry about blood pressure, this is right about the time I'd be pulling out a cuff to check it, because this conversation is achieving the double whammy of pissing me off and stressing me out. "I've talked to two out of three purportedly wronged ex-girlfriends, and everything's turned out to be a bullshit rumor."

"Rumors have to start somewhere," Cooper says.

"Not bullshit ones," I say in return. "Those start in Ian's small, pathetic, boring little mind." Katie looks surprised, and hurt flashes over Cooper's face, but I ignore them, pulling out my phone. "Look, here's Girl Three." I find one of Trissa Jefferson's social media pages, which, yes, I've looked at a time or two. "If it'll get you off my ass, I will send her a message *right damn now.*" Cooper doesn't say anything, so I start thumb-typing:

> Hi. You don't know me but I heard you used to date Ardy Tate.

I go with honesty.

> We just got together and I've heard some things about him. Girl to girl, can you confirm or deny? I'd really appreciate it.

I hit Send and turn to them. "Happy?"

"No." Cooper glares at me. "Not really."

Katie and I watch him stomp off down the hall. "You could just let him be happy," she says.

"You're one to talk," I say, before heading in the opposite direction.

What the hell?

» » « «

It's been a couple of weeks and I still haven't heard from Trissa, not that I've spent any more time trying to track her down. I'm too busy holding hands with Ardy and kissing Ardy and floating on air around Ardy. At least that's what I'm doing when I'm not hunched over my calculus textbook. That class is destroying my will to live. Today, however, it's more interesting. We're starting a chapter on fractals. If I'm understanding it correctly, a fractal—broken down to its most basic definition—is a geometric figure in which every part of it has the same characteristics as the whole. So the patterns of the tiniest part of it repeat themselves both inward and outward. In other words, as the figure increases in size, the pattern is ever expanding.

As Ms. Perkins explains this, my gaze jerks down to where my left thumb and finger are gently tapping on the edge of my desk. I know everyone else is zoned out, but I sit up straighter, paying attention as Ms. Perkins elaborates: wherever a fractal starts, it always multiplies out in versions of itself. No matter where it goes, it always started in one place.

My heart speeds up, like it understands a second before my brain registers what I'm hearing, because now Ms. Perkins is talking about the history of fractals: when they were first discovered and what mathematicians learned about them. She says that not only the cells in our bodies but also the stars in the universe are based on fractal patterns. That all of life as we know it is one giant expanding pattern.

The rhythm of my heart increases to a roar, surging up my chest, through my throat, and into my ears, blocking out all other sound. Is *my* ever-expanding, ever-the-same pattern the key to the patterns of life? It's like it's all connected: the way I do the same things over and over with boys. How I make the same moves, the same mistakes. The way my fingers twitch over and over against my desk. I'm overcome by the terror of it, the responsibility. . . .

And then Ms. Perkins's voice breaks through my whirling thoughts. "That would be cool, right?" She shakes her head. "Except then we learned that, no, cells and the universe are not set up in fractals. It's not as simple as finding that one system that unlocks everything we know."

I slump back in my chair, relieved . . . and also mortified that—though I'm the only one who knows it—for one crazy, brain-whirling second, I kinda thought that maybe I was the keeper of the universe.

Who needs drugs when you have my brain?

» » « «

By now Ardy knows how to find me after school. He's waiting at the flagpoles when I walk out. Leo is also there, and he does not enjoy the kiss I give Ardy when I arrive. "Dude," Leo says, pained, then holds out a hand for my car keys. I give them to him, and he trudges off.

Ardy sets his back against the REACH flagpole, pulling me in and moving his legs apart so I can stand between them. "Did you do fractals today?" he asks.

"It's hot when you talk math." I give him a kiss that's even better than the one I gave in front of Leo.

"Good to know. I'll work on upping my conversational calculus game."

We kiss for a moment, and then I tilt my head back and look at him. "*What* about fractals?"

"All that stuff about expanding patterns. For a minute, I was like *Oh shit, my girlfriend is the queen of the universe!*" He smiles down at me, and my heart contracts. "And then I pretty much immediately realized that I was a huge weirdo for thinking it, which now behooves me to ask . . . did that happen to cross your mind at all?" He watches me, waiting. "What?"

Because I'm grinning a huge, ridiculous, could-not-be-stopped-even-if-I-tried grin. "It might have," I tell him. "Which makes me a huge weirdo, too."

It also makes me someone who has—against all odds—let a boy in. Let him get to know me. To understand me. To see some of my misfit pieces that might not be considered beautiful and appealing by all.

It makes me feel human.

It makes me feel warm.

It makes me terrified that I'm getting in way deeper than I ever dreamed I would have.

But in this immediate moment, outside the school, by the flagpoles, all it does is make me put my hands on Ardy's shoulders and move in for another kiss.

The first text I get is from Leo:

OMG WOULD YOU COME ON.

I ignore it so I can spend a few more minutes with my fingers entangled in Ardy's thick, dark hair.

The second text is also from Leo:

Imma call Mom to come get me.

That's the one that finally convinces me to leave Ardy and head toward my car.

But the third text is the one that stops me in my tracks, that turns everything upside down. It's from Trissa Jefferson, and it's only seven words long:

I need to tell you about Ardy.

CHAPTER SEVENTEEN

Trissa meets me on one of the concrete benches outside Providence St. Joseph's front entrance. She's carrying a giant gold-painted dreidel. "I only have a few minutes," she says. "Everyone had a baby today. There are six balloon bouquets waiting in the lobby." She gestures to the dreidel. "Plus, the Hanukkah gifts are starting to arrive."

As I learned in our exchange before I drove over here, Trissa is fulfilling her high school's volunteer requirements by delivering floral arrangements and balloons to patients at the local hospital. As I learned immediately upon setting eyes on her, she's even prettier than her social media pages led me to believe. Dark brown eyes shining from equally dark brown skin. A blue jewel sparkling from the side of her wide nose. Black hair braided into a thousand tiny strands, each tipped with a glass bead.

Trissa's smile is big and bright and gorgeous, and when she plops down beside me and takes my hands in hers, I'm ready to listen to anything she has to say.

"I really liked him at first," she says. "We hung out at the

Valentine's dance last year, and then he started texting me. He was so funny and so smart. The first time we kissed, it was in the mall."

The wave of jealousy that hits me is more than painful. It might actually kill me. Still, I paddle above it to ask, "What happened?"

"He's different, you know?" Trissa looks thoughtful. "He's not like any other guy I've ever known."

Tell me about it.

"I liked him so much," Trissa continues. "And then . . . I didn't. I don't know why. I guess that sounds awful."

I shake my head because who am I, of all people, to judge the reasons a person's feelings change.

"I hung in there for a little bit," she says. "I thought maybe it was a phase because it wasn't like anything *happened.* I think he could tell something was going on. I made up reasons to avoid him, and he started asking what was wrong, and eventually I ended it." She looks ashamed. "I shouldn't have waited as long as I did, but I hate 'the Talk,' you know?"

Boy, do I ever.

"I broke up with him in a text," she says. "I know it's bad, but I didn't have an answer if he asked *why.*"

On one hand, that sucks for Ardy. On the other, well . . . I understand the urge to do it that way. A clean break, no eye contact while you explain why you want to end things. With every boy I've ever kissed, I've found a way to bail out that allows me to avoid having the conversation about *why.* But to Trissa all I say is "How'd he take it?"

"He ran away."

"What do you mean?" My head tilts to the side. "You said you did it in a text."

"No." Her eyes go wide. "He didn't run away from the conversation. He ran away from *home*."

"He *what?*" That does not sound like the Ardy I know. Not at all. But then again, maybe we're coming back to the same question I've had since the very beginning: *How well do I know Ardy Tate, anyway?*

"He didn't do it right away," Trissa continues. "After I texted him, he came to my house. It was super awkward because I'd told my parents we broke up, and suddenly there he was, on my porch."

Her porch.

"My dad tried to tell him to go away, but I heard them talking and came outside." Trissa gives a tiny shrug. "I said it was okay, that I'd listen to him. Dad said we had to stay right there by the door with the lights on."

The porch light stays on.

"Ardy was upset. He wanted to know why I was making out with him yesterday if I was breaking up with him today." Trissa's eyes go far away. "I guess it was a fair question. I just didn't have an answer." I wait, and after a moment she seems to return to where we are. "It ended awkwardly. I said I was sorry. He said he was sorry, too . . . but he seemed angry. The next day he didn't come to school. The day after that, the police showed up."

I suck in my breath. Ian was right. "The cops came?"

"Yeah, they got me out of math class because he was missing. His mom must have told them we were dating, because they wanted to know everything about the last time I saw him. I told them we broke up. They asked me all these questions, like if he ever seemed unbalanced or if he had talked to me about depression or trying to kill himself." Trissa's voice shakes. "They said . . . they said he left a note."

I stay silent. I can't imagine how I'd feel if that had happened with one of the boys I had dated. If I'd been questioned about his disappearance. If I felt responsible for his whereabouts, his anguish, his mental health. Isn't that why I get them "to break my heart" in the first place? So I don't have to break theirs?

And especially if it were Ardy. Sweet, gentle, careful *Ardy*. I really, really can't imagine that.

"Then they found him," Trissa says. "He was out in the woods somewhere. He went out there alone, but . . . he didn't go through with anything. Thank God." She draws a shuddering breath. "I was glad he was alive and okay, but it really freaked me out. He missed a whole bunch of school—like two or three weeks—and when he came back, he tried to talk to me. I told him no, and he apologized for scaring me and"—she shrugs—"that was it."

"So you never talked to him again?" In its own way, Burbank is a small town. It's almost impossible to avoid someone forever. That's also why I break up the way I do—so that when the inevitable happens and you run into them after the fact, it's not an unpleasant experience for anyone.

"No. I blocked him over all social media. I blocked his

phone number, too. I wanted to be done with it. I think I saw him at the mall one time, but I went behind the cell phone kiosk and waited. When I peeked out, he was gone. If it was even him to begin with." She pauses, searching my face. "I almost didn't write back to you." I nod. It's all I can do. "But I couldn't stop thinking about your text, and I finally decided that if you were asking me . . . there was a reason for it. Like the universe brought you to me. It was my duty to tell you, girl to girl. So you know what you're getting into."

"Thank you." I say it in a small voice, although I don't actually mean it. I'm twisted in knots over what I've heard from her. Ardy's reaction to their breakup was everything I'm afraid of. Big and dramatic and awful. Scary for him, scary for me.

And now here we are. I can wait the remaining six weeks until I'm theoretically supposed to break up with him, or I could do it right this second. It doesn't matter anymore, because either way I'm already in too deep.

Also, I can't figure out what to think about Trissa. I get it—her initial reason for breaking up with Ardy. Or, rather, her non-reason. She's allowed to feel that way. She's also allowed to have a reaction to what Ardy did, but . . .

No matter how violent my allergies to conflict and drama are, I can't imagine a world in which I run in the other direction from someone who's dealing with whatever Ardy was dealing with at the time: depression, suicidal tendencies, anxiety, whatever. He deserved to be heard and helped and understood. Instead, Trissa ran in the other direction. She became part of the problem instead of the solution.

Not. Cool.

Trissa makes a move like she's going to hug me, but maybe my face is what makes her think better of it. "Do what you need to." She stands and gives me a sympathetic smile. "I liked him, too. At first."

And then she's gone. Off to deliver balloons and happiness to people who are broken. Instead of the exact opposite, which is what she did for me.

CHAPTER EIGHTEEN

"End it." Cooper keeps his gaze fixed on the naked gold man before us. He and Katie and I are huddled together on a bench overlooking the fountain at the big outdoor mall in Glendale. The sun is on its way down, so it's chilly, but the buildings all around us are lit up, and the fountain is awash in lights. The gold man is, sadly, only a statue, and to be fair, he's not *completely* naked. He's wearing a little cloth that looks like a diaper. "It's too much for you," Cooper continues. "If Ardy's bringing all that baggage to the table, he deserves someone who's able to cope with it. No offense, but that's never been your strong suit."

"Gee, thanks," I mutter, even though I know Cooper's right.

"We all know you're a genius at breaking up," Katie says. "Use your special Lark superpower and make him think he wants it."

"Tell him you have a brain tumor," Cooper says.

"Or you're gay," Katie says.

"Or you're assholes," I say to them both.

"We're brainstorming," Katie says.

"I know I'm bucking my own trend here." Cooper shifts to face me. "But you've gotten too far into something you're not equipped to deal with. Make something up and get out."

"But it's not fair to him." One freaked-out foray into foliage and no one will touch him? "Me getting out is proving that stupid name true."

"That he's Undateable?" Cooper asks. "You can't be responsible for that."

"And you shouldn't discount that maybe he *is* Undateable," Katie says. "A girl broke up with him and he ran away from home. Do you know anyone else—literally *one* other person—who would do that?"

"Yeah, and it's not like Trissa is the only girl with a weird story about him," Cooper says.

"The other two turned out to be false leads," I remind him.

"Rumors start for a reason," Katie says. "You know I thought he had problems from jump."

"Let's look at the facts." Cooper starts to tick off statements on his fingers. "For a first date, he took you two hours away to go falconing."

"It was a Harris's hawk," I say weakly.

Cooper ignores me. "He expressed his physical intentions toward you . . . *to your mother.*"

"You're making it sound"—I pause, trying to find a way to explain it. "It wasn't like that. He was nice. He was honest. He was *open.*"

"It was *weird,*" Katie says.

"I know, but—"

Katie folds her arms. "And now, like five minutes later, you're all hot and bothered and in love all over the school."

In love?

"Look." Cooper taps me on the knee. "Historically speaking, you have always bailed out for far, *far* smaller offenses. You have literally zero experience with something this big."

I don't say anything. I just stare at the mostly naked gold man standing in the center of the fountain with his back arched and his arms outstretched toward the rapidly dimming sky.

"For what it's worth," Cooper says, "you did it. You stayed in long enough for someone to give a shit."

"This is not a *win*," I tell Cooper. "This is a massive loss. I'm a failure. A relationship failure."

"No, you're human." Cooper's voice goes warm and gentle. "You're human, and . . . there's something going on with him that you're not strong enough to handle."

"But what if I can?"

"What if you *can't*?" Cooper says.

"Think about it," Katie says. "Trissa wasn't even his girlfriend for very long, and when she broke up with him, he ran out into the woods to kill himself. You've already been with him for longer than she was. What's he going to do when you break his heart?"

"Here's a thought," I say to both of them. "What if I don't break his heart?"

Cooper and Katie give me twin looks of concern. "You're not going to marry him," says Katie.

"I'm telling you," Cooper says, "this is perfect timing. One more day of school until winter break. Get out now, and you don't have to see him for two weeks."

I pull my knees to my chest, wrapping my arms around them and setting my chin on top so I can stare out at that golden man.

I don't want to get out.

I want Ardy.

» » « «

Ardy texted me a couple of hours ago, but I haven't responded. I'm not sure if it's as simple as I don't know what to say, or if it's that I want to see what he'll do if he doesn't hear from me. Either way, everything about this is terrible.

I got home from Glendale, beat Leo in two games of chess, and did my homework, and now I'm sitting cross-legged on my bed. Everyone else in the house is asleep, and I'm staring at my laptop. I'm not looking at any of Ardy's social profiles or online pictures. I'm not looking at Krista or Elle or Trissa, either.

Instead, I'm walking down the internet's version of Memory Lane. Taking a stroll through the neighborhoods of Boys I've Kissed Before. Looking at Dax's pic from last week's bonfire. At Wade, one arm casually slung around Keeshana's shoulders. At Rahim, spiking a volleyball over a net in the Santa Monica Beach sand. At Glen . . . Will . . . Kai . . . Elliot. All these boys I've loved and lost.

Except I didn't love any of them, and I'm the one who chose to lose them.

With all of them, disentangling myself was the easiest thing in the world. It almost became a sport, the way I could wiggle out without anyone knowing better. Without hurting anyone's feelings.

Without saying anything remotely resembling the truth.

It was easy.

But what I need to do right now? It's the hardest thing in the world.

»»««

Despite my plans to be brave, I spend all of the next day hiding from Ardy. I enter the school through a different door from my usual one. I stay far away from my locker. I eat lunch in my car, which I park in a completely different location, and then I fake a migraine so I can spend English class in the nurse's office with an ice pack. I'm so clever that I make it off campus at the end of the day without ever catching sight of him. I run Leo home, and then I go to the one place I need to be so I can talk to the one person who I hope will shed some light on it all. I send a message:

Can you talk?

A text comes back right away:

Where are you?

I know it's going to make me look like I'm the one who's a weirdo, but I don't care:

Your backyard.

There are scuffling sounds outside, and then the familiar movement of someone coming up the ladder. I wait in my cross-legged position on the floor until Hope pushes the tree house curtains aside. She stands in the doorway, a silhouette against the sunlight outside.

"I'm so glad you're here," she says.

Ardy told her I've been avoiding him.

"Me too," I say.

"Who'd you hear it from?" she asks.

I cock my head, not sure which part she's asking about: Trissa's story or the Undateable rumors in general?

But then Hope steps fully inside, letting the curtains swing closed behind her. Light shines through the leaves outside the window, dappling her face.

Her blotchy and tear-streaked face.

"Who told you Evan broke up with me?" she asks.

Since no one *had* told me until this exact moment, I shake my head. The source must not matter, because now Hope is sinking to the floor, dropping her head into my lap, the floodgates bursting.

#Heaven is no more.

The world really is coming to an end.

» » « «

I managed to avoid Ardy on the way into Hope's backyard, but I practically run into him on the way out, two hours later. He's carrying a small white dog in his arms, leading a group of jacketed elementary school–aged kids along the sidewalk.

The Watson family again.

When he sees me, he hands the dog to the biggest kid and waves the horde back to their house. He waits while I walk to him. He reaches out like he's going to touch me but then thinks better of it and shoves his hands into his pockets. "Where were you today?"

"Hiding from you." Because apparently when I go with honesty, I don't pull any punches. I steel myself before saying, "I talked to Trissa Jefferson."

Ardy's expression flashes from concern to surprise to . . . what looks like downright anger. "How did you track her down?"

I don't know what to say. If it were me, I wouldn't like it, either. That said, aren't we *trying* to get to know each other? Isn't our history a part of that equation?

"How did you even *know* about her? I never mentioned her in front of you—I know I didn't. You had to go looking for her. That's so . . ." Ardy shakes his head. "Creepy."

Ouch.

"I wasn't being creepy, I swear." Panic rises inside me. This wasn't supposed to turn into an argument. I don't want to fight; I can't have a fight. I'll just use the true-ish story about when I met Krista. "I ran into her at a bookstore. We started talking about schools, and I said I knew someone who went to her school, and it went from there."

Is it true? Was my sweet, sunshiny Ardy really so hurt and so upset that he did what Trissa said? Tears prick my eyes. Ardy must be able to see them, because he reaches for me . . .

And I take a step backward. I don't know why I do it, but I do. He drops his hands, his face darkening.

"Did you do it?" I ask him. "Did you run away to . . ." I can't say the last words; I just can't. "Are you in therapy now? Or are you on medication? Did you get *help*?"

Ardy flinches like I struck him. Like he's in physical pain. His jaw clenches, and his shoulders tense upward. He stares at me for a moment, his eyes dark and angry and hurt, and then he turns. He walks—not into his house but down the street.

Just . . . away.

From me.

» » « «

I want to go somewhere small, somewhere safe, a place where I can huddle into myself and hide from everyone. Where I can go fetal and pretend the world around me doesn't exist. If I had Hope's tree house, I would climb up there and close the curtains and curl up on the floor. But I don't, and I can't stand the thought of going home, where my family could see my face— now blotchy like Hope's—and ask questions. Instead, I climb into my car and I start driving.

At first I don't know where I'm going. I only know I'm driving past house after house decorated with holiday lights, either red and green or blue and white. I don't realize I'm in the foothills until something sparks a memory of being parked on the side of the road in Ardy's minivan and about what he said when we were here. So I keep driving, but now I'm doing it with intention. Now I'm aware of direction. Now I'm going up.

The Ridge restaurant is perched at the top of the hills, surrounded by lush greenery dotted with palm trees. I park in a back corner of the big lot because it seems like a place that would have a valet, and I don't have any cash with me. I walk between the rows of luxury cars and electric vehicles and past the sign to the front entrance, where a man in a shiny vest gives me side-eye as I rush past him into the lobby.

Once I'm inside, a friendly hostess—who doesn't seem bothered at all that I'm here by myself or that I tell her I only want a drink—leads me through a room of white-draped tables to the outdoor patio behind the restaurant. Minutes later I'm seated by the railing, a hot chocolate in hand, looking out at the view.

It's beautiful.

The entire San Fernando Valley is clear, and way in the distance, past the Hollywood Hills, I think I can see the ocean. The Hollywood sign isn't visible from here, but the city it represents is spread out in all its varied, sun-drenched glory. I have been told that every day—literally, *every day*—hundreds of people arrive in Los Angeles, coming for a dream. Usually young people who are aspiring actors or writers or directors, they leave their families and friends behind and cross the Sierra Nevada or travel along the Pacific coast to reach this place of concrete and celebrities, of earthquakes and opportunities. It's a journey that often ends in poverty, in broken dreams, in— worst of all—anonymity.

Me, however. There was no traveling, no turmoil, no trying. I didn't choose it.

Now, as I sit on the deck of the restaurant, jacket wrapped around me, the city before me is huge and incomprehensible and complicated, like my feelings for Ardy. It says one thing but offers another. It has a dark, intense gaze and words of promise, but it holds out a hand filled with regret and confusion.

The fact is, I like Ardy. I like him so much I'm having a hard time thinking straight, and yet I've barely scratched the tip of the iceberg. He's a giant, unlocked mystery. A world yet to know, a world I *want* to know. But here we are, where the depths of who he may have been, who he still might be . . . they terrify me. I don't know if I can handle it.

Nothing in the world makes sense.

I don't know how long I sit there, looking out at the view, but eventually I realize it's been too long since I paid my server, and the sun has dipped low, turning downtown Los Angeles into a dark silhouette on the horizon. I pull out my phone and take a picture of it.

Then, before I can talk myself out of it, I attach it into a text and send it shooting across the hills to Ardy. Along with a message:

You were right, I love it up here.

CHAPTER NINETEEN

Cooper was right: having two weeks to think and breathe was a good thing. Of course, it's not like I saw much of him, because his family is hard-core about Hanukkah, which this year fell right on top of Christmas. Katie, however, basically spent the entire time in my house. Her mom went to New York on some sort of whirlwind romantic holiday with a businessman she met online, and Katie got parked with me. Since we don't have a true guest room, she and I shared my queen bed the whole time she was with us.

Katie said it was great having her mom out of her hair over the break, but she didn't seem great, and once I heard her crying at night. The next day I tried to ask her if she was okay, but all she said was "I think I'm coming down with a cold." I didn't push it, because I didn't want to be pushed on my own family's dynamic. Over those two weeks Katie was an audience to several tense moments between my parents, as well as one full-out shouting match. She had witnessed glimpses of the fireworks throughout our friendship, but this was the first time she had a ringside seat to the true war zone. When twin door-slams—my mother out the front door and my father out the back—echoed through the house, Katie blinked at me. "Dude, that was intense. Are you okay?"

I stayed silent.

Ardy waited three awful days after my text from the Ridge to text me back. When he did, it was simple:

I knew you'd like it.

Under Katie's watchful gaze, I then typed and erased several dozen versions of a return message, finally landing on this:

I'd like to come here again with you. When you're ready.

Of course, Katie thought I shouldn't write back at all, especially after so much time had elapsed. "He's ghosting you," she told me. "He's doing you a favor. Now you don't have to figure out how to end it."

"I don't want to end it," I told her. This time she was the one who stayed silent.

But I only got one more message from Ardy during the winter break:

See you in the new year.

» » « «

January. My final semester of high school. I signed up for Advanced Art, which means that now I get to enjoy a perk. The senior art students are allowed to hang out in the classroom during lunch. Today, once again, I play vending-machine roulette and this time take my haul (yogurt-covered raisins, organic apple slices, sunflower seeds) to the empty art room. I grab a hunk of moist clay from the bin and hunker down at a long wooden table in the back, slapping the clay onto a piece of cardboard to play with after I eat my lunch. I'm almost done when I get a text from Ardy:

Where are you?

Although I was terrified about our first post-break encounter and sort of came here to hide from him, what I was *truly* hiding from was him-with-an-audience. Him solo, on the other hand . . . it's time for that. I text back my location and wait. It doesn't take long. Only three minutes pass before Ardy's in the open door, bag slung diagonally across his lanky body, hair uncharacteristically more mussed than styled. As he lopes toward me, I see that his face looks different, too. I don't know how often he usually shaves, but he's clearly missed a couple of days; there's a fine dusting of shadow over his chin and along his jawline. The greatest change, though, is in his eyes. They're red-rimmed and exhausted.

He pulls back the chair across from me and drops into it. Wordlessly, I hold out my half-full bag of sunflower seeds. He shakes his head.

I shove my food aside, ripping off a piece of clay so I can start rolling it between my hands, trying to give my nervous energy a place to go. "Hi."

"Hi."

Roughly a million years go by before I finally speak again. "Did Trissa lie?"

"No."

My insides twist.

No.

But I don't say it out loud. I only stare at him.

He shakes his head, disgusted. "Apparently, I don't have the luxury of moving on. I *have* to talk to you about it. I don't have a choice."

I flash through my list of ex-not-boyfriends. It would be the easiest thing in the world for Ardy to do some digging of his own, to get a look at the parade of lies that make up my own history. Maybe he's right. Maybe none of this is fair.

"No one is forcing you." I peer at his haunted eyes. "You don't have to say anything."

"Really?" Ardy looks skeptical.

I want to say it would be okay. But we both know that would be the biggest lie of all, so I stay silent. I shake my head.

"Yeah, that's what I thought." We gaze at each other, both of us so hurt, so upset. We don't possess the words to fix what's broken between us. He glances at my hands, then back to my face. "What are you making?"

I look down at the clay in front of me. I've rolled out a flat circle topped with a little room. There are nondescript pieces of furniture around the edges, and in the center there's a little round table with four chairs. Sitting on one is a tiny, crude rendition of a person.

Before I can answer, the bell rings loud and harsh. We

both jump, startled. Ardy gives me a faint smile that breaks my heart. He reaches over and tears off a little piece of the unmolded clay chunk, fiddling with it for a second before setting what he's made onto the chair across from my person. It's another little person, this one with a bag crossed diagonally over its body.

Ardy stands, shifting his own bag as he does. "I'll come over after school." I hesitate because, of course, my house can be a place of serenity or an absolute battlefield. But Ardy's already seen—or at least heard—the war being waged. There won't be any new information for him there. "Please." His voice is low and soft, and my heart breaks again.

I nod, and he turns and walks out of the room, leaving me with my tiny clay Lark and Ardy, still sitting across from each other in Ardy's tiny clay kitchen.

» » « «

When Ardy knocks, Dad is at work and Mom is mowing the backyard. I assume Leo is upstairs or playing video games in the TV room. Since no one is around to see, I motion him toward my bedroom. "Okay if we do this in whispers so we won't get interrupted?"

Ardy doesn't move. "Are you allowed to have boys in there?"

"No, are you kidding me? That's why we have to whisper." I roll my eyes. "Mom doesn't even want Cooper to go in, and God knows he's not going to get me pregnant."

Ardy still doesn't budge. "I'd rather go with parental guidelines on this one."

Right. He's a rule follower. I motion him into the sitting room. "Be my guest."

This room always seems so strange and formal. The chairs aren't very comfortable. There's no TV. It literally is intended just for conversation, which I guess in this case is fine because that's what we're here to do.

Ardy sits in the uncomfortable green chair, and I lower myself into the uncomfortable orange chair, and then we gaze at each other for a long moment. I'm expecting him to start the discussion, but when he doesn't, I ask the one word that means the most: "Why?"

"Of course you're asking that." His lips twist in the faintest approximation of a smile. "You can't imagine a world where you're not beloved by everyone."

Um, who does he think he's talking to right now? Hope?

"You can do no wrong," Ardy continues. "It was different for me." He fixes his eyes on the worn carpet, his fingers twisting a button on his jacket. "In eleventh grade, the kids started saying I was weird. I don't know why. Because I was in the bowling club, maybe. Or because I wore beanies and played paintball? Or just because they needed *someone* to say that about? No idea."

It's not what I expected him to say, and I don't know how to react, so I keep waiting. His face is tense, like he's angry or hurt or both, and I want to hug him. But this doesn't feel like a time when we should be hugging.

Or when he would want that from me.

"I heard the word that was used," Ardy says. *"Undateable."*

I manage not to cringe visibly.

"Still, it seemed like a joke," Ardy says. "Or at least not a big deal. And it didn't matter anyway, because I did date, a little. I went to dances, hooked up with girls."

There's my jealousy again.

"I could call two or maybe three of them ex-girlfriends, I guess," he says. "They were offbeat types. Not like you, you know?"

I *do* know, but only because I tracked down emo Krista and angry Elle before meeting Trissa.

"Is that what you like?" I ask in a small voice. "Offbeat types?"

Ardy pulls his gaze up and levels it at me. "I like people who are interesting," he says. "You fit the bill."

I nod, taking the compliment even though the tone it's delivered in is not exactly . . . complimentary.

"Then Trissa came along," he says. "She was different. Not because she wasn't interesting—she was—but because she's . . . I guess the word is *mainstream*. Everyone liked her, and she liked everyone. I thought she liked me, too." He stops, running a hand through his hair. "This isn't exactly something I wanted to talk about with you."

"Why?"

He cocks his head, staring at me. "Maybe you don't know this about guys, but we tend not to like it when our girlfriend thinks we're a weirdo."

"I don't think that." I say it automatically, but then I scoot forward in my chair, keeping my eyes trained on his. Wanting him to really hear me. "I think you're—"

Amazing.

Adorable.

The best thing that ever happened to me.

"—great." It sounds weak the minute it comes out of my mouth.

Ardy doesn't exactly roll his eyes, but he does something close to it. "Trissa was into me, and then she wasn't. I wish I could explain it more than that, but that's all I have."

Makes sense. That's all she told me, too.

"I was upset," Ardy says. "Not only because I liked her, but the day she broke up with me, her friends doubled down on the *Undateable* assholery. I never heard Trissa say it, but maybe she did—I don't know."

I stay still, searching his face. It sounds awful, all of it: the name-calling, the breakup, not being able to explain any of it. It hurts to think of Ardy being in that kind of pain. The kind of pain that could lead him to . . .

"What did you do?" I ask in a whisper.

"I skipped school for a day or two," he says. "I didn't want to deal with it, you know?"

Oh boy, do I know.

"Seeing Trissa in the hall and not knowing what to say," he continues. "Or hearing crap from her bitchy friends. My mom was shooting a pilot for a cable series, something about a paranormal investigator. She was at work more than usual, so I knew she wouldn't notice if I was gone. I left her a note in case she got home before me, and I drove down to La Jolla."

"For the hawks?" That makes sense. If Ardy was upset, I can see how he'd want to do the thing that he loves.

"Yeah, I was already a volunteer, and they had just started

letting me fly alone." Ardy shakes his head. "Except I went farther than I was supposed to. I wanted to try the *actual* falconing, where you take the bird out to catch animals. Rabbits or mice or whatever."

"Quail?" I ask.

"If you can find them," Ardy says. "But we didn't. And when we were trying, my hawk took off. I guess we weren't bonded enough."

I stare at him. "Your bird flew away?"

"His name was Goliath." Ardy nods. "Into the forest. I ran after him, and I even found him on a tree branch, but he wouldn't come to me. I couldn't get close."

"Were they mad? At the falconry, I mean?"

"Yes," Ardy says. "But I didn't have to hear about it until later. Goliath eventually flew home by himself, whereas I got lost."

"In the woods?"

"Yep." Ardy gives me a wry look. "I got turned around while I was chasing him, and there was no phone service. I don't know if I was going in circles or what, but it got darker, and I couldn't find my way out, and eventually I realized I had to stop until the sun came up the next day."

"Are you serious?" It sounds like the scariest thing in the world.

"Yeah, it sucked," Ardy says. "It was cold and there were noises. Before I stopped walking, I tried to find the ocean so that I could follow the shoreline back to the falconry. Sometimes I thought I could hear the waves, but then it occurred to me that in the dark I could fall over a cliff. So I curled up next to a tree and hoped I wouldn't get eaten by a bear."

I realize my mouth is open, and I close it.

"When the sun came up, it still took a while—maybe three or four hours—but I finally came out by a road. I tried hitch-hiking, and some couple picked me up. Thankfully, they were lovely, law-abiding citizens and not murderers, because I fell asleep in their backseat."

"How far away were you?" It's close to making sense now: Ardy didn't run *away* from Trissa; he was running *after* a hawk.

"Five or six miles," he says. "I got turned around in the forest. In the future you probably shouldn't count on me for any navigational advice."

He's talking about the future.

"I won't." I give him a tiny smile, and this time he returns it. "Was your mom mad?"

"No." Ardy's smile slips. "She was scared. I wasn't clear in the note I left, because I thought I'd be back before her. I figured I'd throw it out and she'd never see it, so I scribbled something about how things sucked at school and I was going to fly away. When she came back and I was gone—and then I didn't come home—she called the police. They read the note and found out I was known as a weirdo who'd gotten dumped. With my dad's history, everyone assumed the worst."

My heart aches for him. It was all a big mistake. The cops coming to school, questioning Trissa, everything. "Why didn't you tell Trissa?" I ask. "I mean, when it was over."

"I tried to," he says. "She didn't want to have anything

to do with me. When I realized she'd blocked my number, I thought . . . why do I care what she thinks, anyway?"

"But everyone else," I say. "You could have told them."

"Tell them what?" he asks. "That it's not just bowling and paintball, but sometimes on weekends I also like to go play with birds? It wasn't their damn business, and I didn't want to hear about how it made me even less dateable."

"You took me to play with the birds." It comes out in the smallest of whispers. "You let me know about it."

"Yeah." His smile is back. It's only a half smile, but it's there. "I guess that was kind of a test. To see if you were too cool for my weirdness."

"I'm not too cool," I assure him.

"I see that now," he says, which I'm certain is intended to be a compliment.

I look at him sitting in the uncomfortable green chair, with shadows under his eyes, and I want to run to him, to hold him and let him hold me. To fix what's broken in each of us, and if it can't be fixed, to acknowledge its existence, laying it gently to the side so we can focus our attention elsewhere. On the good parts, the strong parts, the places where we work, both alone and together.

But it's all jumbled and garbled in my head, and I don't know how to say it.

"I know we said no secrets," Ardy says. "But I should have been able to tell you this one when I was ready."

"I know. I'm sorry."

"I know." His mouth tenses the way it used to before he

started smiling at me, and I start to lift off the uncomfortable orange chair. To go to him, to kiss him, to make him smile for real . . . but Ardy holds up a hand to stop me. "I need a minute, okay?" I drop back, my heart aching. He tilts his head, regarding me. "And maybe you should take a minute, too."

I nod—because what else can I do—and he stands. He walks to the door, turns to give me a final tortured glance, and then goes.

Leaving me sitting there, feeling terrible for both of us.

CHAPTER TWENTY

Although Ardy and I manage to successfully avoid each other for the rest of the week, I catch glimpses of him at the ends of hallways and in English class and across cafeteria crowds. Every time I see him, he's with Hope. They're walking side by side with their heads bent close, or their chairs are practically touching at their lunch table. Even in class, they look only at each other. Never at me. The one time I managed to catch Hope's gaze, she gave me a tiny shrug as if to say, *Sorry, he's my friend.* I think about texting her to see how she's doing after the whole Evan catastrophe, but I don't.

Toward the end of the week, I run into Ardy in the south wing stairwell. We pause on the landing, staring at each other, ignoring the streams of people who have to alter their paths to go around us. His eyes look brighter than the last time I saw him, and the dark shadow around his mouth and on his chin is gone. I want to wrap my arms around him. The urge is so strong that it pushes words up through my body and out between my lips. "My minute's up," I tell him.

The edges of his mouth tense slightly, like he's considering a smile that doesn't quite make it into the world. "I'm close."

It's not great, but it's better.

"Let me know when you're there," I tell him.

"I will." This time the smile becomes more real. Then he ducks his head and edges around me, trotting up the stairs and leaving me to go down.

On Friday after school I meet Cooper at the mall. Of course I've told him what's going on with Ardy, and of course Cooper doesn't approve. "He's still off," he says when I plop across from him in the food court.

"He might be breaking up with me," I tell him. "But for real this time."

"Congratulations," Cooper says. "That would make you a winner."

I can't do that conversation right now, so I pull Cooper's fedora out of my backpack—somehow I ended up with it again—and instead of returning it to him, as I'd planned, I jam it onto my head. I make a face at him. "How's the husband?"

Cooper returns the face. "We're keeping it casual, remember?"

"Yeah, right."

"Lark, I know." Cooper slumps back in his seat with a sigh. "But I like him. Can't you understand that?"

I can. Of course I can. But if I can understand it, Cooper needs to do the same for me. "I need you to get okay with Ardy," I tell him.

"Then I need you to get okay with Ian." Cooper leans across the table toward me. "I said the *L* word to him."

"Shut *up*." I whap him on the shoulder. "This is what

happens when we don't talk enough. I miss everything important. Did he say it back?"

"Yeah." Cooper beams huge, like he's also trying to channel Hope. "Lark, he's so cute."

"I'm going to puke," I tell him.

"Me too. Puke with happiness." Cooper's smile goes goofy and wide and adorable, and I remember why we fell in friend-love with each other. "I'm going to go see him. Want to come?"

"No." Ever since I ran into Ardy in the stairwell, I've been thinking about what I want to say to him, and right now I think I have it perfect in my head. I don't want to wait any longer. "I have to do something," I tell Cooper.

"Cool." He stands, drops one of his Cooper kisses on the top of my head, and takes off. I pull out my phone and start composing a text—or, rather, a series of texts. I start and stop several times before sending them, but finally I think I have it perfect:

An apology—
i'm sorry, i will neve**R** be creepy again
we are goo**D** together
i won't fly awa**Y** from you

I make sure all the messages deliver, and then I shove my phone away, rising to my feet. It's up to Ardy now.

I'm almost to the mall exit when I realize I'm wearing Cooper's hat, and I execute an abrupt U-turn. He's probably still visiting with Ian. I might as well run it back to him. I can practice trying to be nice to Ian, which should engender some good-will among the three of us.

The boutique clothing store is basically dead. Ian is behind the cash register in his standard uniform at the crossroads of boring and bland. There's one old lady browsing a rack of aprons and a dude with an assistant-manager pin hovering by her, I assume hoping to score a commission. Cooper is nowhere in sight.

Ian raises his hand in a greeting when he sees me, and I head up to the counter. "Cooper already left," he says when I reach him.

"Bummer." I pull Cooper's fedora off my head and flop it toward Ian. "I was trying to give him this."

Ian shoots me a weird look. "Why?"

"Because it's his." The minute the words are out of my mouth, I realize my mistake.

"Really?" Ian looks surprised, and I know I should find a way to backpedal, but . . . that seems crazy. And disingenuous. And wrong.

"Yeah. It looks great on him."

Ian doesn't answer; he only stares at me. The assistant manager arrives and gives him a nudge in the side. "Dude, can I get in here?"

Ian scoots over so his coworker can ring up the old lady's purchase: a pink apron covered with little red owls. I meet Ian at the edge of the counter. He takes the fedora from me. "Great. I'll take care of it," he says. "I'll see you later—"

"I know you don't see this side of Cooper a lot," I interrupt.

"But your boyfriend has a personality that is big and fabulous and awesome." Ian opens his mouth, but I railroad right over him, wanting him to understand how great Cooper truly is. "When he is quiet with you, when he's *demure,* that's not who he really is. He really is *this hat.*" I wave it in front of Ian's face. "Please, check him out in it. You will *love* him in this hat."

I flash him a smile, turning to include the assistant manager, the old lady, and the whole world in my new benevolent acceptance. "We should double-date."

Ian nods but doesn't say anything. Satisfied, I whirl and head for the door. There's a chance Cooper will be crabby at me for meddling, but I've done the Lord's work here.

» » « «

Every time my phone—or, truthfully, anyone's phone—makes a noise, I leap for it like a drowning person grabbing for a rope. But I don't hear from Ardy while I drive home, while I do homework, while I eat dinner with Mom and Leo, or while I change into a long-sleeved pajama shirt that reaches my knees. It's one I would never wear at a sleepover, because it's so shapeless and unattractive, but it is the most comfortable thing I own. And tonight I need comfort.

It's only eight o'clock when Mom heads upstairs to watch something on her bedroom TV. I go ahead and brush my teeth and wash my face, even though I figure I have at least a couple of hours of dorking around online: reading romance advice, looking at fashion, and probably a tiny bit of checking up on

Ardy via social media. I pull on my smooshiest socks, tug my hair into a messy tuft on the very top of my head, and am starting to settle into my bed with my laptop . . .

When my phone buzzes.

With a text from Ardy.

Are you home?

I type back immediately:

Yes. You?

Ardy:

Your front door.

I bolt up, shooting out of bed and knocking my laptop to the floor in the process. I start to pick it up and change my mind midbend, then lurch toward my bedroom door in a half squat. I'm out of my room and all the way to the front door of the house before I realize that I look a hot, hot mess.

I pause, but it's too late to backtrack. I can see Ardy's silhouette through the frosted glass of the center window, which means he can see mine, and *that* means I can't rush away to fix myself up. So I don't. I grit my teeth and open the door.

Ardy's gaze travels from the hair fountain atop my head all the way down to my slouch-socked feet before returning to my face, completely devoid of makeup. I manage a weak smile, which he doesn't return. He only looks at me, very serious, and says, "My minute ended."

"It did?" My heart leaps, thudding against my rib cage like it's trying to escape. I step back, swinging the door open wide, beckoning him to come in. As he does, I hear movement from upstairs—probably Mom going to the bathroom or Leo dorking around in his room—and I close the door very, very quietly. I don't want to deal with any family member right now. With the questions and the rules about how long he can stay and where. I just want to talk to Ardy. Alone.

Which shouldn't be a big deal.

I raise a finger to my lips, pulling him toward my bedroom.

"We're not allowed," he whispers.

"I know," I whisper back, continuing to pull him. We make it inside, and I close my door. To be careful, I lock it, too. Then I turn to him.

Ardy's hands are in his jacket pockets, and he's leaning to one side, looking down at me. "Thanks for the text. I would have gotten through my minute without it, eventually, but still . . . thanks."

"You're welcome."

He doesn't move toward me, but it suddenly feels like we're closer to each other. Like my bedroom got smaller, in a good way. Ardy looks me over again. "I've never seen you like this."

Oh. That's right. I'm in my friendless-tween mode.

Now Ardy does take a step toward me. He reaches up to the spray of hair on my head, and he runs his fingers over it. "It's cute." Which makes me laugh a little, because it absolutely is not. My laugh is cut short when Ardy moves his hand off my hair, first running it down the back of my head and neck to my collarbone, trickling off my shoulder before he drops it to his side again. We look at each other.

"What?" I ask, because I can't exactly figure out what we're trying to answer right now. Why it doesn't feel normal yet. Why it isn't mended.

"A week ago it seemed like if I wanted to reach out and touch you, I could just do it." Ardy gives me a rueful smile. "Now I need permission."

"You have permission." I say it quickly, needing him to know I'm okay, that I want *us* to be okay. I take a step forward and reach for his hand. I squeeze it between my own hands for a moment, and then I bring it up to my neck. I slide his hand over my throat, where I'm vulnerable, and then I pull it down . . . a little farther. Ardy's lips part in surprise, and I drop my hands, leaving his where I'd put it on my chest. He stands like that, almost frozen except for his thumb, which is moving in tiny circles against me. "Are you sure?" he whispers, and everything goes electric.

"I'm sure." I gaze up at him, at his dark, intense eyes in the angles of his face. I want to kiss him—I'm *dying* to kiss him—but in this exact moment, I'm living in the anticipation of it. This endless moment of promise. He seems to want it, too, because he takes another step closer. He keeps his right hand where it is for a second, increasing the speed and friction of the tiny circles, until he pulls it away. He starts to take off his jacket, but then he stops.

"Is this okay?"

"Yes." My voice has turned into a whisper. It has nothing to do with my mother upstairs and everything to do with the way Ardy keeps his eyes focused on mine as he shrugs out of his jacket and lays it at the foot of my bed. I let my eyes rove over his crisp white button-up and the sky-blue T-shirt underneath, and then I take a final step forward, touching the belt around his waist. I slide my hand upward, dragging my fingers across each button, and Ardy's abdomen tenses. By the time my hands reach his shoulders, I can't wait anymore. And I've stopped caring about my hair and my sleep shirt and my socks. All I want is Ardy, so I link my hands behind his neck and pull him to me. He comes willingly, and I close my eyes as his mouth covers mine.

Everything else drops away, and I'm lost in the touch and taste of him. Somehow we fumble our way onto my bed, hands and mouths in motion the entire time. Somehow Ardy's shoes come off. His belt, too. Somehow my pajama shirt gets hiked up around my waist. With every new thing—every new movement, every change in an article of clothing—Ardy stops to whisper in my ear: "Is this okay?"

Every time I tell him yes.

"I don't feel blurry," he says between kisses.

"Crystal clear," I manage to say in return.

We're sliding against each other, kissing and rocking and entwining in a way that makes me *need* something I've never known before, when something breaks through the sound of our murmurs and movements. "What was that?" Ardy gasps, lifting his face from my neck.

"I don't care," I tell him, dragging his mouth back to where it belongs: the space just behind and below my left ear.

Ardy kisses me for a second longer before pulling away again. "Someone's coming down the stairs."

"The door's locked," I tell him. "Ignore it." I hold his face directly above my own, assuming that *surely* I look as turned on as he does right now. "For the love of God, ignore it."

I don't want to stop what we're doing. In fact, I'm fairly certain there's a reasonable chance I could actually die if we do stop.

And then we both hear something familiar. It's the muffled sound of Cooper's voice.

"Shit!" It comes out of my mouth even as Ardy vaults from his position atop me. He looks around, panicked, grabbing his jacket and shoes.

"The closet," I tell him in a hiss. "It opens to the TV room. Go through it and out the back door."

He's barely in there with the door closed when my doorknob jiggles. My mother's voice floats from the other side. "Why is this locked?"

I yank my sleep shirt down and kick Ardy's belt under the bed, trying to slow my breathing. I dive across the room to unlock the door, opening it slowly, feigning a yawn. "Sorry, I think I fell asleep. What's up?"

Mom jerks a thumb toward Cooper, who stands behind her, hands on his hips. "No boys in your room. You'll have to come out to talk."

I step out, starting to pull the door closed behind me so

Mom won't hear Ardy opening the door on the other side of the closet, but Cooper holds up a hand. "No need." He's flushed and looks angry. "I can say everything right here. I'll be fast, promise."

Crap. This is not good.

"Why the hell did you go to Ian's work?" I open my mouth to answer, but Cooper shakes his head. "Never mind, I don't care. You ruined everything."

"What?" Now it's my turn to look outraged. "No I didn't. I gave him back your hat and told him that you look great in it."

"Yeah, you told him that his *boyfriend* looks great in it."

"So?"

"So his brother was there."

"Who?" The minute I ask, my memory of visiting Ian flashes before my eyes: the pink apron with owls, the old lady . . . the assistant manager.

I freeze the playback in my memory. The assistant manager, who is *staring* as I make my proclamation about Cooper . . .

"Ian's brother. He didn't know Ian's gay, and he's not cool with it."

"Does he know what year this is?" It seems impossible that in this day and age, anyone could still give a crap who or how someone else loves.

"No, he's an ass." The next piece comes out of Cooper like an explosion. "But even if he wasn't, Ian is supposed to be the one who gets to pick how and when to tell him."

Just like Ardy.

"I'm sorry," I say. "I didn't know that was his brother. I didn't know Ian wasn't *out.*"

"Yeah, things don't occur to you, do they?" Cooper is so far down the road of fury that, even though he's looking straight at me, I can't tell if he can see me. Behind him, I have a vague impression of my mother backing away, giving us our space, retreating to give the appearance of privacy while not actually giving us any privacy at all. "I was happy with him, and things were good, but that wasn't enough. You wanted me to be miserable like you."

"That is not fair—"

Irate, Cooper cuts me off again. "That's why I agreed to your and Katie's stupid game. As long as you could keep it together with some poor sucker, I'd slow my roll with Ian. That's how much I *care* about you. That's how much I *love* you. I was willing to forgo being with the person I love so you could prove your emotional prowess by making a weirdo love you and then break his heart. You were supposed to reel him in, screw around for a while, dump him, and see if he gave a shit. It was a *game*."

"God, Cooper—it wasn't like that."

"It was *exactly* like that." Cooper's cheeks blaze hotter. "*You're* the ass, tracking down all those ex-girlfriends—"

"You're the one who told me their names!"

"—and screwing up my good thing because you didn't know how to have one of your own. Picking the biggest freak show around—"

"Ardy's not a—"

"You *won*." Cooper is too far gone for logic. "You got him to lose his shit. Good job, well done."

"He didn't—"

"That means it's over. Just let me be with Ian." Cooper

stops, hands still on his hips, breathing hard. "But you couldn't do that. You screwed up your own love life, so God forbid I be happy with mine."

We stare at each other. I'm horrified knowing that my mother is somewhere close-by, hearing all of this. A sinkhole is growing beneath me, and my whole life is falling into it. I start to say Cooper's name, but it's too late. He's already storming away. I follow him to the front door, but he yanks it open and is gone before I can sort through everything I need to say. I stand there staring out into the darkness and trying to gather my thoughts before turning to face my mother.

She's sitting in the uncomfortable green chair, pretending to read a book. She sets it down so she can look at me. "Do you want to talk about it?"

"I really don't."

"Okay." She closes her book, standing up from her chair. "But so you know, friendships go through changes. It's totally normal, especially for people like you and Cooper, who have been friends for so long."

I know what she's trying to do, and I appreciate it, but she really doesn't get it. "Thanks." I just want to be alone. "I'm going to bed."

"Okay. Good night, sweetie."

Which should have been the end of it, except then Ardy Tate stalks out of my room. He didn't escape through the closet to the back of the house after all. By the look on his pale, clenched face, I know he heard every word Cooper said. "Sorry," he manages to grit toward my mother. "I know I shouldn't have been in there. I won't do it again." He shoots an angry, hurt look at me. "I promise."

And then he's gone, too.

Leaving me standing there. It doesn't matter that my mother is right beside me. I feel completely and terribly alone.

CHAPTER TWENTY-ONE

I'm grounded, probably forever, and it's perfectly fine with me. Grounded means I can exist in only three places: Home. School. Wheelz.

That's it.

And that's okay.

At first Katie is happy about my situation with Ardy and Cooper. "Good riddance to both of them," she says. "Does that mean you'll start coming to parties with me again?" I remind her about the grounding, and that puts an end to that. "But when you're sprung from prison," she says, "I get you back."

The first few days at school, I basically only see the tops of my shoes. That's where I keep my gaze focused when I'm walking. When I'm in class, I stare at my desk or the teacher. I know Ardy's there in English, over in his corner with Hope, but I don't look at him. I do everything I can to not see him anymore. To not see anyone. This is where all my knowledge of secret make-out places comes to good use. In between classes and at lunch, I can hide in the computer-cart storage room, or the back corner of the library, or that mostly-empty janitor's closet on the third floor.

Cooper's at school, of course, but he literally walks in the other direction when he sees me. I tried calling him later that night, but he hasn't called me back. It's killing me because he's the person I would normally run to so I could talk through everything and figure it out. But each time I get a glimpse of his icy-cold face, I know he's too furious. Too far gone. It's way too late.

I'm so bound up in my own sadness that it takes me a day and a half to remember Hope and our previously budding friendship and the fact that she's going through her own painful breakup with Evan. I take a detour past the French room when I know she'll be coming out, ripping my eyes from my shoes long enough to scan the hall. I'm in luck, because Hope is coming straight toward me. But she veers, heading into French class without saying a word.

It only makes sense. If Ardy's told her any part of it—the game, my plans to win by hurting him—it's no wonder she's over me.

I'm over me, too.

Even the perfect rooms at IKEA don't help.

» » « «

A week into the new hell that is my life, Leo is late to meet me after school, which means I'm at the flagpoles much longer than I normally would be. Thus, when Ardy ambles out the front doors and we make eye contact, both of us freeze, staring across the wide expanse at each other. My heart aches at the sight of him, so familiar and yet somehow new again after this time apart. After a moment I half raise my hand, an awkward attempt at a greeting. He doesn't return the motion. He doesn't do anything but stand there, looking at me for a long, long moment, until he abruptly turns and walks back into the school. I presume he's going to find another way out.

I want a way out, too. Before I can convince myself otherwise, I send him a text:

I'm so sorry.

I wait, staring at my phone. Nothing happens. So I send another one:

It started as a game. It didn't end that way.

Still nothing. I try again, three messages in a row:

Let me explain.
Please talk to me.
Please.

Flickering dots appear on my screen. Ardy is typing. I wait, holding my breath, desperate for communication. For acknowledgment. For anything.

The dots disappear, then flicker back into existence, then disappear again. This time they stay disappeared.

He's not talking to me.

Later that night I try again, this time with a message online. Finally—finally—my phone buzzes with a text from him:

> Stop.

And then with several other texts, all in a row:

> I don't want to block you.
> I know what that feels like.
> But please stop.
> No minute is long enough.

» » « «

Another week passes, and I learn through the grapevine— and by *grapevine,* I mean Katie—that Hope's newly exed ex-boyfriend, Evan, is going to the Not-Prom with Sara Ball. I like Sara okay—she's a ballet dancer and science-decathlon leader who's had a tough go of it because of her last name—but I hate it for Hope.

I can't help but wonder: What does this mean for Hope and Ardy? They're simultaneously available for the first time in years. Is all of this—my terrible judgment, Cooper's treason—a way of making their stars align? Is the big romance of my life story not even about me?

The Spring Fling Thing is on the horizon, and it's all any-one talks about. Except me. I don't talk about it, because I've stopped talking at all. Since I was always either with Cooper or Katie or some boy behind a computer cart, no one else ever expected me to join their conversations, so now no one notices that I've stopped being a part of them. I'm just the girl sitting at a desk or walking through the cafeteria, hearing what people say but not being included. An exile of my own making.

At home Mom and Dad are also talking Not-Prom plans because, of course, it's being held at Wheelz. One evening when I emerge from my room for dinner, I'm shocked to find both of my parents at the table. Leo hasn't been called down yet, apparently so the three of us can have special time together. Mom, like she's giving me some great gift, bestows upon me an "ungrounding" for that night.

"It's fine," I tell them both. "You don't have to do that."

"We know," Dad says. "But we don't want you to look back and regret not going."

I don't tell him that of all the things I can look back on with regret, the fake prom won't even make the list's top ten.

"Besides," Mom chimes in, "it won't look good for Wheelz if our own daughter isn't there."

"Trust me," I tell them. "No one will notice if I'm there or not."

"We will," Dad says.

"Just because things didn't work out with one boy," Mom says, "it's no reason to stop living your life."

"Please don't," I say. This is not a conversation I'm willing to have with her. With either one of them. I cross my arms and wait. Mom and Dad exchange glances.

"For real." Mom's voice lowers, becomes serious. "You *are*

going because we want you to leave this house and start acting like a human again."

"Going to the stupid school's stupid Not-Prom won't change anything."

"We'll unground you for real," Dad says. "Not just for the party."

"I like being grounded."

"You're going," Mom says. "The only thing left to discuss is what you're going to wear."

"Clothing isn't supposed to be part of the equation," I remind her. "No dresses, no tuxedoes."

"I know, but surely people are doing *something* to make it special."

I stay silent. Yes, I've heard people at school discussing wardrobe options. The consensus seems to be on designer jeans and blingy earrings. Sure, no one's going to wear a ball gown, but everyone will put their own stamp on the night. Their own way of making it special.

Not me.

I don't want it.

But it looks like—in all areas of my life—what I want doesn't remotely matter.

CHAPTER TWENTY-TWO

I try to leave the house in cutoff sweatpants and a tank top, but both my mother and Katie insist that I change clothes. It's easy for me to ignore Katie's text instructing me to put on something cute, but it's harder to get past Mom. I consider fighting her on it but decide I don't have the energy. I end up in denim capris with rips along the thighs and a white peasant blouse. Mom would love it if I'd wear heels or a skirt, but I remind her they're not particularly conducive to go-kart racing, and she gives in. What I don't say is that I have absolutely no plans to race. Or to play games or dance or participate in any way whatsoever. I'll make an appearance long enough for my parents to feel like I haven't ruined my senior year or their establishment's reputation, and then I'll bail.

The Wheelz parking lot is already packed when I arrive, but I manage to squeeze my tiny car into a spot. As I'm wiggling out, I notice Ardy's minivan across the pavement. I do a quick scan for Hope's car but don't see it. Did they carpool?

Or . . . did they come together and it's not about carpooling?

Ms. Perkins is stationed at the front doors, I assume to prevent people from going in and out to drink in the parking lot. The rule here is, once you leave the party you can't come back. Also, our parents get a text when we leave, so there's no sneaking out and running around town unsupervised while they think we're at the party.

When I enter, I'm bombarded with a late-nineties pop song. It's way louder than my parents usually pump the music. It drowns out the sound of the karts whizzing around the track, as well as the ever-present beeps and whistles of the video games.

Dad is managing the track. There's a long line for it, which is a good thing—it means people are excited to race—and a shorter line for refreshments. I wave at Leo and Mom behind the counter, fervently wishing I could trade places with them, and then I check the clock on the wall. Nine o'clock. I purposefully arrived an hour after the party started, and I plan to just as purposefully depart several hours before it ends.

There's a big group off to one side. Although some of them are bopping their heads or weaving back and forth a little, Cooper is the only one who is truly dancing. As I watch, he grabs J'shon Frederic and pulls him into some moves.

God, I miss Cooper.

The other person I miss like breathing is with Hope. They've scored two trackside stools and are perched there, heads bent together. The sight of Ardy makes my breath catch in my throat, especially since he *did* dress up for the event. At least kind of. Sure, his jeans are ripped across the upper thighs, like mine, but he's paired them with a crisp white collared shirt and a black blazer. He looks both dashing and rumpled at the same time, and the end result breaks my heart.

"Stop it." It's Katie, arriving at my side. "Distract yourself with a new boy if you have to, but I cannot allow you to stand and stare. It's a cringeworthy offense."

I nod because it's too exhausting to explain that I truly do not care if I'm engaging in cringeworthy behavior.

"Come on." She grabs my arm. "All the delinquents are in the party room."

I allow her to drag me across Wheelz, noticing Sara Ball as we skirt around and past smaller groupings of people. Surprisingly, Sara seems to be joined at the face to Deondray Enos. "I thought she was—" I start to say, but Katie interrupts me.

"Yeah, everyone thought she and Evan were a thing." Katie rolls her eyes. "Evan thought so, too. Karma, right?"

The lights are off in the party room, and even though there are fluorescents right outside, it's dim and hard to see. I squint through the shadows, finding Tilly Thompson and her twin brother, Tyler, whose parents must be worse than mine; at least our *last* name doesn't start with *L*, too. Omar Taylor, Carrie Wright, and Evan are with the twins, all sitting at a table in the back corner. Evan waves us over, and Katie and I pull up chairs.

"What's shaking?" Katie asks the table.

"We hate the music," Carrie says.

"Be nice." Tilly points at me, a reminder that my parents own the place.

"Sorry," says Carrie.

"I'm not the deejay," I tell everyone. "Go request something."

"Meh." Omar shrugs. "Too much trouble."

Tyler pulls out his phone. "I'll deejay for this room. What do you want?"

"Anything but country," Katie says.

"I like country," Carrie replies.

While the others start arguing about music, Evan nudges me. "Hey."

"Hey," I respond.

"How's Hope?" he asks.

I turn to look at him, disbelieving. "You didn't get the memo."

"About you and Ardy breaking up? I heard that. . . . Oh." Evan nods, realizing. "He got Hope in the divorce. Makes sense."

Sure does.

Evan doesn't say anything else, but I turn to follow his gaze out the room to the trackside stools where Hope and Ardy still sit, still together.

Evan shakes it off, turning back to the group. "Let's play a game."

Typical Evan.

"Like what?" Katie makes a face. "Did you bring Monopoly?"

"Something more interesting," he says. "Spin the bottle?"

Tyler and Tilly immediately shake their heads. "You don't play that in a room with your brother," she says.

"I thought we were playing 'Never Have I Ever,'" Carrie says, holding up her lidded cup from the concession stand.

"Shh!" Omar hisses, nodding his head toward me.

My eyes narrow, realizing what he's warning against. I jut a hand toward Carrie. "Hand it over."

"Dude . . ." It's a protest, but she gives me the cup anyway. I slip the straw between my lips and take a long pull. Yep, it's what I thought: her soda's spiked with some sort of alcohol.

"Be cool," Evan says to me.

"Don't be an asshole," Katie tells him. "Her parents *own* the place."

"All the more reason to actually have fun," Evan says.

"No way," I say, and watch everyone's faces fall. "If we get busted, we'll get in trouble, but my parents could actually lose their license. You can't drink here. It falls into the category of not cool."

"Not cool is this dumb Not-Prom," Carrie says.

"It's not like we can go somewhere else," Omar says. "And—no offense, Lark—this is the last place I want to be tonight. My parents made me come to bond with my classmates."

"I know what you mean," I tell him. Carrie raises her cup to her lips, but I give her a stern look, so she lowers it. I look at Evan, but he's staring at Hope and Ardy again. Since I cannot handle being a part of that, I turn back to everyone else. "I can get us outside," I say, and watch their faces light up. "There's a fire exit in the back. It has an alarm, but I know the code to turn it off."

"My car's a block away," Evan says. "We could hang out there."

"In your car?" Katie asks, skeptical.

"Trust me," Evan says. "It's big."

If Cooper were here, he'd say "that's what he said." But he's not, and that hurts. And I don't trust Evan, but I trust myself and my ability to be at the same party as Ardy even less . . . which is why we all end up sneaking out.

» » « «

I wouldn't use the word *car* to describe Evan's vehicle. It's more of a behemoth: a giant silver land yacht with leather trim and three wide rows of seats. Evan starts off in the driver's seat but quickly realizes he's impeded by the steering wheel, so he switches to the passenger side. Katie and I are piled together in the captain's chair behind him, with Tyler next to us and Carrie, Tilly, and Omar in the backseat.

It's been only thirty minutes since we crept out the fire exit, and already things are getting raucous. Unsurprisingly, Carrie wasn't the only one spiking her drink. Slightly more surprisingly, there's still quite a bit to go around. Evan had two fifths of rum in the glove compartment and another two in the trunk. "Where did you get all this?" I ask him.

"Doesn't hurt to have older siblings," he tells me.

Lucky Leo.

"I'm still up for a game," Evan says. He catches my eye, and I shake my head. I am not playing Kiss, Date, Punch with him. Not again. Not when I miss Ardy so much it hurts.

"I'll play something," Katie says. "After everyone takes a shot."

"Did you bring shot glasses?" Carrie asks. "Because if anyone has some in their purse, they win everything."

There's an immediate dive for purses. I have nothing, but

Tilly offers up a contact lens holder. She is met resoundingly with disgust until Katie triumphantly pulls something out. "I win!" It's a single-use Keurig cup.

"Why do you have that?" I ask her.

"I stole it from a hotel." She rips the foil off the top of the cup and opens our side door, nearly knocking both of us out in the process. She dumps the coffee grounds on the curb and then closes the door. "Bottoms up."

Ten minutes later everyone has had at least one coffee-flavored shot of rum, and I'm feeling warm and fuzzy. Although I sometimes go to parties with Katie, I rarely drink alcohol. It doesn't seem worth it: getting in trouble, the lack of control and potential for making bad decisions. However, my life lately has been one giant bad decision. No amount of alcohol could make that any worse.

Katie, smashed against me in our one seat, squeezes my arm and whispers in my ear: "Screw that guy." Then she pulls away, announcing to everyone else, "I have a game."

"I'm not kissing my brother," Tilly says automatically.

"No one wants you to," Omar says.

"The game is called Love Golf." Katie raises both hands to touch the car roof like she's trying to channel something. "Maybe it's called Golf Love. I don't remember."

"I rock at golf," Evan says.

At the same time I say, "I hate golf."

"Listen," Katie says. "You pick two people who we all know, and then you try to get from one to the other in the least amount of strokes."

"Strokes," Tyler and Evan say together.

"Shut up," Katie and I say together.

Tyler takes a swig from the rum bottle and passes it to me. It tastes worse when it's not enhanced by coffee, but I no longer care. Katie points to Tyler, in the seat across from us. "Like Tyler and . . ." She swings her arm in a wide arc until she's pointing at Evan, in the front. "Evan. You have to get from one to the other—through LOVE—as quickly as you can."

We all stare at her. I'm finally the one who asks the question. "What do you mean, through love?"

"Sex." Katie rolls her eyes. "Or kissing or whatever. Like, if you and Tyler kissed, and then you and Evan kissed, you would win in two strokes. Tyler to you, you to Evan. *WHAT?*"

Because I'm laughing so hard I almost can't breathe.

"We did kiss," Tyler says. "In tenth grade."

"Us too," Evan says. "Ninth."

And now both boys are laughing with me.

"Oh, that's right!" Katie exclaims. "I forgot about that. You win, one stroke." She high-fives me. "God, high school."

"Tell me about it," I say. "You and Tyler. Go."

I remember just as Katie bursts into laughter, too. "One stroke, last year."

"See, *you* win," I tell her, and then we high-five again while the boys roll their eyes.

The game doesn't last very long because there's so much giggling, I think; plus, those bottles keep getting passed around. It's all getting blurry and woozy, so I'm not exactly sure why Katie and Tyler went for a "walk" outside or when everyone else went after them.

Or how I ended up in the front seat with Evan.

All I know is that now it's murky dark and we're alone and I keep wondering if there's an earthquake because it feels like his car is lurching, but then I remember the rum and remember *that's* the reason everything is off-balance.

Evan is looking over the console controls at me in the dimness. "Why did we break up?" he asks.

"You and me? We were never dating," I tell him. "We were only kissing a lot, and then I found out I had mono, so you said we had to stop." I lean closer to him, giggling because it's suddenly so funny. "Wanna know something?"

"Sure." The streetlight glints off Evan's teeth when he smiles at me.

I say it in a stage whisper. "I didn't have mono."

Evan cocks his head. "So why'd you say you did?"

"To trick you into breaking up with me," I tell him. "I make evvvvveryone break up with me. It's my superpower."

"Huh." Evan leans back in his seat, staring at the car parked in front of us. "I don't remember that."

I think I'm too drunk to be offended.

"Why did you break up with Hope?" I ask him. There's a long silence. "You don't have to tell me." I say it too late.

"It wasn't about sex." Evan keeps his eyes straight ahead. "I don't know what she told you, but it wasn't that. It was . . . she was perfect and I wasn't, and . . ."

He pauses and I wait for the rest of his answer, hoping it'll make some sort of sense in my spinning head, something I can use for my own screwed-up life. There was a time when I was prepared to hate Evan on behalf of Hope, back a thousand years ago, when Hope and I were friends, but now it doesn't matter anymore. And anyway, Evan breaking up with her isn't that bad. It's not as bad as me. Not as bad as the person who fell in love with a perfect boy and ruined things, hurting her best friend in the process. That person is pretty crappy. That person doesn't *deserve* to have someone good, someone nice.

Just as that concept breaks the surface of my brain, I realize Evan has grabbed my hand. I look down at where his fingers are gripping mine and then back to his face. But he's still looking out the window . . .

At Ardy and Hope, stopped under a streetlight by the side of Wheelz. They're talking, and as we watch, Ardy leans closer to her. . . .

I can't look anymore, which is why I turn my head to face Evan. That's why, as my heart cracks and breaks inside me, I reach for him.

That's why it happens.

CHAPTER TWENTY-THREE

We've all seen it before in movies and on TV. The heroine awakens to find herself flung atop her twisted bedcovers like last night's trash. Her clothing is rumpled, and caked mascara glues her eyelashes together. Her tongue is a shriveled corn husk, you could physically shave her teeth, and a miniature freight train with spiked wheels and a shrieking horn grinds along inside her skull.

Check.

I remember Evan's mouth. And then his hands, sliding over my body . . .

I rub my eyes, succeeding in impaling my left cornea with what I assume is a particularly sharp flake of dried mascara. The pain makes me sway to a sitting position, and the resulting nausea from *that* makes me stagger off my bed and out my door to the bathroom.

I'm there for several minutes, during which I throw up my body weight. When I emerge, Leo is standing outside. He hands me an open bottle of purple Gatorade.

"I can't," I tell him.

"Trust me," he says.

"What do you know about hangovers?"

"Only what I read online. Here." I accept his offering, taking a wary sip. It doesn't make me want to die, so I take another, bigger this time.

"Thank you," I tell Leo. He trails me back to my room, where I collapse in my bed. "How mad are they?" I ask from where my head is burrowed in my pillow.

"Less mad than you'd think," he says. "At least, not at you."

"Fantastic." Because that means they're fighting, probably *about* me. I raise my head to look at him and instantly regret it because the sun coming through my window might be trying to kill me. "Leo, I'm sorry."

"It's actually a win for me," he says. "You've made my high school life awesome." I manage to crack my eyelids open. Leo is grinning. "I could murder someone and I'll still look like the good one."

"You're not helping." Normally I would put him in a headlock, but that's clearly not going to happen right now. I flap a hand at him. "Go away."

When I wake again, my father is entering my room. He opens the curtains and sits on the edge of my bed. I squint against the light. "It's so bright."

"Some parents would ground you for being drunk," he says. "Or I guess I should say *re*ground you."

"But you believe God is punishing me enough?"

"I haven't decided yet." I use my fingers to open my eyes for a second so I can see him shaking his head. "In the plus column for 'punishment enough,' you do look like hell."

"I feel worse than I look," I tell him.

"Also in the plus column, we shouldn't have made you go in the first place. You did tell us you didn't want to." I stay silent, and I hear my father give a heavy sigh. "And I do appreciate you taking people outside to drink, although it would have been better if it hadn't happened at all."

"It was happening before I showed up," I tell him. "It was either move them outside or narc them out."

"Your mother called everyone's parents," he says. "Maybe we should have told the school, too, but since no one tried to drive after drinking, and you seem to be the worst offender, we decided to leave it at that. Here." I raise my head to see what he's setting on my nightstand: a piece of dry toast on a paper towel, a cup of coffee, and two Tylenol tablets.

"I don't know if I can get that down."

"You'll be happier if you do." The bed lurches as Dad stands up, and I valiantly refrain from barfing again. "I have to go back to work. Please don't asphyxiate on your own vomit."

"I'll try."

"Good." I feel his hand land lightly on the top of my head. He strokes my hair for a moment. "Hang in there, Larks. Things get better."

And then he's gone, leaving me alone in my misery.

Later I'm in my bathroom, rinsing out my mouth after puking (again), when there's a knock on the door. My mother doesn't wait for me to answer; she barges right in. I look past my watery, red-rimmed reflection in the mirror to the image of her standing behind me. "You don't have to ground me more right now," I tell her. "I'm not going anywhere."

"I'm actually here to unground you."

"What?" I spin to look at her, immediately regretting the quick movement.

"Your father and I think you've had enough punishment." Mom tilts her head to the side, assessing me. "And for the record, it was never our goal to make you miserable."

"You're not making me miserable." I take several careful steps to the bathtub so I can teeter carefully on the edge. "I did that all myself."

"I kind of got that." She comes over and perches beside me. "But our job as your parents is not necessarily to increase that misery." She pats my knee. "So consider yourself ungrounded. Also, consider yourself warned not to ever drink like that again."

"Don't worry," I assure her. "This is miserable."

"I know." She stands and heads out.

"Mom." She stops in the doorway to look back at me. It's on the tip of my tongue to ask if she's going to fix her life, too . . . but I can't. And maybe it's not my job to ask that question of her, anyway.

» » « «

I feel almost human again by late afternoon. I say *almost* because although my head doesn't hurt and I'm no longer nauseated and the world finally stopped spinning . . . all the physical pain has tightened and coalesced and focused into a heavy spot around my heart. After I eat something—and fend off questions from Leo about what punishment I've received—I escape him and my parents and my house. I get into my car, and I drive to Griffith Park.

The picnic table is warmer than the last time I was here with Cooper, and I have no mango smoothie along for the ride. It's just me, my thoughts, and the California sun. I sit on the table, feet on the bench, gazing out over the park. Many yards away a group of kids play soccer in the grass. I envy them their freedom. From where I'm sitting, all they have to care about right now is whether or not a ball gets into a net.

God, that sounds amazing.

I think back to what Cooper and I talked about when we were here, about the idea of losing one's self on purpose, like while watching a movie. Because . . . isn't that what love is?

All along I've tried to control everything. With Ardy, with everyone. But at the end of the day, I couldn't do it. The thing about falling in love is that, no matter how you rail against it, a *fall* is involved. And you can't control the world around you when you're in free fall. You have to let the wind and the sky and the air take you where you're going to go.

I watch the soccer players for a while, and then I go somewhere else. Downtown Burbank. To the theater.

Cooper—in his little red vest and button-up shirt—looks surprised to see me when I walk in and hand him my ticket. I don't even know what movie I'm seeing. It was the one starting next after I marched up to the ticket counter.

Cooper rips my ticket and hands half of it back to me. "Meeting someone?"

I'm immediately grateful that he's deigning to talk to me at all. "No." I smile at him. "Flying solo."

"Surprising." Cooper doesn't smile back, but . . . there's something in his eyes. A hint of amusement or solidarity or *something*. "I hope you enjoy it." He even sounds sincere.

The movie—a romantic comedy—is entertaining enough, but it's not like it changes my life. That's okay, though; it's not why I'm here. I'm here to prove that I can go out and see a movie alone. That I can sit in a crowd of strangers and not be attached to one of them. That I can lose myself, even into something as superficial and meaningless as a fictional couple's story on a big screen. That I can loosen my grip on the steering wheel.

When the movie's over, I again pass by Cooper. I give him a half nod and keep walking, but he calls my name, so I stop.

"I hear you were one of the degenerates who got busted last night," he says.

"Who told you that?"

"Katie."

It reminds me I need to text her back. Earlier today she sent several messages in a row:

You okay?

Your parents called my mom. She was like, whatevs.

So screw her.

Hope you're not too busted.

And then several minutes later:

Did you hook up with Evan?

I'm not sure how I'm going to answer that last question.

"Okay," I tell Cooper. I almost leave, but then I stop so I can say one last thing. "The movie was okay. Not as good as others, but watchable."

"That's the point," Cooper says. And then he's off to tear more tickets.

I leave the theater and make my way up San Fernando to the mall. I take the escalator to the second floor and head straight to where I need to go: a store proudly displaying a *NOT STRAIGHT* T-shirt in the front window.

Glen greets me with his customary hug. When he returns me to the floor, he looks around. "Where are your partners in crime?"

"Cooper and Katie?" My heart sinks, and—out of nowhere—tears glaze my eyes because one of my partners in crime can now barely look at me. I turn away from Glen, pretending to be occupied with a rack of striped vests. "Oh, they're around."

"Looking for something in particular?"

My self-respect.

My life.

The boy I love.

"Nope," I tell Glen.

"Those are ten percent off." He gestures to the vests. "But I can give you fifteen."

I take a pink-and-yellow vest off its hanger, slipping it over my T-shirt. "What do you think?" I ask Glen, trying to buy time.

"Huh." He susses me out. "I don't know that I would have picked it for you, but—"

"I'm not in chess club." My interruption makes Glen stop. "I'm not in marching band, either. I never was. And I didn't make the track team. I didn't even try out. I don't like to sweat."

"Okay." He looks confused, but he's listening.

"I said all that stuff because I wanted you to think I wouldn't have any time for you once we started high school. I wanted to make you break up with me."

"You mean . . . at camp that summer?" Glen's brows knit together. "Is that what you're talking about?"

"Yes. You broke up with me on the bus. Because I lied to you."

"Really?" Glen's eyes go faraway, like he's trying to remember. After a moment, he returns to the present, setting his large hands on my shoulders. I shrug them off. He peers into my eyes. "Why are you here?"

"I'm trying to set the record straight."

"It's been three years." He doesn't move from his position in front of me. "You know I'm with Allie, right?"

My mouth drops open. "Yes! This is not about trying to get back together with you!"

"Okay, cool." He raises his hands in a *don't blame me* gesture. "Then I guess I don't know what you're getting at."

"I'm getting at . . ." I pause. What *am* I getting at? "I'm trying to apologize. For lying."

"No problem." Glen shrugs his shoulders. "Apology accepted."

It's *so* anticlimactic that, five minutes later, I'm leaving the store with a bag of merchandise. Which Glen sold to me with, of course, a 15 percent discount.

CHAPTER TWENTY-FOUR

Evan is waiting by the flagpoles when I step onto the school property. It's infuriating, both that he would wait for me and also that he would wait for me *here*. I alter the trajectory of my path, but he immediately steps into it, so I sling my backpack to the front of my body, tucking my arms around it. Making it a barrier between us.

"We should talk about it," he says.

"No thank you." I take a step to the side, but he blocks my path. "Please don't do that."

"Lark." Evan's green eyes look softer in the morning light. Almost mossy. Serious. "You cried."

Yes. Yes, I did. I may not remember everything clearly, but I do remember the crying. We had been kissing in the front seat of Evan's car for . . . I have no idea how long. One second? One minute? I have no idea, because it was so messy. Blurry. I didn't even realize I didn't like it, that I wasn't into it, until I registered Evan's hand sliding up my side.

Then, with no warning, I burst into tears and pushed him away. He tried to talk to me, but I couldn't stop. I kept crying when he left the car, and I was still crying when he returned with my dad.

Now, standing by the flagpoles, I fight my natural reaction—to apologize for my tears, for making it weird. Instead, I say the thing that's honest. "Thank you."

I don't finish the sentence: *for finding my father . . . for getting in trouble . . . for not hurting me.* But I think he understands.

"You don't like me," he says. His voice is low and gentle. "I mean . . . romantically."

I shake my head. "You don't like me, either."

"Yeah." Evan looks at the ground, scuffing at it with his foot, before meeting my eyes again. "But we both miss the people we *do* like."

I unhook my hands from each other, allowing my backpack barrier to slide away. "Yeah."

"Sucks," he says.

"I know." The smiles we share are tentative, but they're there. A reminder that we all make mistakes.

» » « «

Katie is the next person to talk to me about that night. She snags me in the hall and drags me to the second-floor girls' bathroom. "Dude, I caught Tyler and Carrie having a convo about whether you let Evan go *there* at the Not-Prom."

I'm horrified. "People know?"

"No, I made sure." She shakes her head. "I told them not to let it get around, because you and Evan want everyone to think you had sex—"

"What?"

Katie holds up a hand—*hush.* "But really you guys had a mutual sobfest about your breakups. You're both embarrassed because it was so pathetic."

I stare at her, begrudgingly appreciative. "I kind of hate you, but that was genius."

"I know, right? They'll spread it everywhere." She gives me a pinched smile. "It's just enough truth to make everyone believe it."

"You never told me what happened with Tyler," I remind her. "You guys left to 'take a walk.'"

"We did take a walk." Katie plasters a nonchalant look on her face. "We walked to my car and spent the night in the backseat. It was fine."

"Do you like him?"

She shrugs. "I liked him that night." She waves her hand in the air like she's brushing away the memory, then fixes me with a look. "I can't believe I'm going to say this, but . . . don't you want to work your crap out with Cooper?"

"I'm trying," I tell her.

"Good." She makes a face. "He's so mopey when you're not around."

"You and Cooper are hanging out?"

But Katie's over the conversation. "Whatever," she says, before fleeing the bathroom.

» » « «

That afternoon, I hijack my ex-hookup Dax Santos outside the boys' locker room. Actually, that's another lie. Hijacking him is what I *intended* to do. What really happens is that I watch dozens of athletes parade out until finally I get tired of waiting, so I barge in, interrupting Dax in the middle of toweling off. He's none too thrilled to be seen in all his glory, and less so when I launch into a monologue about how—when I got him to end things between us—I hadn't actually entered the world of plant-based cuisine. In fact, I was the exact same girl he started kissing in the first place; I was just pretending not to be.

Unlike Glen, Dax isn't nonchalant about the whole thing. He's *pissed.* "Why would you do that?"

"I thought . . . it would make it easier."

"For *you.*" He glares at me. "It was so weird when I thought we were heading toward something. I thought maybe I'd given you mixed signals. I blamed myself for not providing clarity about being a dude who's into partnered wellness—"

Okay, he's not wrong about how I handled it, but *partnered wellness*? Really? Freaking California . . .

"I told my friends about it," he continues. "I told my sister. I told my *guru.*"

"You have a guru?" Obviously, we never knew each other in the first place. "I'm saying I'm sorry."

"And I'm saying I'm not interested in making you feel better about what you did, about how you lied." Dax looks disgusted. "Actually, let me be a little more clear. What I'm saying is—go screw yourself."

Ah. There's all the conflict I tried to avoid.

» » « «

The days blur by and Cooper continues to ignore me. Sometimes we make eye contact in the hall, but then he always looks the other way. It's better than Ardy, who somehow manages to avoid my eyes completely. One day, I'm feeling extra-sad about Ardy when I see Cooper outside Calculus class. I'm about to try to talk to him, because maybe he'll take pity on me if I tell him how heartbroken I am, when Will Hartsook marches up to me. The minute I lay eyes on his pink face, I know there's going to be trouble. Will only goes pink when his emotions run high, and right now he doesn't look like someone who's in the throes of delight. I scan my brain, trying to remember exactly what lie I told him. Before I can reach the memory, Will yells out a question: "Where is Cleopatra buried?"

"Dude, chill." It's Keeshana, walking past us. "Obviously, Egypt."

Will doesn't glance in her direction. He folds his arms over his chest, glaring at me. "Well?"

Oh. Right. He's talking about Cleopatra, my tragic, fictional dog who tragically, fictionally died the week Will and I were kissing in parks and mall elevators, spiraling me into a tragic and fictional depression, one that had no space for another person to fit in. I try to remember what I said at the time. Maybe I buried her in the backyard? Maybe under the maple tree?

But instead I say, "Will, I have to tell you something."

"Is it that you're a giant liar?" Will's eyes flare bright green in his pink, pink face. "I had an interesting conversation with Dax last night. I used to think I couldn't stand that guy, but once we started talking, it turns out we have a lot in common. And all of it has to do with how much you suck."

He's not wrong, but it's not fun to hear.

"I'm sorry." Maybe there's a chance an apology will head off his anger at the pass.

"Why lie?" Nope. Not headed off at all. "Why not act like an actual human being and *tell* me you don't want to make out anymore? Why go through an elaborate lie about a stupid *dog*?"

"I don't know." Normally I would flutter my eyelashes or stick out my boobs or something, but I don't have it in me right now. "I was afraid."

"Of *what*?"

"Of this fight." My voice trembles, but I stand my ground. "Of making you mad. Of having to argue or defend myself. And I'm sorry." Will shakes his head and starts to turn away, but I grab his arm to stop him. "I'm really, really sorry. What can I do to make it up to you?"

"Nothing."

"Will, I was wrong. Tell me, what can I do?"

He pauses. After a long moment, he turns back to face me. "Actually, I could use some help with something. I mean, if you want to dig yourself out."

"Seriously?" I'm thrilled at the chance to prove myself a better person than who I've been in the past. "Yes!"

"It's shitty work." Will smiles. "You're not going to like it."

"I don't like you being mad at me," I tell him. "If this will serve as my apology and you'll accept it, I don't care. I'm in!"

Will nods, his face fading from very pink to slightly less pink.

It turns out that Will wasn't exaggerating when he said it was shitty work, because what he needs me to do is help with *actual shit*. Horseshit, to be specific. Will's family owns one of the riding stables on the edge of Griffith Park, which means that—like me at Wheelz—Will often gets roped in to help out. This afternoon, however, he's hunkered on a little wooden stool nearby while I—Lark Dayton, queen of loving and leaving—am shoveling out a stable.

Blisters are rising along the pads of my hands, and I'm sweating through my T-shirt as I lift the shovel again and again and again, throwing hay and horse poop into the wheelbarrow that Will helpfully brought in for me to use. I know my face has to be at least as pink as his was earlier, when he yelled at me. "I thought you were going to go somewhere else while I did this," I say through gritted teeth now.

"That's what I thought at first, too." I glance over to see him beaming, holding up his phone. "But this is so much more fun."

Flash.

He takes a photo. "Dax is going to love this."

"Awesome," I mutter. If only Cooper could see me now.

I keep shoveling the shit.

It quickly becomes evident that word has gotten around. My exes are coming out of the woodwork: accosting me at my locker, at my car, outside the girls' restroom. The only one who seemingly can't stand to look in my direction is Ardy. Even though all I want to do is talk to him, I don't. Instead, I apologize to everyone else. At first I'm surprised by how little belligerence and anger is directed at me. After Dax and Will, I expected nothing but fury. However, when Wade shows up, when Rahim comes around, when it's Peter's turn to accost me . . . none of those guys seem mad. Sure, some of them start things off by saying I wronged them, but they quickly turn the conversation to how I can get back into their good graces now. How I can *help* them in some way.

Since I'm not in a position to say no—at least not without feeling like more of an asshole than I already do—I agree. That's how I end up editing the speech Rahim wrote for our upcoming graduation. And how I spend an afternoon supervising Wade's little brother's lemonade stand outside the local pet store. And why I find myself on Peter's roof, helping him pull gunk out of his gutters.

It's apparently also why Morris Blair swings into line behind me at the cafeteria. "Hey, Lark."

"Hey." I continue trying to make a decision between steamed cauliflower or roasted brussels sprouts to go with my tilapia, until Morris taps me on the shoulder.

"I was hoping I could tag you in after school today."

"Huh?" I turn to him, confused. "Tag me in for what?"

"My car needs an oil change. And one of the tires is shot."

"And?"

"Can you do it for me?"

My eyes narrow. This had better not be what I think it is. "Why?"

"You know." Morris slouches casually against the sneeze-guard. "Because of that time in seventh grade."

"*What* time?"

"When you . . ." Morris looks a little less sure. "When we broke up. You know, that time. When you . . . lied. About stuff."

All right, that's it. I might kill someone.

Morris must see it on my face, because he takes a quick step backward. "Maybe . . . maybe that wasn't you after all."

"You *know* it wasn't me. You and I have never been to-gether." I poke him in the chest, hard. "You go out there and in-form all your little friends that I am not on some sort of amends *tour* for the general public!"

"Do you *want* to hook up?" He gazes at me. "You are kinda hot."

"No!" This is infuriating. "Go away!"

"Eh." Morris shrugs. "It was worth a shot."

Oh. The. Hell.

» » « «

Later that day I discover how word has gotten around so fast. It's because—thanks to Will and his photography acumen—I'm now all over the various social media outlets. I even have my very own special hashtag.

#larkkarma

Really—I might kill someone.

» » « «

We're a week out from graduation when I put a stop to it. It's because I catch Will and Wade glance at me before high-fiving in the hall outside the chemistry lab. I glare at them and start to turn away but then think better of it. Instead, I march straight to them. Wade gives me a wide grin. "Hey, do you think you can help with my brother's cookie stand next week?"

"*No.*" It comes out of my mouth adamant and strong, but both boys crack up. "I've atoned," I inform them. "Enough is enough."

They look at each other. "I don't know," Wade says. "Do *you* think it's enough?"

"I've got horseshit forever," Will answers, and they both laugh again.

"I hate you both," I tell them.

I start to stalk away, shaking my head, when I hear Wade call my name. I turn back to find them both smiling at me. "It's all good," Wade says.

"Yeah." Will gives me a little wave. "You're a cool chick."

"Thank you." I double down on my glare, but it's got some humor in it. Now I only halfway mean it. "But you can tell everyone else, too—*enough.*"

"We'll spread the word," Wade says. "And if you ever need something—"

"Yeah, like if your family buys horses or something," Will chimes in, "I'm your man."

"Or if you're thirsty." Wade's smile widens. "We have lemonade."

I roll my eyes and walk away.

Ding-dongs.

Still—it's one of the few times I've come close to smiling since Ardy.

CHAPTER TWENTY-FIVE

Exam week is looming, along with graduation, along with Real Life, along with the last days that will offer an opportunity to even get a glimpse of Ardy. And then I round a corner and literally run into him. I'm hurrying so fast on my way to Art class that there's an actual impact.

Ardy catches me by the forearms when I charge into him. "Whoa!"

We both freeze, and I mean *freeze.* Paralysis City. Two statues, locked into place, gazing into each other's eyes. Ardy's fingers are wrapped around my arms, hard and narrow and familiar. His pupils are wide, the brown of his eyes a warm ring around them.

Ardy swallows. His hands loosen, and he starts to take a step back. . . .

But I step forward, moving with him, moving closer, turning my hands to grasp his arms, "Ardy, wait." And now we're standing together, holding on. It's either romantic or really weird. Ardy's mouth twitches up on one side. He gets the humor of it, too, which gives me hope. "I'm holding your elbows," I tell him.

"You are." A lock of hair slips out of place and tumbles onto his forehead. Instead of letting go of me and using one of his hands, he pushes out his bottom lip and puffs the lock of hair away. It seems like a good sign. "What do you want?"

He says it matter-of-factly, but now it seems not so good after all.

"I want to talk to you. I want to explain what happened. I was never trying to hurt you—"

"Lark." It comes out of his mouth so softly that I can barely hear him. "I want to believe you."

"Then *believe* me. Ardy, I . . ."

I love you, I love you, I love you. But I don't say it, because that would be too much risk, too much exposure, too much everything.

Besides, Ardy says, "You have a history of lying to your boyfriends."

"No." I shake my head. "Not always, and they weren't really boyfriends. I just lied at the end, when I didn't know how to end things." I'm panicked now, rambling. "I won't ever do that again, I promise—"

"Lark." He's trying to break through what has turned into one giant run-on sentence of panic.

"I *learned,* I'm *better* now, and anyway, I can't imagine *wanting* to end things with you, so please—"

"*Lark.*" I stop because Ardy is letting go of me, thrusting my arms away from his. He takes a step backward, and this time I let him. He gives me the saddest, most wistful smile. "Hashtag Lark Karma."

He shrugs because what else is there to say.

And then he's gone.

» » « «

There's only one place to go from there, so I do. After Art and Advanced Biology, after driving Leo home and changing clothes, I hop back into my car and head to the mall.

I hide behind a skin-care kiosk, peeking around the corner, until Ian appears to enter the store where he works. I watch him greet the assistant manager—his brother—while wearing his traditional Ian outfit. His hair is slicked back in his traditional Ian way. I glance at my teeny-tiny skirt and my tall, tall boots. I take a second to hike my shirt down an inch and my boobs up an inch. The lady working the kiosk gives me side-eye, and I narrow my gaze at her. "It's my body, okay?"

Then I'm off, my boots clacking on the tiled mall floor.

When I walk in, a middle-aged man is browsing the rack of aprons while a young woman flips through a pile of screen-printed T-shirts. Ian's brother is by the front door. He practically leaps on me, launching into a greeting. "Welcome! We're having a spring sale this week. Dresses by the wall are half off—"

"Thank you," I interrupt, which I might have done anyway, even if I didn't have important business to take care of. I keep my eyes fixed on Ian, who is counting money at the cash register. "But I'm not here to *shop*." My voice rises on the last word, loud enough that Ian looks up from behind the counter. I continue, as loud as I can. "I'm here to apologize to the love of my life!" Ian's eyes go wide, and in my peripheral vision I see the other customers' heads swivel toward me. "I lied when I came here before!" I proclaim for my audience of four, hoping everyone important remembers what I'm talking about. "Ian, I'm sorry! I wasn't trying to deny our love. I just wanted your attention!"

I saunter toward him, hyperaware of how much thigh and upper boob I have on display. Ian's eyes are wide and horrified. He slams the cash register drawer closed and hurries out from behind the counter. I glance at his brother as I pass by. His eyes are identically wide, but less horrified and more intrigued.

Ian meets me in the center of the store. "What are you doing?" he hisses.

"Fixing this," I hiss back. Out loud I proclaim, "I miss you! I miss your voice and your presence and your . . . mouth."

"You miss his mouth?" It's Ian's brother, who has moved closer to us. He looks wildly interested.

"Yes!" I tell Ian's brother. "Yes!" I also tell Ian. Then, because I'm really trying to sell this, I grab Ian by the head, I surge at him, and I smash my face into his for a mind-blowing kiss.

At least, that's what I hope it looks like from behind me. In reality, I share a mind-blowing kiss with the back of my thumbs that I have pressed against Ian's mouth. To his brother, it should look like I'm passionately cradling Ian's head, instead of going for broke on my thumbs, channeling every first kiss and every last. They've all prepared me for this moment. When I finally pull back, Ian is staring at me like I've grown horns.

"Wow," his brother says.

Ian makes a swipe for my hand. "Come on." Then he glances at his brother. "I'm going on break."

"But you just got here—"

Ian doesn't even pretend to listen. He rushes me out of the store at the speed of light. Or at least he tries to . . . but my boots have very spiky heels, and when we cross the entrance, I trip on the flooring strip and almost twist my ankle. Ian grabs me and we cling to each other, resulting in a very weird hobbled gait as we make our way to the closest bench. "What the ever-loving hell was that?" he asks as soon as we're seated.

"Cooper told me I'd outed you." I try to convey the intensity of my atonement with an earnest gaze. "I'm so sorry. It was wrong, and I would never, *ever* do that on purpose. I'm just trying—"

"I know," Ian says. "I never thought it was on purpose."

"I'm sorry."

"I know that, too." We sit there in silence for a moment, until Ian breaks it. "Thanks for the kiss, but Brody—my brother—isn't gonna buy it."

"No?" Come on, I put my heart and soul into that fake kiss.

"I already told him everything about Cooper. Told our mom, too."

"How'd that go?" I'm not sure what else to ask.

"Not awesome." Ian looks at his carefully laced shoes. "But it was time."

"Maybe, but it should have been in your control."

"Oh, I'm not arguing with that. I wish it had happened differently." Ian glances over at me and manages a slight smile. "But it didn't. So now it is what it is, and everything I'm dealing with at home—my brother and everyone—I'd be dealing with at some point, whether you pushed it to happen or not."

"I'm so, so sorry." Because there's nothing else to say.

"I know," Ian says. "I forgive you."

It's the thing that makes me realize he *is* good enough for Cooper after all.

Not that it's my decision.

It's not.

"Cooper told me about you and Ardy," Ian says. I tighten up. I *cannot* stand to hear more about Ardy's problems at Ian's school. Except Ian doesn't look triumphant or like he's telling gossip. Instead, he looks compassionate. "I shouldn't have repeated what people said about him. I didn't know him. It wasn't fair."

And that's what makes me love Ian. Because not only did he forgive the unforgivable, but he admits his own wrongdoing.

"I forgive you." I mean it. I so mean it.

"Still." Ian leans—just the tiniest bit—toward me. His shoulder brushes mine. "I feel bad."

I also lean toward him, just enough that I can feel the warmth of him against my skin.

Because I am showing a *lot* of skin.

Ian pulls back and turns to give me and my skimpy outfit a once-over. "So, this is what you thought I'd like if I were a straight boy?" I shrug, and Ian smiles. "Wanna hear something great?"

"Please."

"My little sister, Claire, heard me arguing with my brother and Mom."

"That's the opposite of great." My heart sinks for that sweet little kid, hearing such an ugly grown-up conversation. Knowing that some people can have such a hardness in their heart, even for people in their own family.

"No, listen." Ian touches my arm. "She was like, 'What's the big deal? It's how his heart was made to love.' It shut my mom and brother down. I think they at least heard her." He smiles. "Kids don't show up hating other people on their own. That has to be taught."

That, at least, is a sunny spot in this day. "I'm glad Claire has you to teach her."

"Yeah, me too." He scans my face. "You know Cooper misses you, right?"

"I miss him, too." God, I miss him. I scoot closer again, sliding my arm around Ian's waist, and give him a quasi hug. "You might be okay."

"Yeah, the jury's still out on you."

It makes me laugh. It's nice to laugh again.

》》《《

I dork around the mall for a while, and then I head for home. When I get there, Cooper's waiting on my porch. That fedora is on his head, jammed down almost to his eyebrows, and the sight of it—and him—makes me smile. I get out of my car and he rises, stepping to the ground. "Got something to say to me?"

"Ian has a big mouth," I tell him.

"Can't argue with that."

"No, I mean his mouth is actually big. My hand spent some time in very close proximity to it—which I presume he's already told you—so it should know." I hold up my hand to talk like a puppet saying the words: "He's a terrible kisser."

Cooper's lips turn up at the corners. "I beg to differ."

Dropping my hand, I shrug. "However, he does seem to be reasonably good at making you happy."

"He has his moments."

I step onto the bottom porch stair and turn so I'm looking Cooper in the eyes. "You should be happy. Be with him and be happy and be yourself. I never should have asked you to be anything else."

"Here's the thing." Cooper runs a hand through his hair, sending it straight up in the air. "I might be trying on a couple of different versions of me. Next year, college, a whole new crop of people. All bets are off. I might be 'cute librarian.' Or 'emo hipster.' Or 'clove cigarette cool.'"

"Not that one." I make a face at him. "I don't want to visit a dorm room that smells bad."

"I'm just saying, I might try some new things, so be aware of that." He takes a step away from the porch so he can look over my revealing outfit. "Speaking of being aware, are you aware you're barely dressed?"

"Ooh, that reminds me—stay right here." I make it to my room and back to the porch in under a minute. I wave a plastic bag at Cooper. "Got a present for you."

He takes the bag and opens it wide. The late-afternoon sun hits the T-shirt inside, blazing the white letters to life: *NOT STRAIGHT.* Cooper can't stop his grin. "This is badass."

"Fifteen percent off." And then I throw my arms around him. "Let's not break up anymore, okay?"

"Okay." We hug for a moment, and then Cooper says, "So how are you going to get that boy of yours back?"

"I don't think I am." My shoulders droop all of their own accord. "I broke his heart when I didn't mean to. I'd need an army to convince him to trust me again."

Cooper looks at me thoughtfully. "I have three words to say."

I smile at him. "I love you, too."

"Nope." He doesn't return the smile. "Three different words."

I puzzle for a moment. "I give up?"

This time Cooper's smile is huge and bright and all-encompassing. "Hashtag Lark Karma."

What?

CHAPTER TWENTY-SIX

There's a thing that California people say when summer hits: *It's a dry heat.* As if that makes it okay for the hot air to slam into you like a wall when you come out of your air-conditioned house, or for the handle of your car to scorch your fingers when you try to open it.

Graduation day is a dry heat, proving the rule instead of the exception. I don't hear movement in the house, so I assume Dad is off to work and Mom is off to her day. Leo's supposed to help at Wheelz this morning, so he's gone, too. I shower, get pretty, and head out. There's at least one thing I can do for Ardy that he can't do himself.

It takes a total of eleven minutes from when I pull into the hospital parking lot to when I return to my car. Either my mission is accomplished or I've sent the impossibly gorgeous Trissa Jefferson back into Ardy's orbit.

No matter which one it turns out to be, it was the right thing to do.

» » « «

When I get to Wheelz, Leo is perched on a trackside stool, a cardigan draped over his shoulders as he watches the handful of early kart drivers. "It's a thousand degrees outside," I tell him.

"It's cold in here."

Not to me. The air still feels good after being outside.

"Warning." Leo jerks a thumb toward the back. "All hell is breaking loose." He pulls his cardigan closer. "She says she's putting his things in the guest bedroom."

I take a seat next to him. "Do you want me to take you home?"

"I don't know." Leo doesn't look at me. "Sorry I texted. It's supposed to be your big day."

"Yeah." I don't tell him the real reason why that's true. "What got them started this time?"

"Everyone in the community loved the Spring Fling Thing so much that all the other schools are approaching them for special events. Some church groups, too. People are putting down deposits in advance, and there's all this extra money. Dad's hiring an extra assistant manager, for real this time."

"Then why are they fighting?"

Leo sighs. "Because that's what they do. It's never been about the hours or the work or the money."

It's like the world makes a sudden lurch beneath me. I grab the edges of my stool for support, flicking my gaze to the track so Leo won't see my inner turmoil. Before us, the vehicles continue their rotations. Some fast, some slow, all moving along the same path. Many cars, one pattern: around and around. Not getting anywhere but broken, only to be fixed and sent back to go around and be broken again.

I turn to my wise little brother, everything falling into place. "It's never been about anything at all."

Leo nods. "I don't think they'd know what to do if they agreed on things. They like it this way."

"Or they're used to it. They can't imagine anything different, so they keep things the way they are."

"Yep."

It's something I've avoided forever, that conflict. While my parents choose it, continue it, perpetuate it.

"Hey, Leo." He looks at me. "How are we remotely functional human beings?"

"Who says you're functional?" Then he grins to show he's kidding. I sling an arm around him.

"Doofus."

"Sister to a doofus."

» » « «

Our caps and gowns are shiny yellow. When the entire senior class is gathered in the hallway behind the gymnasium to await the ceremony, we look like the surface of the sun. I'm huddled in a corner with Cooper, facing out so I can surreptitiously scan the crowd for Ardy, but I don't see him in the moving, blazing swarm of yellow. I do see Rahim, though. He catches my eye and winks. "You ready?" Cooper asks me.

A tremor of terror runs through me, but before I can answer, Katie appears, shoving between us. "Ugh," says Cooper. "Buzzkill Barbie is here."

"Shut up." Katie says it as a reflex, but she's looking at me. "Are you really doing this?"

"Yes," Cooper says.

Katie doesn't act like she even heard him. She keeps her violet eyes trained on mine. "Lark?"

"Yes," I tell her, and am surprised to see sudden tears shimmer from behind the barely visible glow of her contact lenses. "Are you okay?"

Katie nods, reaching out to grip me by the shoulders. She blinks, and a tear spills from each eye. "You are the weirdest person I know." Except the way she says it, all tender and quiet, it sounds like a compliment.

She lets go, spinning abruptly and walking away. Cooper and I stare after her.

"What's up her ass?" he asks.

"I think that's how Katie does love." I look at him and grin. "She should try something different."

"Like a game," we say together, smiling.

Just then Wade and Will pass behind Cooper and glance at me. Wade grins, and Will shoots me a thumbs-up sign. I look back at Cooper. "I'm ready."

I see Ardy when we start lining up outside the gymnasium doors. Our bright yellow sleeves brush as we pass each other. We both stop walking, which makes Tyler bump into me from behind and say, "Dude." Neither Ardy nor I say anything; we only look at each other. It's like outside the art room, except this time we're not touching . . . but every bit of the ache and longing is still there.

At least it is for me.

Then the doors are opening and we're being ushered inside. I take a deep breath in preparation for my uncertain future, and I head in. One of three hundred yellow rays of light.

CHAPTER TWENTY-SEVEN

The gymnasium is a swaying, whispering blur around me. I know my parents and Leo are out there in the bleachers, but I haven't seen them. I'm sitting ramrod-straight in my hard plastic chair between Aaron Daniels and Jessica Dent. Wade Collins is in front of me and to the left. Ardy must be many, many rows behind me.

But I can't think about that now. I can't worry about where he is. I need to focus on . . . oh, I don't know . . . not fainting, maybe. I feel as hard and plastic as my chair. Petrified by what's about to happen.

Our principal already made her opening remarks from the podium at the center of the stage. The junior marching band played our fight song, and our valedictorian gave her speech. Then we were treated to a medley of current pop songs blasting from the gym speakers while a slideshow of the past four years of our lives played across the giant screen behind the stage. It came to a close, the final image of our entire senior class fading to darkness, and our salutatorian spoke.

And now that's all over. It's actually happening. The real thing. The true event. Why we're all here . . .

Xena Abernathy is the first to walk across the stage. Principal Barlow leans over the microphone, and a second later we hear Xena's name echo throughout the gymnasium. Our principal shakes her hand, giving her a rolled-up diploma tied with a yellow ribbon, and Xena flashes us all a quick peace sign. There's a sprinkling of applause, and then she's leaving the stage. Principal Barlow is focused on the next student.

As Valerie Addison walks toward her, I realize my hands are tapping against my left leg. I force them into stillness, but it reminds me—one went first.

One always goes first.

Every time, one person has to go first.

Rahim Antoun—third to walk across the stage—is supposed to kick everything off. As he mounts the stairs, I hold my breath. It all hinges on him. If he bails, if he makes a last-minute decision not to follow through, I'm dead in the water.

Our principal leans forward, Rahim's name reverberates, and they do the shake-and-diploma thing. Rahim keeps walking, my heart basically ceases to beat, and he pauses by the two flagpoles on the left side of the stage. I think most people are focusing on Amy Amherst, who's ascending the stairs on the opposite side, so they're not paying attention to Rahim easing a hand into his yellow robe. They're not watching him pull out a cardboard square.

I don't think anyone notices—except maybe Rahim's parents, I have to assume—until Rahim reaches high on the school flagpole and slaps the cardboard against it. Allowing the entire gymnasium to see what's there: a blank yellow square.

There's a collective head turn from the crowd, followed by a gust of whispered questions. I can hear some of them around me: "What's Rahim doing?" "What's that mean?"

I keep my eyes fixed firmly on the stage. I pretend I don't hear the questions, and I *definitely* pretend I don't know what the hell is going on. Principal Barlow glances at the flagpole and the yellow square, falters in her pronunciation of Carolyn Arnold's name, and then shrugs. I slump back in my seat, relieved. Either the principal thinks it's a harmless senior prank, or she's empowering our emotions, like we do here. She's not going to stop it.

Excellent.

The ceremony is uneventful until—as I'm standing in my row, ready to line up for my turn—Wade Collins takes the stage. After he receives his diploma, he also pauses by the flagpoles. A second later there's a new square under the first. This one is turquoise.

"I guess it's our school colors?" Jessica Dent whispers from my right.

This time Principal Barlow doesn't miss a beat. She calls out Shiri Crosby's name. When it's my turn to shake her hand, she makes eye contact and gives me a warm squeeze, like she's done with everyone before me. She has no idea I'm the one orchestrating the off-script part of the event.

I'm back in my seat when Cooper Felder earns a round of cheers for his cartwheel—which he somehow manages to do, even in his gown—before he smacks the next square onto the pole. Another turquoise one.

Will Hartsook is the next to place a square. Yellow.

I keeping my gaze firmly fastened on the podium, clapping loudly when Katie Levitt walks. I'm gratified to see that, a few rows up, Cooper is doing the same.

It's a while until Dax Santos takes the stage. He was the hardest sell, but eventually I convinced him. It may have had something to do with the photo of me shoveling horseshit that I printed on a canvas and signed for him. At first he laughed really hard, and then, finally, he agreed that I'd been put through enough.

Now I watch closely as he stops in front of the flagpole. Dax pulls out his square and smacks it up there beneath the rest. Turquoise.

Then he faces the audience and gives a full-body eye roll before trotting off the stage. Around me the whispers start anew. "Is it a football thing?" "Spirit club?" "No one asked me to do it."

That last comment was from Jessica Dent, but I don't answer. I can't, because Ardy Tate is now in line to get his diploma. I can't, because this may be the last time that I can unabashedly stare at him, that I can admire his tall, lanky figure and the angle of his jawline and the swoop of hair cresting back from his forehead. I wonder if he has figured it out, what the squares mean. I wonder if he's amused or touched . . . or if he's angry and resentful. Or maybe he's focused on graduating and doesn't care about the culmination prank of a high school he barely attended.

"Gerard Tate," Principal Barlow says into her microphone, and Ardy swings across the stage.

Watching him, everything inside me hurts.

Ardy doesn't pause at the flagpoles. He does the shake-and-take, then keeps right on going. The only time he stops is right before he descends the steps, and it's not to look at me. It's to gaze out into the audience and give a fast nod, I assume to his mom.

He doesn't see that I'm clapping so hard my hands sting.

It's ten more minutes before the last student is waiting at the edge of the stage. It's Joe Zola, who I flirted with last year but never kissed. When I approached him this week about helping me, he was startled and amused . . . and he had a question. "Why didn't we ever hang out?"

"You didn't seem interested," I told him.

"We weren't in the same classes. I never really knew you."

I looked up at him, realizing something as I said it: "I didn't really know any of the guys I hung out with."

"That's a bummer." Joe gave me a slow smile. "A lot of nice guys here."

Now, as I watch him cross the stage, I know he's right.

Principal Barlow speaks his name—"Giovanni Zola"— and they shake hands. Joe accepts his diploma and heads off the stage, stopping at the edge. A moment later a final square graces the flagpole. This one is bright pink. A splashy break in what was shaping up to be a familiar pattern. Familiar to me, at least, and hopefully one other person.

If Ardy got it. Who knows.

As Principal Barlow waits for Joe to get back to his seat, I tap the pattern against my left leg, for good luck. Then I silently forgive my parents—or at least I try. I can't explain why they keep choosing the worst version of themselves, but I know I can't break their pattern. I can only break my own.

I hope.

Principal Barlow leans forward toward the microphone, a big smile on her face, to pronounce us all "commenced." There's a hushed expectation throughout the gymnasium. The families are ready to stand and applaud and take pictures. The seniors are ready to cheer and throw their hats in the air. . . .

Except Principal Barlow doesn't have a chance to say anything, since suddenly the giant screen behind her comes to life. It must cast a glow over her podium; she stops speaking before she's even started. She turns around to see what the rest of us are looking at.

It's a video that is now dozens of yards high, on full display for everyone here.

"What the hell is that?" Jessica Dent asks.

"That's a fractal," I tell her. Because, thanks to Peter Talbot, we are all watching a swirl of rainbow colors grow in an ever-expanding, ever-evolving, ever-the-same pattern. "We learned it in Calculus."

"Okay, but *why?*" Jessica asks.

I don't answer her. I don't need to; the words I wrote are about to do it for me. They appear, starting tiny from the bottom of the screen in a slow scroll à la *Star Wars,* because of *course* that's how Peter would program it.

On the edge of the stage, Principal Barlow is engaged in an animated whispered conference with Assistant Principal Longley and Ms. Cole, whose job has something to do with the school computers. Ms. Cole is gesturing around the gymnasium while both principals shake their heads violently. I don't know who's fighting for what, but it doesn't matter. My message has crawled up high enough to be visible to all:

REACH high and break all patterns.

The gymnasium explodes into applause, since of course it seems like a celebratory message to the first-ever graduating class of REACH.

Those words continue their scroll up the screen, and suddenly there's a stark, cold terror in my chest. Every heartbeat pumps ice instead of blood. I'm horrified by what I've done, but there's no way to stop it now. It's already happening.

But I don't have to watch it.

I jerk to my feet and start to edge out of my row.

"What are you doing?" Jessica whispers.

"I have to pee," I tell her.

I could have ended it right here, with the pattern and the fractal and the message. Ardy probably would have known it was me. Or maybe he wouldn't have, but at least the rest of our class and the teachers and our families wouldn't have, either. But now they will. When Cooper and I came up with the idea, I wanted to do the scariest thing possible. I wanted Ardy to see me being my most honest and my most exposed.

And, frankly, my most *weird*.

I head across the wide expanse of gym floor between the senior seats and the double doors we all marched through an hour ago. I'm about there when the final words pop onto the screen. I don't turn to look, but I know it's happened, because there's a collective gasp from the hundreds of people in the giant room.

I love you, Ardy Tate.
I'm sorry.
#larkkarma

As I yank the doors open, Principal Barlow's voice echoes from the speakers:

"As seems only appropriate for the individual and creative nature of our fine school, that was, uh, an unorthodox ending to our graduation. And now please join me in congratulating the graduating class of—"

That's when the doors slam shut behind me.

CHAPTER TWENTY-EIGHT

I go to the flagpoles outside because it seems like the natural place to wait for Ardy, but when after fifteen minutes he still hasn't shown up and I've fielded several very confused texts from my parents, I head for my car. Everyone is going to start coming out of the gym soon, and I don't want to answer the questions. I don't want congratulations or reprimands.

I just want Ardy.

I slide behind the wheel and then shoot him a text:

Call me.

Of course, I don't know if he'll get it. He might have blocked me, after all. He might even have done it in the fifteen minutes since I put his name in ten-foot-tall letters for everyone to see.

Ardy's street is quiet when I pull onto it. There's no minivan in his driveway, so I park in front of his house to wait. Except he's not the one who comes home.

Hope is.

Her parents' sedan pulls into her driveway, and all three of them get out. I slink down in my seat, but of course she's already seen my car. I watch her have a conversation with her dads before they go into their house and she heads toward me. I get out to meet her.

Hope stops a few feet away. Her hair is even shinier and blacker than usual against the yellow of her gown. We regard each other for a long moment until she breaks the silence.

"Ballsy."

"Necessary."

"Get this: Evan wants to get back together."

Well, that's news. "Are you going to?"

"I don't think so." She gives me a half smile. "I don't think it'll ever be right with him, and I don't want to die a virgin."

"I don't either." I return her half smile. "At least I want to *know* if I am or not." My phone buzzes in my pocket, and I reach underneath my robe to find it.

"I'm always going to be friends with Ardy," Hope tells me.

"Good." I locate my phone and pull it out.

"That's all it is," she continues. "But I'm not going away."

"I don't want you to," I tell her. "One of the best things about him is how he does friendship." I check my screen for the text that just came through. There are no words, only a photo. I look back up at Hope, my half smile growing into a giant grin.

"I have to go."

"Good luck."

Although I'm sure she meant it all along, this is the first time I actually believe it.

» » « «

Ardy Tate is standing at the railing, looking out over the valley, when I arrive on the Ridge patio. I'm far enough away that he couldn't have heard me among the chatter and the clinking of silverware of the diners, but he turns around anyway. He watches me thread my way between the tables and chairs to him.

I had pulled off my gown as I was handing over my car to the valet. I'm surprised to see that Ardy is still wearing his.

I can't stop myself from asking the question.

"You didn't want to take that off?"

Amusement shines from his brown eyes. "You know there was talk of the senior class going naked under the robes, right?"

"I did. Sounds unhygienic." I look down to where I can see his shoes peeking out from beneath the hem of the gown. Surely, *surely,* Ardy is wearing clothes under there. . . .

His voice brings my head back up. "That was a ballsy move."

"Funny, that's what Hope said."

"I'm always going to be friends with her."

"She said that, too." I gaze at him, trying to make my sincerity visible on my face. "I want that for you both."

"I got a text today."

"Yeah?"

"From Trissa." For the first time in what seems like forever, he smiles. "She apologized for not hearing me out after the forest fiasco."

Warmth blossoms inside my chest. "I'm glad."

"Me too." His smile doesn't waver. "Another ballsy move on your part."

I shrug. Everything I've done seems more desperate than ballsy.

"And weird," Ardy continues, stepping closer. "Really weird."

"Yeah, I know." I also take a step toward him. "I think maybe I'm weirder than you think I am."

"Nah." He cocks his head, staring at me. "I think maybe you're exactly as weird as I think you are."

"I'm sorry." I reach out to touch his wrist. "I should have been honest with you from the beginning. About everything."

"Honesty is hard." He finds the zipper at the top of his graduation gown and starts tugging it down. Okay, he *has* to be wearing clothes, because there's no way Ardy Tate is about to get naked at this restaurant. I keep my eyes on his face. On his thick dark hair and his angled jawline and the sunlight glancing off the frames of his glasses.

I can't believe how badly I messed things up with this boy, or how badly I want him now.

Ardy's zipper reaches the bottom of his gown, and he looks back into my eyes. "Want to see?"

There's no way to answer, because, truthfully, no matter what's under there, the answer is yes. I swallow and nod.

Ardy pulls his robe open and shrugs it off his shoulders, revealing ripped indigo jeans and a plain white T-shirt. Except it's not plain. Written on it in thick black lettering is a sentence. It's broken up and posted vertically, in chunks, with some of the letters missing:

___et me tell you
___bout the
gi___l I love who is beautiful and
___ind.

I tear my eyes up from the shirt. A small smile crosses Ardy's face. "Can you read what's missing?"

I nod, an absurdly huge grin forming across my face. Ardy was planning to give me a message, too. Each of us was trying to tell the other the same thing. "Too cheesy?" he asks.

"I think it might be perfect," I tell him. "Also, I love you, too."

And then Ardy's mouth is on mine. It's warm and delicious and perfect. It's better than every other kiss that's ever happened, because this time nothing is blurry.

Everything is crystal clear.

Finally.

ACKNOWLEDGMENTS

There was this time when I spent three years as a writer on ABC's *Grey's Anatomy.* Three years knowing and loving (and sometimes fighting) and working (and sometimes crying) with a big, wonderful, dysfunctional, and yet fully functional group of writers whose names are, INPO*: Bill and Stacy and Naser and Ariel and Dan and Jim and Michelle and Zoanne and Lauren and Azia and Nayna and Charles and Jalysa and Bridgette and Parriott and Ellen and Fred and Austin and Barbara-Friend-who-really-likes-seeing-her-name-in-a-book and Andy and Meg and Tia and Drizz and Finch and Darren and Shonda.

I wrote four books while hanging out with these nerds. This is the last one, and the reason I need to give some extra-special love to my sweet gingers—Karin Gist and Elizabeth Klaviter—who still talk me through the days when the world spins in the wrong direction. Thank you.

Also, a heaping dose of gratitude to the following:

My shining-star editor, Chelsea Eberly, for asking the hard questions and helping find answers.

Lisa Gallagher, who continues to be an agent extraordinaire.

The whole team of wonderful, talented, supportive people

---

* INPO means "in no particular order."

at Random House: Mallory Loehr, Michelle Nagler, Jenna Lettice, Barbara Bakowski, Angela Carlino, and Josh Redlich.

Racer's Edge in Burbank, California. Especially that guy named Drew who gave me a tour of the facility.

Sky Falconry near San Diego. They're all about raptor education and conservation, plus you can fly a bird of prey in real life.

Everyone who participated in the "Ship Name" game on Twitter, but the loudest shout-out to Samantha Sirsky for #Heaven.

My friend and fellow writer Clyde Morgan—on behalf of us all, thank you for the story about your unfortunate kiss. You will always be Snapper Doodle to me.

One more thing: The original concept for this book wasn't a game but rather a bet. It was loosely based on a thing that happened a long time ago with now-theatre-teacher Maria Used-to-Be-Smith Moore. Yes, it was about boys. No, I won't tell you what it was. Neither will she.

ABOUT THE AUTHOR

JEN KLEIN is the author of *Shuffle, Repeat; Summer Unscripted;* and *Hearts Made for Breaking.* When she's not writing YA novels, Jen is an Emmy-nominated television writer. She's written on *Grey's Anatomy* and *Star* and is currently writing on the series *The Resident.* Jen lives in Los Angeles.

jenkleinbooks.com

MEET OLIVER + JUNE.

Oliver is being forced to drive June to school each morning,
and these opposites are fighting over music, life—everything.
And maybe falling for each other?

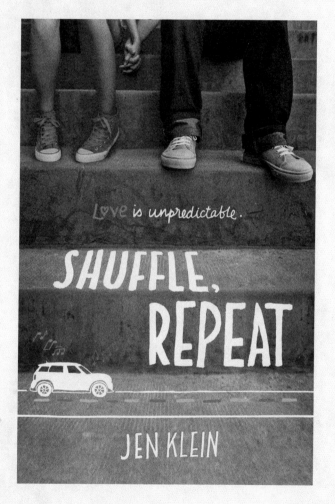

Love is unpredictable.

SHUFFLE, REPEAT

JEN KLEIN

AVAILABLE NOW!

GIRL looks for a SIGN. ENTER: BOY

Girl follows Boy. ENTER: SECOND BOY

Girl NEEDS TO FIGURE STUFF OUT. Enter: Drama

JEN KLEIN

Summer
Unscripted

FATE FOLLOWS
NO PLAN.

AVAILABLE NOW!